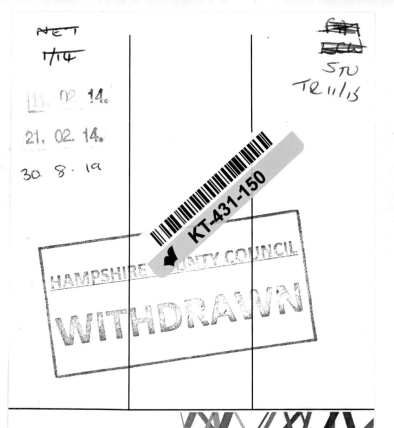
Get **more** out of libraries

Please return or renew this item by the last date shown.

You can renew online at www.hants.gov.uk/library

Or by phoning 0845 603 5631

 Hampshire
County Council

C015357433

A QUESTION OF GUILT

A QUESTION OF GUILT

Janet Tanner

This first world edition published 2012
in Great Britain and 2013 in the USA by
SEVERN HOUSE PUBLISHERS LTD of
19 Cedar Road, Sutton, Surrey, England, SM2 5DA.

British Library Cataloguing in Publication Data

Tanner, Janet.
  A question of guilt.
  1. Women journalists–Fiction. 2. Arson investigation–
  England–Somerset–Fiction. 3. Romantic suspense novels.
  I. Title
  823.9'14-dc23

ISBN-13: 978-0-7278-8234-9 (cased)

All Severn House titles are printed on acid-free paper.

Severn House Publishers support The Forest Stewardship Council [FSC],
the leading international forest certification organisation. All our titles that
are printed on Greenpeace-approved FSC-certified paper carry the FSC logo.

MIX
Paper from
responsible sources
FSC® C018575

Typeset by Palimpsest Book Production Ltd.,
Falkirk, Stirlingshire, Scotland.
Printed and bound in Great Britain by
MPG Books Ltd., Bodmin, Cornwall.

One

Have you ever seen an avalanche? I have. I've heard it too, and it's the most awesome, terrifying thing. The roar of it vibrates in the air and that wall of snow rushing down the mountainside makes the whole world shake and tremble. I only saw it briefly, over my shoulder, as I skied for my life, and I promise you, I never want to see it again. But that roar, like a wild animal about to devour you, I still hear that in nightmares.

I could so easily have died that day, buried beneath goodness only knows how many feet of snow. I try not to think about it, but I know it will be a long time, if ever, before I can get up the nerve to ski off-piste again. And I'll probably never be up to it physically, anyway. I shattered my leg as well as breaking my wrist and my collarbone when I shot over the overhanging rock that saved my life and where I lay stunned whilst the snow roared past, a foaming white ocean I could no longer see.

When I woke up in hospital I was grateful for the pain because I was alive to feel it and I might so easily not have been. Later, as the weeks and months dragged by, I became awfully tired of it, and frustrated. Let's face it, I'm no saint. When my leg throbbed relentlessly and I had to have more surgery I had to work very hard to keep reminding myself how lucky I had been. I had. I had! But there were times when I felt I was being sucked down more surely than if I'd been buried alive that day.

I never did find out what started that avalanche, but I know it could have been something quite insignificant. Like a pebble starting a landslide, when a little shower of rubble becomes a cascade, so that ocean of snow may have begun with one little breaker. But of course it didn't end there. Long after the snow had settled, the chain of events that avalanche started was rolling relentlessly on. Leading me, though I didn't realize it, into a web of blind alleys and dark secrets towards a nightmare that would put my life in danger all over again.

Everything that happened began with the avalanche. My questionable decision to go off-piste that day was the catalyst. If I'd stayed on the slopes, I wouldn't have ended up badly injured; if I hadn't been injured, I wouldn't have been at home in Stoke Compton, bored and frustrated, looking for something to help the days pass more quickly. I'd have been simply getting on with my life. Tim and I might still have been together, and I'd have been too busy with my job – a reporter on the regional daily, *Western News* – to think of anything beyond Crown Court cases and the regeneration plans for the city docks area and the occasional interview with some local celebrity. I would never have begun asking questions about an old case of arson that had happened in my home town, thirty miles away.

Would I have pursued it if I'd known what lay in store? The answer to that has to be yes. I'm a journalist first and foremost; I'm nosy and persistent. And I have a strong sense of justice. But I had no idea, none at all, of the nightmare I was letting myself in for. Or that I was to discover, the hard way, that sometimes the very people you think you can trust turn out to be those you can't trust at all.

But I'm going too fast. If I'm to tell you what happened, make any sense of it, I have to start at the beginning. Well, what was the beginning for me, anyway.

When I got out of hospital I was still incapacitated to a certain degree, and definitely in need of some tender loving care. Coping by myself in the city flat I shared with Tim was barely practicable given the way things were. If he had been in a nine-to-five job within striking distance, I could probably have managed, but he wasn't. He's a captain with one of the budget airlines, which means he works irregular shift patterns and is often away overnight. Tim in a luxury hotel in Malaga or Madeira with the rest of the flight crew wouldn't be a great deal of help to me if I needed urgent help.

I wasn't sure, in any case, if I wanted to rely on Tim. For some reason I was having second thoughts about whether he was the right one for me. I couldn't actually pin down what had changed, only that it no longer felt right. Perhaps it was just that I was unsettled after the accident, depressed and seeing things through a dark haze; that was probably it. But I would have expected to want to cling to security, not push it away. I looked at Tim and felt this nagging doubt in the pit of my stomach; wondered if it had been the glamour of his job that had attracted me, not the real man inside the smart black uniform with gold braid on the shoulders. All sorts of things about him started irritating me, just silly little things really, like the way he raised a critical eyebrow and turned down the sound system whenever he came into the room, as if I was noise-polluting the planet all by myself, or tidied the magazines and newspapers I'd been leafing through into a neat pile or even whisked them away altogether. Once upon a time I'd found such habits endearing, now I prickled with annoyance. And I didn't like it. If I was going to spend my life with this man, it didn't bode well.

I couldn't help wondering if I was irritating him too. There was an impatience in his manner, as if he blamed me for what had happened – and perhaps he did. He hadn't wanted me to take the skiing holiday at all and I knew he didn't think I should have ventured off-piste. He'd said so often enough. Foolhardy, he'd called it.

'Surely there must have been weather warnings?' he'd said. Weather warnings loomed large in his life as a pilot. 'Surely you checked?'

'Of course I did. I'm not stupid.' I sounded petulant, I knew. Being incapacitated and in more or less constant pain wasn't doing much for my temper, however hard I tried to remain positive.

Tim's expression told me he wasn't altogether sure he agreed.

'The trouble with you, Sally, is that you don't always stop to think about the consequences of your actions. When you get an idea in your head, you do tend to jump in with both feet.'

'Not any more,' I retorted ruefully. 'Not with a metal pin in my leg and a plaster cast.'

'That,' Tim said, 'is a bit like shutting the stable door after the horse has bolted.'

'Oh, give it a rest Tim, please! We can't all be perfect like you.' I snapped. And immediately felt guilty and miserable. I wasn't the only one affected by this. It wasn't a lot of fun for Tim either. And however much I might protest that I'd taken all the right precautions, that the avalanche was a fluke and I hadn't been the only one caught out that day, I still felt like a naughty child who'd brought all her troubles on herself by her disobedience, and inconvenienced everyone else into the bargain.

'The best thing would be for you to go home for a while, until you're stronger and more mobile,' Tim said, and I knew he was right.

Twelve years ago I'd been only too ready to leave; the family farm on the outskirts of a small country town, which my father ran himself with the help of just one regular farm-hand in winter and some casual local labour in summer, had felt like a prison when I was eighteen. Now, battered and bruised mentally as well as physically, I longed for peace and tranquillity and the time and space to consider my future. I looked forward to Mum fussing over me, cooking the delicious meals I'd sorely missed, putting hot water bottles in my bed, bringing me a mug of warm milk with a tot of whisky in it. I thought nostalgically of cows in the lane, jostling as they were driven in for milking, instead of city streets with nose-to-tail traffic. And I pictured the night sky inky black and studded with stars instead of the orange street-light glow I'd grown used to.

'It would be the answer, wouldn't it?' I said.

Mum had offered, of course, when she and Dad had come to visit me in hospital, but I hadn't been quite ready then to sacrifice my independence. Now I was. And the fact that Tim seemed pretty relieved at the thought of getting shot of me and the difficulties I was causing him made up my mind.

I went home to Rookery Farm, Stoke Compton, ensconced in the rear seat of Dad's comfortable 4 x 4 and for the first few weeks it was heaven on earth, balm for my battered body and soul. But as I began to get better the rural idyll began to pall, and I found myself remembering just why I'd been so keen to leave in the first place.

I missed my job as a reporter on a regional daily; I missed my friends; I missed the hum of the city; I even missed arguing with Tim. I was going crazy with boredom – there's a limit to how much daytime television you can take – and I was even fed up with reading, though it had been such a luxury in the beginning. When I moaned about it to him on the phone, Tim suggested I should use the time to try to do some freelance journalism, maybe a magazine article instead of the hard news that was my bread and butter when I was at work, and I did toy with the idea. But I couldn't think of a single thing to write about. Nothing ever seemed to happen in Stoke Compton; I couldn't imagine editors falling over themselves to buy pieces on Mum's WI meetings, or the price of animal feed, and the same torpor that was driving me crazy seemed to have sapped my ability to think outside the frame.

And then fate took a hand.

It was a wet February day when rain was pouring down relentlessly from a leaden sky. The gusting wind threw it in angry flurries against the windows and roared like a dragon in the chimneys. Last year's leaves lay in sodden piles in the farm-yard, mixed with filthy bits of straw and silage and the gateway leading to the lane was ankle-deep with churned-up mud. There was no way I could take my usual constitutional – a short walk to exercise my leg and try to get some strength back into the muscles – and I was feeling even more fed up than usual.

By four o'clock it was almost dark outside, hardly surprising, since it had not been properly light all day. It was warm and bright in the kitchen, though, where I was helping Mum prepare the vegetables for supper. The Aga emitted a comforting glow and the hidden lighting Mum had had put in when they were redecorating a couple of years ago supplemented the big old central fitting that had been there, I sometimes thought, ever since the farm house was built, and which I imagined had once supported an oil lamp.

The small digital radio on the window sill was tuned to the local news programme, but I was only half listening. I'd been away from Stoke Compton so long that the items really struck no chords with me at all, and I found it hard to summon up any interest in road works on the bypass, or a traffic light failure in town. I was far away, in a world of my own.

It was my mother's voice that caught my attention.

'You have to admire that woman, don't you?'

'What woman?'

For a moment, Mum didn't answer; she was clearly listening intently to the broadcast, and, curious, I began listening too.

'I'll never stop fighting for Brian. I'll never give up as long as he's in jail for something he didn't do, while the real culprit is still out there walking free.' There was fervour and determination in the disembodied voice, a fervour that rang out over the air waves. 'Brian is innocent. I know that as surely as I know anything!'

'What was all that about?' I asked as the interview concluded.

'That was Brian Jennings' sister. The chap that started that terrible fire in the High Street – you remember.'

I scraped a satisfyingly long ribbon of skin from a carrot with my vegetable peeler. 'Vaguely.'

'Oh, you must remember! It was a terrible to-do.'

I stripped another peeling from the carrot. 'Mum, I've covered dozens of fires. After a while they all blur into one.'

'Well, you should remember this one!' Mum sounded a bit put out. 'Two girls almost burned to death in your own home town! And I'm surprised you haven't heard about the campaign Brian Jennings' sister is running to try and get the case looked into again. She's often on the radio, trying to get someone to listen to her. She's even got the local MP involved, I think, but it doesn't seem to be getting her very far.'

The first little prickle of interest stirred somewhere deep inside me, a sensation I hadn't felt in months.

'She thinks he was wrongly convicted?'

'That's what she thinks. I suppose she would, being his sister. And she says she won't rest until justice is done. Like I say, you've got to take your hat off to someone who just refuses to give up, whether they're right or wrong. It can't be easy for her, taking on the powers-that-be as she has.' Mum cocked an eyebrow at me. 'Have you finished those carrots?'

'Last one.' I chopped the carrot into roundels and scooped them into the casserole. 'There you go.' I wiped my hands on the big navy-blue cook's apron I'd borrowed from its place behind the larder door, and perched on one of the high kitchen stools, looking at Mum quizzically.

'Tell me about the fire, then. What the story was. I know you think I should know, but just refresh my memory.'

'Let me get this in the oven, and then we'll have a cup of tea and tell you all about it.'

Mum was smiling faintly. I think she was pleased and relieved that at last I was actually taking an interest in something!

The terrible fire started late at night, in an electrical-appliances shop in the High Street, apparently the result of petrol-soaked rags being pushed through the letter box, and had quickly become an inferno. Two girls who shared the flat above the shop had been lucky to escape with their lives. They had been in bed and asleep when the fire started, and if it had not been for a baker on his way to work raising the alarm and managing to get a ladder up to one of the rear windows, the fire would almost certainly have had the most tragic consequences.

'There was never any doubt but that the fire was started deliberately and eventually Brian Jennings was in the frame,' Mum said, sipping her tea. 'To begin with everybody assumed it was down to yobs – they were always smashing up the bus shelter or putting a brick through one of the shop windows, that sort of nonsense. Most of the shops in the High Street had got those metal security blinds, but not that one. All he had was a row of concrete bollards to stop ram raids. I think he was struggling, to tell the truth.'

'So perhaps he started it himself, for the insurance money,' I suggested.

'That was another theory that was going around, of course,' Mum said. 'I never did believe it myself, though. He wouldn't risk it – not when he knew there were two girls asleep upstairs.'

'People do awful things if they're desperate,' I said. I'd come across quite a few instances of unbelievable ruthlessness in the course of my career.

'Well, it wasn't that, anyway,' Mum said. 'It turned out he'd let his insurance lapse – couldn't afford to keep up the payments. The fire ruined him – the shop never reopened, not as an electricals store anyway. It's a café now. Very nice, too, they say. They do quite a trade on a Saturday, coffee and cakes, and toasted sandwiches. It's one of the girls who used to rent the flat upstairs that's got it, funnily enough. You'd think she'd have wanted to get as far away from the place as possible, wouldn't you? I know I would, if I'd had an experience like that . . .'

'Mm, yes.' I shuddered, imagining how terrifying it must have been for them. 'But what made the police think it was this Brian Jennings and not the yobs? And what on earth possessed him to do something like that?'

Mum shook her head. 'Who knows? He was a strange one, by all accounts, a real loner, and he'd had a crush on one of the girls for ages. It was a case of "if I can't have you, no one else will", I think. They found a lot of stuff in his flat, strange stuff, you know what I mean? Pornography, lots of photographs of Dawn that he must have taken with a long-lens camera – and she reckoned he'd been stalking her, hanging around outside, just watching the place, and following her if she went out. I think a couple of witnesses said they'd seen him lurking about on the night of the fire, which put the police on to him. But the final nail in his coffin was when they found traces of petrol in the pocket of his jacket. They had him up in court, and he was found guilty. Arson and endangering life, I think it was. He got put away for a good long time.'

'But his sister maintains he's innocent?' I said.

'She does. Poor soul, she's put her life on hold trying to get the case looked at again. She's given up everything, from what I hear, to fight to prove his innocence, and like I say, it's all been for nothing.'

I sipped my tea, but prickles of excitement were darting in my veins as if it were champagne and my brain had gone into overdrive.

It was so long now since I'd been able to go after a story, I'd almost forgotten the adrenalin rush, the singing anticipation. But I was feeling it now.

I didn't know if this Brian Jennings was guilty or not; it could very well be that his sister's love and loyalty was misplaced. But her fight for 'justice' was a compelling story, and who knew what I might discover if I did some digging into the facts? For the first time in months, I had something other than my own aches and pains to think about. It was a great feeling.

Two

I could hardly wait to begin looking into the case, but, before speaking to Marion Jennings, I needed to have all the information that was out there at my fingertips and decided the best starting point was probably the local newspaper office, where it was sure to be archived. I might have been able to discover most of the facts by going online, but Dad was busy on the computer, bringing his accounts up to date, and in any case I thought I'd get more of a feel for things if I could chat to the reporter who had covered the case. Even if he or she was busy, the girls in the office would probably be able to fill me in on most of the background; the premises occupied by the *Stoke Compton Gazette* were practically next door to the shop that had been petrol bombed.

'There's no chance you're going into town today, I suppose, Mum?' I asked, as we shared a cup of coffee in the kitchen.

'You mean *you'd* like to go into town?' Mum gave me a straight look, but the corners of her mouth were turned up into a half smile.

'Well . . . yes . . .'

'I usually do my supermarket shop on a Friday . . .' This was Wednesday. 'But if you give me half an hour to check the cupboards and see what we need, I don't suppose there's any reason why I shouldn't do it today.'

'I wasn't really thinking of going to the supermarket,' I said.

'No, I know you weren't. But if I dropped you off in town, did my shopping and popped back to pick you up . . . How long would you need?'

'How long does it take you to do your shopping?'

'A couple of hours, usually.'

'That would be great.'

I still hated being dependent on other people, even my mum, but I wasn't going to think about that now.

'OK,' Mum said, and then, as if she'd read my thoughts, she

added: 'You'll soon be able to drive yourself again. And your dad's car is an automatic. You'd better start wheedling your way into his good books.'

My spirits lifted another notch. She was right. I probably could manage an automatic. And though Dad could be crusty, and he'd always been fiercely possessive about his car, I could usually twist him round my finger.

'Not this morning, though,' Mum said with a smile. 'He's never in the best of tempers when he's got to do the accounts, and he wouldn't thank you for interrupting him.'

She found a pencil and one of the envelopes discarded from the morning's mail and began opening cupboards.

'Go and get ready, Sally. This won't take me long.'

The rain had stopped overnight, but the sky was still grey and leaden, and the air felt cold and clammy. As Mum drove slowly up the track that led to the lane beyond, the wheels sunk into patches of thick mud and splashed through puddles. The lane was not much better; a delivery van came up behind us, tail-gating in his impatience to overtake, and splattering grime all over the rear windscreen of Mum's little hatchback.

'White-van man,' I said, through gritted teeth. 'I didn't know they'd infested the country too.'

'Oh yes.' Mum shook her head as the van finally took his chance and roared past. 'I just hope we don't round the corner and find him crashed into a tractor or a hedge cutter.'

'Or some innocent motorist coming the other way.'

'He's headed for trouble in these winding lanes, that's for sure,' Mum said.

But this time, it seemed, white-van man had got away with it. We didn't see hide or hair of him again, and soon we were approaching the outskirts of Stoke Compton.

'Where do you want me to drop you?' Mum asked.

'The High Street would be good.'

As we turned into it, Mum nodded her head to the left.

'That's where the fire was; like I said, it's a café now.'

I looked in the direction she was indicating and saw a large plate-glass window bearing a bright, arched logo – *Muffins*.

'They put tables and chairs outside on the pavement in the

summer,' Mum said, but I was looking up at the windows above the café frontage, small casements, and the dark, funnel-shaped stain still evident on the grey stone of the wall.

For all that I'm a seasoned reporter, used to remaining uninvolved no matter how traumatic the scenario I'm faced with, a small chill prickled over my skin. Perhaps because this was my hometown, the place where I'd grown up and always felt safe; perhaps because I was going soft. It was a year now since I'd had to deal with the harsher side of life – apart from my own problems. I hadn't had to attend road accidents where people were trapped in cars, I hadn't been standing on the bank when bodies were pulled out of the river, I hadn't had to try to interview grieving relatives or horribly mutilated soldiers wounded in Afghanistan. This was nothing compared to some of the stories I'd covered in the past. Just a fire – nobody had died. And yet it was getting to me.

Fire has always frightened me, I must admit. There is something about the relentless roar of flames and clouds of thick black smoke, the crash of falling masonry and roofs caving in, the awesome power of a blaze that has really taken hold, that gets to me on a very primitive level. And afterwards, the charred devastation, dripping water, the smell . . . it frightens me and also fascinates me. But even so . . . it was weird that I was reacting so strongly to the scene of a fire that happened five years ago. I really needed to toughen myself up again!

Mum pulled into a space by the kerb.

'Will this do?'

'Fine.'

'I'll see you here then – or as close to here as I can get.' She checked the dashboard clock. 'Midday – OK?'

'OK.' I opened the car door and got out, holding on to it while I retrieved my crutches from the rear seat. Managing without crutches was something else I was going to have to get used to, but this morning, not being sure how long I was going to be on my leg, or how far I would have to walk, I'd brought them with me.

Mum waited until I set off down the High Street in the direction of the newspaper office, then pulled out and drove off with a toot and a wave.

The newspaper office had once been a shop. Through the plate-glass window I could see a girl sitting behind a reception desk. I juggled my crutches, pushed open the door and went inside.

The receptionist was on the telephone, taking the details of a small ad, from what I could make out. Whilst I waited for her to finish I looked around with professional interest. The long, narrow room was lined with work stations, at two of which girls were busy on computers; at the rear an office had been partitioned off, plaster board up to waist height, glass above. Inside was a man I assumed must be the chief reporter. His back was turned towards me, so I couldn't see his face, just a dark head of hair and a country-style checked shirt. Then I was denied even that paltry view of him as he sat down and disappeared behind the plasterboard partition.

Taken all in all the newspaper office could hardly have been more different from the one I worked in. The *Western News* took up a whole building, and every department from the news room to the family announcements had its own separate space. Yet in spite of that the atmosphere was somehow exactly the same, the frenetic buzz that comes from deadlines to be met, the feeling of being at the heart of things, even the smell of fresh newsprint emanating from the latest editions that were stacked on a rack close to where I was standing.

'Can I help you?' The receptionist had finished her call and was flipping the docket she'd been writing on into a wire tray as she spoke, ready to be delivered, I guessed, to the mother paper's main office in town.

'I hope so,' I said. 'I'm interested in the case of Brian Jennings, who was convicted of arson here in the High Street five years ago. I was wondering if the reporter who worked on the story could spare me a few minutes?'

The receptionist looked startled, then recovered herself though I could see her trying to work out just who I was and what my interest in the story was.

'You'd need to speak to Belinda Jones, our chief reporter,' she said crisply. 'She's not in today though.'

'Ah.' My heart sank.

'Belinda is never in on a Wednesday. The paper comes out

on a Wednesday, so it's our quietest day, with no deadlines to meet.'

'When will she be in again?' I asked.

'Well, tomorrow. But I'm not sure . . . She has a very full diary . . .' She gave me a narrow look from behind dark-rimmed spectacles. 'Perhaps it would be best if you were to leave me your name and a contact number I'll get her to give you a call.'

Immediately I was on the back foot. I might not be exactly the most famous reporter in England but the *Western News* does sell in the Stoke Compton area and I have occasionally had a byline. Plus there's quite a network of journalists who move from paper to paper. If my name was recognized then it was quite possible lines of communication would rapidly shut down. Far from practising professional solidarity, the chances were that the chief reporter on a local paper would think the 'big boys' were muscling in on her territory, which she would guard like a lioness with her cubs. But my mobile number would mean nothing to anyone but my friends and family. Safe enough to give her that, and if I used my mother's maiden name it wouldn't shriek 'competition' to anyone.

'Sally Jacobs,' I said without batting an eyelid, and followed on by dictating the number of my mobile. She wrote it down.

'What about your archives?' I asked, mindful of the two-hour wait I'd have before Mum came back for me. 'I'd really like to take a look at the reports that appeared at the time of the fire and the trial.'

'Oh, they're all on microfiche,' she said. 'You could access them at the library. It's just down the road.'

Again my heart sank. I loathe microfiche — it takes forever finding what you're looking for, pulling it up to a readable size and then flicking from page to page.

'You don't have original copies of the papers?' I asked.

'You must be joking! We've hardly any storage space here.' She was looking at me curiously again. 'Are you part of Brian Jennings' legal team?'

'No, I'm not.' I was thinking on my feet now. 'I'm doing a thesis on questionable convictions for my degree,' I lied. 'I was really hoping I might be able to . . .'

'Belinda has a cuttings file on the Jennings case,' a man's voice behind me said.

I swung round and found myself looking into an angular face and a pair of hazel eyes. From the checked shirt he was wearing I knew instantly he was the man I'd seen in the partitioned-off office, whom I'd assumed was the chief reporter, but clearly wasn't. Besides the shirt, he was wearing brown denim jeans and trainers – the reason I hadn't heard him come up behind me as the soft soles had made no sound on the carpeted floor.

'Oh, but I don't know that we should . . .' The girl receptionist's mouth had tightened disapprovingly.

'Where's the harm? It's all published material. Nothing more or less than could be found on the microfiche. And it looks to me as if this young lady doesn't want to be walking any further than she has to.' He indicated my crutches and flashed me a grin.

'That's hardly the point,' the girl said crisply.

'Oh, lighten up, Tara!' He grinned at me again. 'Come with me and I'll sort you out.'

The phone on the reception desk was ringing again.

'On your head be it,' Tara said grimly and turned away to answer it, effectively distancing herself from what was going on on our side of the desk.

The young man led the way between the work stations towards the portioned-off office and I followed, swinging on my crutches, something I'd become proficient at by now, though the calluses on the palms of my hands were testament to the chafing it had inflicted on them.

The office was small but uncluttered, the desk clear but for the computer, a notepad and a pot of pens and pencils. Files were stacked neatly on shelves and a large calendar, a clock and a corkboard adorned the walls. The only jarring feature was a table at the rear of the office on which a number of photographs had been spread out haphazardly.

'This is very kind of you,' I said inadequately.

'Consider it part of the service.' The young man was running his finger along a row of box files, all neatly labelled. 'I'm Josh Williams, by the way. And in case you're wondering, I'm a staff photographer.'

'Oh right.' That would explain his cavalier attitude – and also his easy charm.

'And you are . . .?'

'Sally . . .' I almost said Sally Proctor, but caught myself it time. 'Sally Jacobs,' I said, and immediately felt guilty for the deception.

'Here we are.' Josh Williams pulled out a box file, placed it on the desk and rifled through, extracting a purple folder.

'Belinda likes to keep files of important local stories for easy reference,' he explained, 'and this one seems to run and run. Pretty well everything we've ever printed about the Brian Jennings case should be here – and a few more bits and bobs besides, I shouldn't wonder. Belinda's hot stuff as a chief reporter. Not much gets past her.'

Certainly the file was encouragingly fat.

Josh Williams pulled out the chair – a high-backed, comfortable-looking swivel covered in brown faux leather – from the well in the desk.

'Will this be all right for you, or would you prefer an ordinary upright?'

'This will be fine.' I lowered myself into it, glad to take the weight off my leg.

'You look as though you've been in the wars,' Josh said conversationally.

'Skiing accident.' I pulled a rueful face. 'You don't want to know.'

'Skiing, eh? Never done it myself. A group used to go every year from my school but my parents didn't have that sort of money to throw around.'

'It's not that expensive a holiday,' I said, a bit defensively. 'And it's terrific fun.'

He cocked an eyebrow. 'Yes, I can see that,' he said, his tone heavy with irony. 'But I think I'll stick to sailing in Greece, thanks all the same. That's what I call a holiday. Anyway,' he tapped the purple folder, 'I'll leave you to it. I'm off to take some pictures of a couple who are celebrating their diamond wedding. Sixty years – can you imagine it? When you've finished just leave the file on the desk. I'll put it away when I get back. Keep Belinda happy.'

He reached for a leather bomber jacket that was hanging on a hook on the back of the door and shrugged into it.

'If you need anything, just ask Tara, Her bark is worse than her bite.'

'I'll believe you.'

'Honestly. She's only been here a couple of weeks, and she's very much in awe of Belinda. Don't take any crap from her and you'll have her eating out of your hand.'

'Hmm.' I could well imagine Josh could wind the redoubtable receptionist around his little finger – he was a very likeable character. Whether I could do the same I rather doubted. And I had not the slightest intention of pushing my luck.

When he'd gone, closing the door after him, I opened the purple file on the desk in front of me, glad that the plasterboard meant I was now out of sight of the receptionist. With her suspicious gaze on me I would have found it difficult to concentrate and I suspected the other girls working in the outer office would probably have me under surveillance too. As a journalist myself my skin should be thick enough to work despite it, another sign I was going soft. But perhaps that wasn't such a bad thing. Sometimes in the past I'd taken a good hard look at myself, the professional trying to piece together stories that often exposed vulnerable people to the glare of publicity, and not much liked what I'd seen. But this was different. It might well be a chance to right a wrong. The idea of becoming a crusader buoyed me up again, adding to the excitement that always went with starting on a new and juicy assignment and I felt alive for the first time in months. With a sense of anticipation I slid the wodge of cuttings out of the file.

Belinda Jones was obviously as methodical in her filing as she was meticulous about the tidiness of her office. The cuttings were all in date order, with the latest ones, relating to Brian Jennings's sister's efforts to clear his name, on top. Since that was the end of the story so far, and because Belinda's interviews with her were a reiteration of what I already knew, I turned the whole pile of cuttings over and started working from back to front. Soon I was totally engrossed.

The reports of the fire had apparently been front page news, the banner headline 'GIRLS ESCAPE BLAZE – LUCKY

TO BE ALIVE' appeared directly below the stylized title of the newspaper – the *Stoke Compton Gazette*. The story confirmed what Mum had told me, that the fire had taken hold in the early hours of the morning when the two girls who shared the flat above the electrical goods shop were asleep in bed. The alarm had been raised by a Paul Holder, who was on his way to start an early shift at the bakery further down the street, but by the time the fire brigade arrived the shop was an inferno. The two girls had been trapped in their upstairs flat, but, thankfully, the baker had found a ladder which was being used for repainting the windows at the rear of the bakery and rescued them. Though shocked and suffering from some smoke inhalation they were otherwise unharmed, though both had been taken to hospital and were still being kept in for observation.

The girls were named as Dawn Burridge and Lisa Curry, and there were photographs of both of them, clearly taken in happier times, before their ordeal. Dawn was an exceptionally pretty girl with dark shoulder-length hair that tumbled in waves and curls about a heart-shaped face. She was a leading light in the Stoke Compton Players, the report said, and there was an additional photograph, apparently reproduced from an earlier edition of the Gazette, showing her appearing as principal girl in their annual pantomime. She had been deputy head girl at her school, and worked for a local estate agent. All in all it was easy to see that she was just the kind of girl who would attract admirers without even trying.

Her friend and flatmate, Lisa Curry, was apparently a sous chef at Compton Grange, a rather expensive country hotel a few miles outside Stoke Compton. She was less striking than Dawn, with a round, rather plain face and hair that was either cropped short or pulled back into a ponytail, from the picture it was impossible to tell which. She was also several years older – twenty-three to Dawn's twenty. She had been active in the local ATC as a teenager, but was no longer a member. The antisocial hours her job entailed had put an end to that, I surmised.

The first mention of Brian Jennings was in a cutting dated a few weeks later, though as yet no names were named. 'Police have arrested a local man in connection with the suspected arson attack in the town High Street,' the report read. It then went on to regurgitate much of what I had read before, adding that the two girls who had been victims of the blaze had made a good recovery, but that Dawn, shaken by what had happened, had decided to leave the town and return to her parents' home in Dorset.

With hindsight it was easy to understand. She would have already known what was only to emerge publicly at a later stage – that the fire had been deliberately started by the weirdo who had been stalking her. She must have been totally spooked by his unwanted attention, and realizing he was capable of trying to burn her in her bed when she rejected him would have been the last straw.

I flipped back to the next cutting – a brief mention of Brian Jennings' first appearance in court – not a lot to go on there – and then found the much meatier report, some nine months later, of the actual trial.

As Mum had said, the evidence against him was damning.

Without a doubt, he had been obsessed with Dawn. When police searched his flat they had found, amongst other things, a horde of photographs of her that he had clearly taken without her knowledge by means of a telescopic lens, programmes, posters and newspaper cuttings relating to her appearances with the Stoke Compton Players, a pair of her briefs, presumably stolen from her washing line, a cigarette butt stained with her lipstick which he had apparently taken from a pub ashtray, and a journal recording his sightings of her, together with disgustingly explicit descriptions of his fantasies concerning her. Dawn had given evidence of his persistence – how she could scarcely move but he was there, behind her, and that was backed up by a number of her friends.

There was evidence from a couple of witnesses that they had seen him hanging about in the High Street on the night of the fire, and, most damning of all, the police evidence of traces of petrol found in the pocket of his jacket.

The fire had been his way of getting revenge when Dawn continued to spurn him, the prosecution had claimed. In the end, as Mum had said, it seemed to have come down to a case of 'if I can't have you, no one will.'

The case for the defence, by contrast, was pathetically weak. Brian Jennings had no real alibi for the night of the fire, and his explanation of the petrol traces found in the pocket of his jacket – that he'd filled a can with petrol at a local garage for his sister's lawnmower and wiped his hands on his handkerchief after spilling some – had cut no ice with the jury. He had been found guilty unanimously, and received a lengthy prison sentence.

'You are a scheming and dangerous man,' the judge told him. 'I have no hesitation in committing you to a place where you can no longer endanger the public for the maximum time the law allows.'

I shook my head, a bit deflated by the open-and-shut nature of the case. Really, there seemed no holes in it at all. There was no doubt that Brian Jennings had been obsessed by Dawn Burridge, and entirely believable that she had rejected him utterly. His photograph showed a pasty-faced man with lank, greasy hair who, judging by the folds of flesh around his neck, was probably also unfit and overweight. There was no way the stunningly attractive Dawn would have given him a second glance. And with the dark side to his nature revealed by the cache in his flat, it was easy to imagine how that adoration could have turned to blind hatred and the desire for revenge when perhaps she slighted him once too often.

And yet, in a funny sort of way, it was almost too convenient. Was it possible that in fact the circumstantial evidence had led to the wrong conclusion? Had someone else entirely been the arsonist – someone who had escaped scot free? Was Brian Jennings innocent as his sister claimed? Unlikely, I had to admit, but the bit was between my teeth now, and I was determined to try to find out.

Three

'So how did you get on?' Mum asked, pulling back into the stream of High Street traffic.

The two hours since she dropped me off had sped by; when I'd glanced up at the wall clock in the *Gazette* office I was shocked to see that I had only five minutes before she was due to pick me up again.

I'd packed Belinda's file together and left in on the desk as Josh, the photographer, had said I should, hoping he wasn't going to get his nose bitten off for allowing me access to it. But I suspected he was well capable of taking care of himself, especially where a female was concerned, even one as feisty as a chief reporter probably was, and wouldn't care much about her disapproval in any case. In my experience photographers were a law unto themselves more often than not.

I thanked the receptionist on my way out, but got only a frosty nod in return. Well, I could handle that. Thanks to Josh Williams I was now pretty well up to speed on the background to the story. But I was doubtful as to how much more help I could expect from the staff of the *Gazette*. Belinda Jones might well turn out to be as uncooperative as the tight-lipped receptionist.

I'd only been waiting a couple of minutes when Mum drove down the High Street. There were no spaces in the lay-by now, so she double-parked for the time it took me to load my crutches into the back seat of the car and climb into the front. Then, as she pulled away, I told her what had happened.

'I've got sheafs of info,' I said, tapping the notebook which lay on my lap. 'But you were right, it does look like an open and shut case.'

'Most local people thought so,' Mum agreed. 'But then, they would, wouldn't they? It's much more comforting to think a strange character like Brian Jennings went a bit peculiar than it is to wonder if there's a pyromaniac wandering the streets.

At least with him locked up people could feel safe in their beds. But . . .' She shook her head.

'But what?' I asked.

Mum slowed down to join the queue waiting at the traffic lights at the end of the High Street. 'Well . . .' She hesitated. 'Since she started her campaign I must admit I've sometimes wondered whether it wasn't all a bit convenient, having someone like him who made the perfect scapegoat. I mean . . . I do trust the police, of course I do. It's come to something if you can't. But with all this business of them having to meet clear-up rates for crime and that sort of thing, and him being such an easy target . . .'

I nodded thoughtfully. 'I know. I must say I feel the same. And whatever, it's a cracking story.'

The lights had changed to green; the traffic was moving again.

'So what's your next step going to be?' Mum asked as we cleared the junction.

'Well – go and see Marion Jennings,' I said. 'Get her side of it. If I can persuade Dad to lend me his car, or *someone else* to give me a lift . . .' I cast her a sneaky sideways look and grinned pleadingly.

The corners of Mum's mouth twitched.

'Oh, I expect you'll get lucky one way or another.'

'I don't want to let this go, Mum,' I said, serious again. 'It's so good to have something to get my teeth into. You and Dad have been great, but to be honest, I've been going quietly mad.'

'Understandably! Two old fogies like us . . .'

'You are not old fogies!'

'That's a matter of opinion. But seriously, Sally, you've had a pretty rough time. And that boyfriend of yours has been no help at all.'

'It's difficult for him, with his job . . .' I didn't really know why I was making excuses for Tim.

It was, of course, perfectly true that the demands of being a pilot meant strange working hours and periods of being out of the country, but that in turn meant he often had several days off at a stretch. Yet in all the time I'd been at Stoke

Compton he'd only been to stay two or three times and made a few fleeting visits. Recently, when he'd arranged to come over something always seemed to crop up at the last moment to prevent him from coming. An unexpected call to duty, a problem with his car, a heavy cold or flu.

Given that prior to my accident the gilt had gone off the gingerbread where our relationship was concerned and I'd begun to wonder if Tim was the one for me, I'd been ridiculously upset by his inattention. Looking back now I can see that it was probably all part of the depression that had slowly but surely closed in around me. I was isolated – some days I saw no one but Mum, Dad, and old Sam, Dad's pretty well monosyllabic farm hand – incapacitated, and bereft of all the things that used to make up my busy life. Apart from visits from my oldest friend, Rachel Parsons, who still lived in Stoke Compton, seeing Tim was about the only thing I had to look forward to. He was my link to the world beyond the comfortable but boring and predictable hours that my days now consisted of. It was the only explanation for me desperately hanging on to a relationship that I knew in my heart had run its course, and probably the reason I was making excuses for him now, to Mum – and to myself.

'It's a long way for him to come and see me,' I said now, lamely. 'Thirty miles each way . . . when he has start times in the middle of the night . . . I can't expect him to do it.'

'Hmm.' Mum's lips made a tight line.

'What?'

'If he thought anything of you he'd find a way. I'm sorry, Sally, I know it's not what you want to hear, but it's my opinion you deserve better. You should kick him into the long grass once and for all and find someone who treats you properly.'

I pulled a wry face.

'Easier said than done. I'm not twenty any more – or even thirty. Most of the eligible men out there have been snapped up, and the ones of my age come with a lot of baggage.'

'You're a lovely girl, Sally!'

'You would say that. You're my mother.'

'It's no more than the truth. You're pretty . . .'

'Have you noticed the crow's feet round my eyes?'

'You're bright and kind,' she went on as if I hadn't spoken. 'Don't try to tell me that there isn't someone out there who would treat you a whole lot better than Tim does.'

'Oh Mum . . .'

''I'm saying no more on the subject.' Mum checked her mirror, overtook a removals van that was taking up most of our side of the road. 'Just don't put all your eggs in one basket, is my advice.'

'Did you say that it was one of the girls who lived in the flat who has a café now in what used to be the electricals shop?' I asked, anxious to change the subject.

'That's right,' Mum confirmed.

'Do you know which one? No – hang on, I think I can answer that myself. The one Brian Jennings was stalking worked in an estate agent's office, but her flatmate was apparently a chef.' I flicked open my note book, checking. 'Lisa Curry.'

'I really wouldn't know,' Mum said. 'I'm not one for stopping for a cup of coffee and a bun in the middle of my shopping.'

'No.' I smiled. Socializing in High Street cafes wasn't Mum's style, and in any case the cake tins at home were always full of delicious cakes she'd baked herself. Mum's Victoria sandwiches and rich fruit cakes were to die for.

'If I'd finished at the newspaper offices in time I'd have popped in for a coffee myself,' I said.

Mum sucked in breath over her lip.

'I wouldn't think she'd want to start talking about the fire when she's got a café full of people.'

'Maybe not, but I shall definitely want to speak to her sometime, get her take on what happened,' I said 'I need to find Dawn Burridge too. One of the newspaper reports said she'd gone home to Dorset, but I suppose it's possible that once the trial was over and Brian Jennings locked up she might have come back. Her job was here, after all.'

'I really couldn't say, Sally. But it's five years ago, remember, since it all happened. She's probably married with a family.'

'Maybe. Is Lisa? Married, I mean?'

'It's no good asking me, Sally. I don't know anything about them really. I'm not going to be much help to you, I'm afraid.'

'Never mind. I can find out.'

My journalistic juices were running, my head full of the story. For the moment I'd forgotten all about Tim.

Which was really just as well since I had a nasty feeling he'd forgotten all about me too.

I spent the afternoon sorting the notes I'd made and organizing them on to Dad's computer. He'd finished working on his accounts now, the relief evident when he came down for a scratch lunch of bread, cheese and one of his favourite boiled onions – well, microwaved, to be more accurate, but the result was much the same.

'Well that's the paperwork brought up to date,' he said, wiping his hands on the seat of his baggy cords as if they'd been soiled by contact with bills and catalogues. 'The computer's yours now if you want it, Sally. Just as long as you don't mess up what I've done.'

'I won't, don't worry. I shan't go anywhere near your accounts. I just wish I had my laptop,' I added.

But of course, I didn't, because, strictly speaking, it wasn't mine. It belonged to my newspaper. I'd had to leave it at the office when I went off on the skiing holiday and there it had been ever since, being used, I presumed, by whoever was doing my job in my absence.

'Actually I think I might treat myself to one,' I said, and wondered why I hadn't done so before. It would certainly have gone some way to easing my boredom if I'd been able to surf the net, and it was a measure of the depression that had descended on me these last months that I hadn't stirred myself to get a computer of my own. I had, of course, access to the Internet on my phone, but the 3G signal I could get in the countryside was so poor as to be useless in comparison to what was available at home.

I saw Mum and Dad exchanging satisfied glances.

'This is doing you the world of good, Sally,' Mum said, and I had to agree.

When I'd finished typing up my notes and transferred them on to a memory stick Dad lent me I started preparing a list of how I was going to proceed.

Top of the list, as I'd said to Mum, was paying a visit to Brian Jennings's sister, Marion. Mum told me she lived in Newcombe, a village just a few miles from Stoke Compton. I found her address and telephone number in the phone book and added it to my notes. Since she was campaigning to try to prove her brother's innocence I hoped she would be glad enough of my help to share with me whatever information she had, including the name of Brian's solicitor. It was my hope that he too would welcome any publicity I might be able to generate, and perhaps take me on board as an extra investigator who might be able to learn something to strengthen his client's case.

Number two on my list was talking to Lisa Curry and Dawn Burridge. They might be convinced that the arsonist who had almost cost them their lives was behind bars, of course. But they might also be able to tell me something that would give me an alternative explanation for what had happened.

I went on to transcribe the notes I'd made from the newspaper cuttings – the names that had come up as witnesses when the case went to court, and the people who had been mentioned in the press reports – Paul Holder, the baker who had first spotted the fire and rescued the two girls, the captain of the fire brigade, the tenants of neighbouring flats. As something of a long shot I included the girls' employers at the time – the country house hotel where Lisa had been a sous chef and the estate agent's office where Dawn had worked. I didn't hold out much hope that the hotel employees would be the same ones now as had been working there two years ago – it was my impression kitchen staff moved about pretty frequently. But estate agencies were a different matter. Staff often stayed with the same firm for a very long time. Two years would be nothing in their world.

Now that I had the use of the computer I took the opportunity of looking the girls up on Facebook but I couldn't find either of them. Chances were, then, that they were married and would be using their new names. Or perhaps after her experience of being stalked by Brian Jennings, Dawn wanted to keep a low profile. I did find a page for Muffins, Lisa's teashop, but it wasn't very informative, just a picture of the cheerfully decorated interior and another showing a display of scrummy-looking cupcakes.

My scrutiny of the web was interrupted when the telephone on Dad's desk began ringing. I didn't answer it, as I didn't imagine it would be for me, and I knew Mum would pick up in the kitchen. She did, but a moment later she was calling through: 'Sally – it's for you! It's Rachel.'

As I think I mentioned earlier, Rachel is one of my oldest friends. We met on our first day at primary school, two little girls trying very hard to be brave and grown up when we actually both felt rather lonely and lost, and the bond we formed then had lasted. We sat beside one another on the same work table each year, we went to one another's birthday parties and spent time in one another's homes. I'd loved having Rachel for sleepovers, and even better was when I got to stay with her. She had an older sister and she lived on a new estate in Stoke Compton where there were other children to play with – a real treat for me, an only child whose home was a couple of miles out of town. Rachel, of course, loved coming to the farm because of the hens, the ducks and the baby animals, not to mention the barn where we could hide behind the bales of hay and make believe we were just about anywhere we wanted.

When we moved on to 'big school' – the local comprehensive – we stayed friends. Homework and holidays, first dates and heartaches, we shared them all. Even after we left school we remained close for quite some time, keeping in touch by letter and phone calls – and later emails and texts – and meeting up when I was at home. But life was taking us in different directions; I landed my dream job with the regional daily and moved away, while Hannah stayed in Stoke Compton, working as a cashier with one of the banks. I had my own flat in town; she remained living with her parents. And then she got together with Steve Brice, and for the first time in almost twenty years a chasm opened up between us. I was happy for her, of course I was – she'd had a crush on Steve for as long as I could remember – and when he asked her out she wrote excited letters filling me in on every detail of their burgeoning romance. But as their relationship progressed from the casual to the committed she wrote less and less often and volunteered less and less information. I understood that what she and Steve were sharing was too private now to be reported on in girlie letters, but I missed our former closeness all the same.

I was chief bridesmaid at her wedding, organizing her hen party, shepherding the small attendants up the aisle and somehow managing to keep them from treading on her flowing train, and holding her bouquet while she made her vows. But not so long afterwards, Rachel was not only a wife but also a mother. A baby girl, born just eleven months after her wedding day, was followed within two years by twins and this meant her time was fully occupied and we had even less in common. Apart from Christmas, Easter and little Megan's birthday – I was her godmother – I rarely saw Rachel.

Since I'd been at home convalescing, though, Rachel had turned up trumps. Though she was incredibly busy, working part-time as well as being a mum to her growing brood and all that entailed, she'd somehow managed to phone regularly as well as come and see me,

'How are you doing, Sal?' she asked now.

'I'm fine.' I wasn't in the habit of taking such questions literally. 'And you?'

'The same. Hey, listen, the reason I'm ringing is to see if you fancy a night out? 'Steve's offered to babysit, and there's a special promotion on at Ricardo's – pizza and a glass of wine for ten pounds. What do you think?'

'Sounds good to me,' I said. Ricardo's is a trattoria and wine bar in Porton, our nearest big town; they do the most delicious pizzas and the lovely Italian waiters who make a tremendous fuss of us whenever we eat there gave it a holiday atmosphere – if it weren't for the damp and cold outside you could almost believe you were living it up in some balmy foreign resort.

'I'll pick you up then – about seven?' I could hear children's voices clamouring in the background. 'Oh, Alistair – no! I'm on the telephone!' Rachel exclaimed, exasperated. And to me: 'I'll have to go, Sally. Alistair's knocked over Abigail's poster paints . . .'

'OK – go!' I said good-humouredly. 'I'll see you later.'

'Yes, with bright blue hands, I expect. Children!'

But she loved being a mum, I knew, and I envied her that, though I wasn't at all sure how I'd cope given the same situation.

I put down the phone, reached for my crutches, propped up within easy reach, and went through to the kitchen.

'Don't cook for me tonight, Mum,' I said. 'I'm going out on the razzle with Rachel.'

'That's nice.' Mum looked pleased for me, and I was feeling pleased for myself.

Taken all round, this was turning out to be rather a good day.

Four

Rachel arrived, a little harassed, at about twenty past seven.

'Sorry I'm late, Sally. You know how it is . . .'

'Don't worry about it.' As she ran a distracted hand through her hair I could see she did indeed have traces of bright blue paint ingrained around her cuticles, and I smiled to myself. 'I'm just glad you could get away at all.'

'Me too. It will be heaven to eat a meal I haven't had to cook myself. There's only so much cottage pie and macaroni cheese I can take.'

'I must admit I'm looking forward to a pizza myself,' I said. 'Mum's a wonderful cook but it's all good old-fashioned casseroles and roasts. What with the way she's been feeding me and no exercise to speak of I must have put on a good half stone!'

'You still look fine to me.'

'Hmm – a matter of opinion. I'm dreading getting back on the scales.'

It's about half an hour's drive from the farm into Porton, but we didn't talk much on the way. Rachel is something of a nervous driver, especially in the dark, which makes me nervous too. She's prone to waiting at roundabouts and junctions when there's no need and then going when she shouldn't, so she was busy concentrating hard and I was reluctant to say anything to distract her.

She did begin to tell me she was rather worried about her sister, Becky, who had, it seemed, recently split up with her husband, but I gently suggested she wait until we were in the wine bar when we could talk more easily.

We never did get around to it, though, because by the time she'd let me out outside Ricardo's – I couldn't open the door myself because of the childproof locks on the inside – and she'd gone off to find somewhere to park and then rejoined me, she was far more concerned about the fact that she'd managed to scrape her wing mirror while trying to manoeuvre into a bay in the multi-storey car park.

'I was so worried I might clip somebody else's car I didn't notice I was too close to the pillar!' she groaned. 'Steve's going to kill me.'

'Is it just the mirror?' I was feeling horribly responsible – if it weren't for me it wouldn't have happened.

'Yes, but you know what Steve's like about the car . . . Oh shoot! How could I be so stupid?'

'I'm sure it's not nearly as bad as you think,' I said. 'Come on, choose your pizza and try to forget about it.'

Ricardo, attentive as ever, had already put little dishes of olives, bread and dipping oil on the table, and I was enjoying a big glass of red wine. Rachel ordered a spritzer, we debated the relative merits of the huge selection of pizza toppings, and then settled back on the leather banquette.

'So, what have you been up to since I saw you last?' Rachel asked, a good deal calmer now. 'No – don't tell me . . . you've been bored silly.'

'Actually no,' I said. 'I've got myself a project.'

'A project. Oh – not a calf! You haven't got a baby at home to bottle feed, have you? Because if you have you can send him over to me.'

I laughed. 'I'd have thought you had quite enough to do already! But no, it's not a calf. It's work . . . sort of. A story I'm following up on.'

'Tell me more,' Rachel said. 'I thought you said nothing ever happens in Stoke Compton that's worth writing about.'

'It did, though, didn't it – five years ago. The big fire in the High Street.'

'Well, yes, but surely that's old news?' Rachel sipped her spritzer. 'The weirdo that did it was caught and convicted. He's in prison, isn't he?'

'But his sister is convinced he's innocent and I thought . . . oh, I might be flogging a dead horse, of course, but miscarriages of justice do happen. Wouldn't it be fantastic if I could find something out that meant the whole case had to be reopened?'

Rachel looked doubtful.

'I don't know how you'll manage that. Surely if there'd been anything to find out the police would have been on to it?'

'They had Brian Jennings, didn't they? An easy target. Just the sort of person everyone would like to believe was responsible, and not really bright enough to be able to defend himself, from what I gather. Once he was in the frame I bet they didn't look any further. A good result for their crime statistics.'

'He was obsessed with Dawn Burridge,' Rachel argued. 'They found dozens of photographs of her in his flat. And there was the evidence about the petrol, too, wasn't there?'

'Traces in his pocket, yes. But he said he'd bought petrol for his sister's lawn mower and she backed him up. It's all circumstantial, Rachel.'

'Hmm.' Rachel looked unconvinced. She dipped a chunk of ciabatta into the aromatic oil.

'So, Miss Marple, how are you going to beat the police at their own game?'

'Well, to begin with, I'm going to talk to everyone concerned. Brian Jennings' sister, maybe Brian himself . . .'

'You're going to visit him in prison?'

'If I can.'

'Rather you than me!'

'But first I want to talk to Lisa Curry and Dawn Burridge – see if there was anyone they'd upset who might have wished them harm.'

'Surely they'd have told the police at the time if they'd suspected anything like that?' Rachel said.

'Maybe they did. But Brian Jennings was an easier target. Or maybe they were too shocked to think straight. Then, when Jennings was arrested, they assumed, like everyone else, that it must have been him.' I speared an olive and popped it into my mouth, chewing on it thoughtfully. 'Do you know them at all?'

'Lisa and Dawn?' Rachel shook her head. 'No, not really. I think Lisa went to our school, but . . .'

'Did she?' I said, surprised. 'I don't remember anyone of that name.'

'Well, you wouldn't, would you? She'd have been several years below us, and you don't notice the ones who are younger than you. I don't remember her either. But when she and Dawn were in the news, Becky – my sister – said Lisa was in her year.'

'Really?' I sat forward, interested.

'They weren't friends or anything. I don't think Becky liked her much.'

So, no hope of an introduction there, then.

'And Dawn's not from round here, is she? According to the newspaper reports she went home to Dorset after the fire.' I frowned. 'Strange, though. Why would she come here in the first place?'

'For her job, I suppose,' Rachel said reasonably. 'She worked at Compton Properties, the estate agent's in the Square.'

'I know . . . but why *here*? I wouldn't have thought there'd be much about Stoke Compton to attract a girl from Dorset. If she wanted a change of scenery, I'd have thought she'd have headed for somewhere with a bit more life.'

The pizzas arrived, bubbling tomato, cheese and anchovies on thin, crispy crusts, and for a few minutes we were too busy eating to talk.

'I'm just going to have to drop into the café and try to get talking to Lisa,' I said between mouthfuls. 'Hopefully she'll be able to give me an address for Dawn too.' A thought struck me. 'I suppose it's possible she might have come back to the area when the trial and everything was over and she'd had time to get over what happened. Presumably she had other friends here besides Lisa – a boyfriend, even. That might have been the reason she came here in the first place. In time being with him would take precedence over her unpleasant memories of what happened with Brian Jennings, wouldn't it?'

'I suppose . . .'

'Well, *Lisa* certainly seems to have been able to put it all behind her,' I went on. 'The café is in the very place where the fire started. I do find that a bit surprising. I wouldn't have thought she'd be comfortable with that at all.'

'Lisa is a pretty tough nut, according to Becky,' Rachel said. 'My guess is she saw an opportunity and took it. Properties on the High Street don't fall vacant very often. And of course, the fire would have very different connotations for her, too. Quite apart from the fact that it was Dawn who was the target for the attack, and not her, the whole episode must have something of an aura of romance for her.'

'Why?' I asked, the last forkful of pizza poised halfway between my plate and my mouth.

Rachel cocked me a look.

'She married the baker who rescued her. There is something pretty romantic about that, you must agree. The hero and the damsel in distress, getting together and living happily ever after. It's like something out of a fairy story.'

'Mm.' I nodded, feeling rather pleased about this unexpected twist. Even if my efforts to find a fresh suspect for the fire-raising came to nothing, there should at least be a feel-good feature in the story of Lisa and her baker.

'Talking of happy ever afters, how are things going with Tim?' Rachel asked.

'You haven't mentioned him lately.'

I shrugged. 'Nothing to say, really. Actually I don't think it's "going" anywhere.'

'Oh Sally.'

'And I'm not at all sure I want it to.' It was the first time I'd actually said it out loud to anyone.

'In that case best call it a day. I can thoroughly recommend married life, but not if it's with someone you don't want to be with one hundred per cent. That's a recipe for disaster. Besides which, you're just wasting time when you could be meeting someone else. The love of your life.'

'Like I've had the chance to meet anyone this last year!'

'True. But you're well on the road to recovery now. If you don't think he's the one you want, tell him so.'

It was almost an echo of what Mum had said, but I didn't want to think about it right now.

Rachel glanced at her watch.

'Look, I'm sorry to bring this party to an end, but I don't really want to be too much longer. I've got to be up early in the morning.' She grimaced. 'And I've got to face telling Steve I've scraped his wing mirror . . .'

'Oh Rach, he'll be fine about it, I'm sure.'

'Hmm, I wish I was! I'm going to be in the doghouse and no mistake.' She signalled the waiter for the bill.

'This is on me,' I said.

'Oh Sal, no!'

'Yes. Fair's fair. You drove. I'll get the bill.'

'Well, if you insist. Thank you.' She slipped into her jacket. 'I'll get the car. Be outside in – say – ten?'

'I'll be there.' I grinned wickedly. 'And don't hit any more pillars.'

She raised her eyes heavenward, mimed an exaggerated shiver, then headed for the door.

I took some notes from my purse and laid them on the silver dish the waiter had provided along with a tip, then settled back in my chair with one eye on my watch and one on the road outside in case Rachel was quicker than she expected. But soon my mind was wandering as I thought over what Rachel had told me about Lisa Curry. I hadn't realized she was local, and it opened up a whole new way of looking at what had happened, supposing that Brian Jennings had been wrongly convicted.

If he hadn't started the fire and if it hadn't been an accident or the work of yobs, then whoever was responsible must have had a motive. So far, I'd been thinking of Dawn as the intended victim, but it could just as easily have been Lisa. From what Rachel had said, I'd got the impression she might not be a very nice person.

A sharp toot attracted my attention and I came back to earth with a jolt, feeling horribly guilty. Rachel had pulled up outside and I hadn't noticed; by the light of the street lamps I could see her leaning over, peering anxiously into the trattoria looking for me.

I struggled to my feet, grabbed my crutches and headed for the door as fast as I could. The waiter was there before me, holding it open, and I swung out on to the pavement.

'Sorry, Rach!' I apologized as I slid into the passenger seat.

'Not to worry. At least there aren't any traffic wardens about at this time of night.' She grinned, letting in the clutch and moving off with a bit of a jolt. 'I'd hate to have to tell Steve I've been done for parking too!'

'You weren't parked,' I pointed out.

'Well, obstruction, then. Come on, missus, let's head for home.'

Though it was after ten by the time Rachel dropped me off, lights were still burning at the downstairs windows, small, warm oases in the dark shadow that was the rambling old farmhouse. I was quite surprised – given how early they had to get up, Mum and Dad liked to be early to bed too, and though she usually left a hall light on for me, Mum almost always turned off the ones in the kitchen and living room. She didn't like wasting electricity, and when anyone entered the farmyard the security lights came on, making it bright as day. They were blazing out now, illuminating the barn and outbuildings, and throwing dark contrasting shadows across the cobbles. As the car turned in, Scrumpy, the collie who followed Dad every-where by day but slept at night in her kennel, set up a frenzied barking and I called to her softly to let her know I wasn't an intruder.

Rachel waited for me to make it to the door, doing a three-point – or, more accurately, a six-point – turn while I fitted my key into the lock. Then, when I turned and gave her a wave, she drove off. I stood for a moment watching her tail lights disappear down the track, and breathing in the cool night air, still faintly scented with the unmistakable smell of home.

In summer that smell could be overpowering at times – slurry and manure, the sweet aroma of silage, all mingling with the heady perfume of the honeysuckle that grew like a weed over the front door. The smells were fainter now in early spring, but still easily detectable as they rose from the damp earth and the clots of mud left by the tractor and the array of boots abandoned in the porch. Somewhere in the darkness an owl hooted, a low, eerie call that pierced the night and floated on silent wings above the fields beyond the barn. For some reason it made me feel sad, though perhaps sad is not quite the right word. Nostalgic, maybe, brushing against half-forgotten memories and making me ache for a time when life had been sweet and simple.

'Is that you, Sally?'

Mum's voice from inside the house snapped me out of my reverie.

'Yes, I'm home,' I called back, stepping inside and closing the door.

Mum was in the kitchen doorway, a mug of hot chocolate cupped between her hands. She was in her dressing gown, ready for bed, and again the nostalgia nudged me. She'd had that dressing gown as long as I could remember – no-nonsense dark grey wool with a sash that tied around her middle so that she resembled a sack of potatoes. One Christmas Dad had bought her a crimson velvet one – I'd gone with him to help him choose it – but she'd hardly ever worn it. The grey wool was warmer, and 'comfy' she said – a bit like Mum, I thought.

'I didn't expect you to still be up,' I said.

'I thought I'd wait until you got in.' Mum headed back to the kitchen and I followed her. 'Do you want a hot drink? Cocoa? Ovaltine?'

I couldn't face the thought of anything milky on top of pizza and wine.

'Maybe a cup of tea. It's OK – I can make it.'

'No, you sit down. You don't want to overdo things.'

'I'm not.' But Mum was already bustling to fill the kettle and I gave in with a sigh. Actually I did feel pretty tired now and my leg was aching quite badly.

'Did you have a good time?' Mum asked, popping a tea bag into a mug.

'Yes. It's a nice place, that trattoria. Rachel had a bit of a disaster, though. She managed to bash the wing mirror on the car, and she's worried to death about telling Steve.'

'Oh dear, poor Rachel. She's not much of a driver, is she? Didn't she lose her bumper not so long ago?'

'In the supermarket car park, yes. She went up over the kerb and got it stuck. She is a bit accident prone. But at least she hasn't killed anybody.'

The kettle was boiling; Mum made my tea and put it on a leather coaster on the table in front of me.

'Here you are.'

'Thanks, Mum.'

'Now – the reason I stayed up.' Mum sat down opposite me. 'Tim phoned.'

My heart should have leapt with pleasure. Instead it sank.

'Ah. And I wasn't here. I don't suppose he was very pleased about that.'

'He did sound a bit short,' Mum conceded. 'But then he always does. Either that, or patronizing. I don't think I'm quite good enough for him.'

'Oh Mum! I never heard such rubbish!'

'Hmm . . . I'm not so sure,' Mum said archly. 'He does like the high life and all that goes with it . . .' She smiled at her unintentional pun. 'Oh, you know what I mean, Sally.'

I said nothing. I did know what she meant. Sometimes I thought it was the glamour of his job that Tim liked more than the actual flying – he often complained about the tedium of computerized flights, but he wouldn't give up the perks of being a captain of a scheduled flight to go back to flying the mail or tutoring pupils at a flying school. The gold braid on his shoulders and the admiration of the passengers meant too much to him. And perhaps he had developed an exaggerated opinion of his own importance that made him look down on the simple life my parents led.

'Anyway,' Mum went on, 'he said he's coming to see you tomorrow. Asked me to tell you.'

'Oh! Just like that! And why didn't he call me on my mobile?' For some reason, I was thoroughly affronted. How dare Tim assume he could neglect me for weeks on end and then expect me to be at his beck and call when he deigned to fit me into his busy schedule without even bothering to make another call to speak to me.

'I'm only repeating what he said.' Mum didn't actually sniff, but her disapproval didn't escape me, all the same. 'He'll be here about ten. Apparently he's rostered for an evening flight to Tenerife.'

'Honestly, he's the limit!' I snapped. 'I suppose he thinks I've got nothing better to do, and he couldn't be more wrong.'

Mum raised an eyebrow at me and though she said nothing, the look she gave me spoke volumes.

'I know, I know,' I muttered.

'I'm off to bed then.' Mum rinsed her mug under the tap and loaded it into the dishwasher. 'Your dad says he can never settle properly until I come up.'

'Yes, right.' I grinned. I'd heard Dad's snoring often enough when Mum was still downstairs finishing up in the kitchen.

'You shouldn't be too long either. You don't want to overdo things. And just be careful on the stairs.'

'I will.' But I'd become pretty adept at hauling myself up with one crutch and the banister to support me. 'I'll just finish my tea and then I'll call it a day. I am pretty tired.'

'Night, then, love.'

'Night, Mum.'

After she'd gone I remained sitting at the kitchen table, my mug cradled between my hands, thinking not about my project but about Tim. The way I'd reacted when Mum had told me he was coming to see me tomorrow was confirmation, if confirmation was needed, that my feelings for him were not what they should be. We couldn't go on like this, it wasn't fair to either of us, and the time was coming when I was going to have to tell him it was over. But still I shrank inside at the prospect. Finding the right words – and the courage to say them – would be bad enough; I hated the thought of hurting him, even though he had been less than supportive to me these last months. Worse, there would be the practical aspects – moving out of the flat we shared, finding somewhere else to live. At least we weren't married, but our lives were still tangled together in so many ways, and I found myself regretting having agreed to live with him.

Thinking of that brought on a wave of nostalgia. It was painful to remember how happy and excited I'd been, buying little things to make the flat a home – bright cushions, a way-too-expensive lamp that I'd fallen in love with, a new cover for the duvet on the bed we were going to share. I'd bought domestic bits and bobs, too – a rolling pin and pastry cutters (unused except for mince pies at Christmas), a roasting pan, even a blowtorch to toast crème brûlées when we had friends for dinner. Looking back now it felt as if I'd been playing at house, and perhaps I was. But we had been happy. Very happy. For a time. Falling asleep in the arms of the man I loved, waking up beside him, making plans together, making love whenever and wherever we wanted within our own four walls . . . it had been wonderful while it lasted, and recalling it now brought tears to my eyes.

But it wasn't working, and if I was honest with myself, it hadn't been working for a very long time. If I could feel so resentful of Tim, if I preferred to be free to carry on my investigation instead of spending time with him, if I could no longer make excuses for him, and, more importantly, didn't want to, then I really had to tell him it was over.

How would he take it? Would he be relieved, or would he be upset? If he promised to change and pay me more attention, should I give it another chance? I honestly didn't know.

I wasn't looking forward to tomorrow.

Five

Typically, Tim was dead on time. He would have allowed for rush-hour jams getting out of town, factored in unexpected delays such as temporary traffic lights that might have sprung up since he last came to see me, and then, if it didn't happen, he'd slow down on the last stretch so as to pull into the farmyard exactly when he'd said he would. I suppose such precision would be reassuring if you were a passenger on his plane, but as a blueprint for normal everyday life it could be a tad irritating.

By contrast, I was running late. Everything still took a little longer than it used to – getting in and out of the bath being a case in point. Mum and Dad didn't have a walk-in shower, just a sort of hose attachment that sprouted from the tap, which was less than ideal for me in my current state. I'd been a bit late getting up, too – I hadn't slept well, I'd had too much on my mind, but I'd fallen into a heavy doze around dawn. I was still in my room drying my hair when I heard the doorbell, and by the time I'd stuck on a bit of make-up and headed downstairs, Mum had made Tim a coffee. He was sitting at the kitchen table drinking it, and making what sounded like rather stilted conversation.

Mum was right, I thought – he did speak to her in a patronizing way, as if he was talking to someone less bright, less informed, than he was. And it struck me, too, how incongruous he looked sitting there at the gnarled and marked old table in his perfectly ironed black denims, pristine open-necked shirt, leather jacket and shoes polished to a blindingly bright shine. He got up as I came in, and greeted me with a chaste kiss of the sort he deemed suitable with Mum hovering. He smelled of the expensive duty-free aftershave he always used; once that scent had made me go soft inside but now it left me cold.

'Sorry I wasn't ready,' I said.

'It wouldn't be you if you had been, Sally,' Tim said. Though he was smiling, pretending to tease, I sensed that the underlying criticism was real enough.

'So, are you going to go out somewhere?' Mum asked – hopefully, I thought. 'It's a nice day. It would be a shame to waste it.'

She was right – it *was* a nice day, the sun shining, the sky a clean-washed blue that had the promise of spring. But I still couldn't manage to walk very far, and even had I been able to, Tim's highly polished shoes were not really suited for trekking along the muddy lane.

'Suppose we drive up to Deer Leap?' I suggested. Tim cracked a questioning eyebrow, and I explained. 'It's only about half an hour from here, and there are some fantastic views. It gets quite busy in the summer, but on a Friday at this time of year I wouldn't imagine there would be too many other people about.'

The sort of place where we can talk undisturbed . . .

'And there are plenty of nice country pubs where we can get a drink and a spot of lunch if we feel like it.'

If we feel like it being the operative phrase . . .

'Good idea,' Mum said, and I guessed she was relieved she wouldn't have Tim turning up his nose at her scratch lunch of hearty soup or the remains of the weekend roast.

While Tim was finishing his coffee, I got my coat. My heart had come into my mouth at the prospect of saying what I'd more or less decided needed to be said and my nerves were twanging. We set out in his Audi with Classic FM playing on the radio, and when Tim asked me what I'd been up to I told him a little about my investigations, but my voice didn't sound entirely natural and it was difficult to summon any enthusiasm for the subject that had been consuming me with the conversation we needed to have hanging over me. I wondered if Tim would notice I wasn't my usual self, but when I gave him a sideways glance I had the oddest impression that he wasn't really listening to what I was saying.

Deer Leap is a high spot on the Mendips, a broad parking area overlooking a beautiful valley, with paths angling off along the crest of the hill. There was no way we could walk them today, though – they were accessed by stiles in the drystone walls that bordered the parking area that I would have struggled to manage, and in any case, the fields beyond would still be soggy from the recent rain. Instead we remained in the car, parked to give us a panoramic view of the valley below.

Right, I thought – this was it. No more putting it off. Time to take the bull by the horns.

'Tim,' I said, 'we need to talk. About us.'

There was a silence. I glanced at Tim. He wasn't looking at me, but still staring out at the view. He was chewing his lip and there were lines of tension in his face, as if he sensed what I was going to say. Then he reached across, switched off the radio, and turned towards me.

'I know we do. I'm really sorry, Sally. I've been neglecting you, haven't I?'

'I realize it's been difficult. With your job and everything, and me not able to lead a normal life.' I was trying to do this gently, to avoid recriminations and bad feeling if at all possible. 'I do understand that, Tim . . .'

'You do?' His eyes snapped up to mine. There was an expression in them that puzzled me.

'Yes, of course I do. But . . .'

But it's not just that, I was going to say. *It's all kinds of other things as well* . . .

I never got the chance.

'I am truly sorry,' Tim said again, and it occurred to me suddenly that he was apologizing rather too much for simply not coming to visit me as much as he might have done.

'Tim, there's no need . . .'

'There's every need. I should have confessed a long time ago. But with you in the state you were, I couldn't bring myself to upset you. It didn't seem right.'

I frowned. 'What are you talking about?'

His eyes fell away again, his fingers played with the knob of the gearstick. By the time he looked at me again I had a pretty good idea what he was going to say.

'I'm sorry, Sally, but there's someone else.'

Still it shocked me. Tim had someone else!

'Oh!' I said stupidly.

'I met her through work and things have . . . developed.'

For a moment I couldn't think of a single thing to say. Then something inside me exploded.

'A trolley dolly, I suppose.' I was astonished by how hurt I felt – hurt enough to refer to an air stewardess by such a derogatory term.

'Actually, no. She's my first officer,' Tim said, almost apologetically.

That took the wind out of my sails all over again, but of course, it made perfect sense. Women weren't only flight attendants now, they were also pilots. And I could just picture the scene – Tim in the left-hand seat, some glamour girl with gold braid on the shoulders of her uniform in the right, cocooned together in a cramped cockpit for hours on end. And then the two of them wheeling their suitcases through customs together, being bussed to the same hotel for overnight stays, sharing a meal and a drink – no, not a drink; eight hours between bottle and throttle was the golden rule. But getting very cosy, nonetheless.

'How long has this been going on?' I asked tightly.

Tim shrugged. 'Does it matter?'

'Yes, actually.'

And it did! Had Tim been seeing her when we were still together? When I was in hospital and he was visiting me, pretending concern? Was she the reason he'd been so ready to suggest I should come home to Stoke Compton to convalesce when I was discharged? Had she moved in with Tim? Was she sleeping in the bed we had shared? It mattered a great deal. And explained a whole lot more.

'I met her last summer,' Tim said.

'So she's the reason you haven't been able to find the time to come and see me. And there was I believing you when you said you just couldn't fit me into your busy schedule. I suppose she's the reason you wanted me out of the flat, too.'

Tim said nothing, and I knew I'd hit the nail on the head.

'What a fool I've been!' I said bitterly. 'Making excuses for you to everyone. Even to myself. I knew things weren't good between us, but I never imagined you were cheating on me . . . well, not to this extent . . . How could you do it, Tim? How could you just string me along? And don't say it's because you felt sorry for me, please. Because that would just be adding insult to injury.'

From the way Tim's mouth opened and closed I knew he'd been on the point of saying exactly that.

'You bastard,' I said softly. My hands were tightly clenched on my knees because what I really wanted to do was hit him.

'We didn't get seriously involved until a couple of months ago,' he said lamely.

'And that makes it all right?'

'Well, no, but . . . I've said I'm sorry, Sally, and I am.'

I shook my head, laughed without humour.

'You know what is so funny about this? I was actually going to tell you that I wasn't sure that I wanted to be with you any more, and I was worried about doing it. Worried about hurting you. Well, more fool me.'

'*You've* met someone else?' Tim looked, and sounded, as shocked as I had felt a few minutes ago.

'Hardly,' I said dryly. 'But if I had I'd never have done this to you. I'd never have crept about behind your back, lied to you, cheated on you . . .'

The look of relief on his face was so palpable I had to once again restrain the urge to hit him. The conceit of him! He couldn't bear the thought that I might have actually decided that I preferred to be with someone other than him – his ego simply couldn't stand it. What on earth had I ever seen in him?

'So,' I said, getting my temper under control. 'I suppose the reason you're coming clean now is that you want to set up home with this . . . woman.'

Tim had the grace to look a bit shamefaced.

'Well . . . yes.'

'And you want me out of the flat. Permanently.'

'Oh, good gracious, no! I wouldn't expect you to leave, Sally. The plan is for me to move in with Paula. She has a cottage in Winton – very convenient for the airport. But don't worry, I'll pay my whack of the rent on the flat until you can find someone else to share with you, or are in a position to afford it yourself.'

'Well thanks, but I couldn't possibly accept it,' I said stiffly, my pride kicking in.

'I insist. I wouldn't leave you in the lurch while you're incapacitated.'

'Hopefully that won't be for much longer. I mean it, Tim – I don't want your money.'

'We'll see about that. But thanks for being so understanding, and taking it so well, Sally.'

I snorted. Actually, I hadn't taken it well at all. Given that I'd been agonizing over how I was going to end things myself I should have been grateful that he'd handed it to me on a plate. Instead, I was surprised how hurt I was, knowing he'd been sneaking around with someone else – falling in love with her – while I was coping with the devastating consequences of my accident.

I had no intention of letting him know that, though. His ego was quite big enough already.

'Right,' I said, sounding far calmer than I felt. 'I suggest we go and have a drink and a spot of lunch somewhere and sort things out.'

'All right, if you feel up to it . . .'

'Might as well get it over with,' I said. 'Then we can both get on with our lives.'

Things were reasonably civil between us by the time Tim took me home to Rookery Farm, and we'd sorted out a lot of the practical issues. Tim would move out of the flat we shared, and would be gone by the time I was fit to return. I was still stubbornly refusing to accept any financial help from him with regard to the rent and so on, and I knew I'd have to sit down and do my sums as to whether I could afford to keep it on alone or whether I'd have to look for a flatmate – something I'd really prefer to avoid if at all possible.

Mum was in the kitchen, cleaning eggs ready for her stall at the farmers' market on Saturday morning.

'No Tim?' she enquired as I went in.

'No. Nor likely to be again.'

'You've decided to call it a day.' Though she was trying to sound non-committal, I could tell she was actually relieved.

'Tim beat me to it,' I said ruefully. 'He's involved with someone else.'

'I knew it!' Mum stripped off her Marigolds, leaning against the big stone sink. 'I told you he was making excuses about why he wasn't coming to see you. Well, good riddance, I say.'

'I know . . . I know . . .'

'So who is she? How long has it been going on?'

'Mum – I really don't want to talk about it any more right now. I'll tell you all about it later.'

Though I could see Mum was bursting to hear all the details, she simply nodded.

'When you're ready, my love. But I will say this. You're a lot better off without that one, so don't go upsetting yourself. Now, why don't you sit down and have a nice cup of tea?'

'A cup of tea would be good. But . . .' Not only did I not want to talk about what had happened with Tim, I didn't want to think about it, either. And there was one sure fire way of taking my mind off the break-up.

'Is Dad using his computer?'

'No. He's out seeing to one of his cows. He had to have the vet to her this morning.'

'Oh dear!'

'Yes, he's a bit worried about her. So you can be sure he won't be wanting to get on the computer for the next couple of hours, at least. Go on, you have it. I'll bring your cup of tea in to you.'

'Thanks, Mum. You're a star.'

I logged on to Dad's computer, pulled up the notes I'd made so far, and read through them. Mum brought me the promised cup of tea and a slice of her famous lemon drizzle cake and I nibbled on it as I added the information I'd gleaned from Rachel last night, including the name of the estate agency where Dawn had worked, and the fact that Lisa had married Paul Holder, the baker who had rescued the girls. I also made a note of the thought that had occurred to me that it might have been Lisa, not Dawn, who was the intended victim of the arson attack, and, armed now with her married name, I had another look for her on Facebook. This time I found her, but her page stated that 'Lisa only shares some information publicly', and her photograph wasn't a photograph at all, but a white silhouette on a blue background. Could it be that she was a bit paranoid because of what had happened? I didn't know, but it was important that I kept an open mind.

I sat back in Dad's comfortable swivel chair, nursing my mug of tea, and trying to think about this logically. Top of my list of people to see had been Brian Jennings' sister, Marion, but I was having second thoughts about that. It was unlikely that she would be able to tell me anything more than the basic facts, which I already knew – if she'd learned anything of any interest, then almost certainly she would have taken it to Brian's solicitor and an appeal would be under way. Almost certainly that was not the case – it was only a few days since I'd heard her radio interview, and she'd not mentioned any new evidence. What was more, I rather thought that the moment she knew a newspaper reporter was taking an interest she'd go public with the fact, as she would see it as support for her cause. I really didn't want that. Far better if I could talk to the people concerned first. I'd have to admit to an interest in the fire, of course, but if it was known that I was actually trying to find another suspect doors may well slam in my face. I wanted to ask questions as discreetly as possible, and if I became high profile it would be no help at all.

Time enough to speak to Marion later. My first port of call should be Lisa Curry – or Lisa Holder, as she now was – and Dawn Burridge. And before I could do that I needed to know where she now was.

Lisa should be able to tell me that, I imagined, but the other line of contact with her was the estate agents' where she had worked – or maybe still did if she'd come back to Stoke Compton when all the hoo-ha had died down.

I skidded my chair back to the computer, Googled 'Compton Properties', and in no time at all their website was on the screen in front of me.

My first impression was that Compton Properties appeared to be a thriving business. There was page after page of houses for sale, ranging from humble terraced cottages to large family homes, and even the odd barn conversion. Some of them bore the banner 'Sold' or 'Under Offer'. There was also a section of property to rent and a page explaining what the company could do for prospective landlords in terms of managing the lets. Another wing of the business appeared to be house clearance – a service required when the homeowner had died, presumably, or was moving abroad. The furniture and effects from such clearances then went into a monthly auction, also run by Compton Properties, which was held in a warehouse-style building on one of the local trading estates.

I took a look at the 'About Us' page and was surprised to see that the business was owned and run by one man – a Lewis Crighton. 'Lewis Crighton has twenty years of experience in the property market,' the blurb proclaimed. 'After working for an old-established agency, he founded Compton Properties, his own business, in 2001, and has thousands of satisfied clients.'

The photograph showed a good-looking man of perhaps forty seated behind the wheel of what looked to be an open-topped sports car. Dark hair sprung from a high forehead, the features were strong in a narrow face, the mouth wide and smiling above a neatly trimmed beard. It was the sort of face, no doubt, that would inspire trust in clients, but I couldn't help feeling it was also the face of a man who knew exactly where he was going, what he wanted, and how to get it. The sort of man who would find talking easy – I could just imagine the convincing patter that would flow from those full lips.

But would he talk to me? If I could get myself into Stoke Compton tomorrow, then perhaps I would find out.

'Any chance of me getting into town tomorrow?' I asked.

Mum, Dad and I were seated around the kitchen table eating tea. Dad was still worried about his cow, I could tell, but it didn't stop him tucking into an enormous plate of toad in the hole. Farming is the sort of job that makes you hungry – all that fresh air and physical effort. I, on the other hand, had very little appetite.

Mum gave me a knowing look. 'I suppose you want to get on with looking into this story of yours.'

'I do really,' I said.

'Are you going to want your car tomorrow, Jack?' Mum dished

up seconds on to Dad's already empty plate. 'I reckon our Sally could manage that, what with it being an automatic.'

Dad came out of his reverie.

'Well, I wasn't planning on going anywhere. You're welcome to borrow the car if you think you can handle it, Sally.'

'Oh Dad . . . are you sure?'

I was a little nervous of taking responsibility for the 4 x 4, but I was also anxious to be independent. I couldn't expect Mum to go on ferrying me round forever.

'I will,' I promised.

'I hear you were on my computer again this afternoon, too,' Dad said.

'I was, yes,' I confessed.

'Hmm, quite like old times, eh? My car, my computer – anything else you want?' His tone was dry, but his eyes were twinkling, and it occurred to me that Mum and Dad were actually enjoying having me at home again.

I grinned.

'That'll do nicely for now. Thanks, Dad.'

'So what exactly is it you plan to do in Stoke Compton tomorrow?' Mum asked.

We'd finished tea, the dishwasher was stacked and the kitchen tidied. Dad had disappeared into the living room to watch the national news from the comfort of his armchair and Mum and I were lingering over a cup of coffee.

'For starters, I want to talk to Lisa Curry. Try to find out if there was anyone else who might be in the frame for starting the fire.'

'That's not likely, surely?' Mum sipped her coffee. 'Why on earth would anyone do something like that? Brian Jennings . . . well, he was known to be an oddball. But it's not the sort of thing that would even occur to a normal person, let alone actually do it.'

'You'd be surprised what people do,' I said. 'I've come across all sorts of cases where someone has committed murder for what seemed like the most trivial of reasons. But to them, it had gone right out of proportion and pushed them over the edge. That's what I want to find out. If there's anyone else who might have had a motive for starting that fire.'

Mum still looked unconvinced. 'What sort of motive?'

'Anything, really, that seemed important enough to them. Greed, jealousy, the feeling they've been betrayed, you name it, it could be the trigger. Suppose, for instance, that one of the girls was having an affair with a married man and she threatened to tell his wife. That could result in him losing his family, his home, his reputation, perhaps even ruin him financially. If he was sufficiently frightened, he might have thought the only way out was to get rid of the threat.'

'It doesn't seem a very sensible way to go about it,' Mum argued. 'Never mind that it would be a terrible thing to do, there was no guarantee of the outcome. As was the case. The girls were rescued.'

'Desperate people don't always think rationally,' I said. 'I've come across it more than once. And then, of course, there's jealousy. That's always a powerful motive. Dawn was a very pretty girl, very much in the limelight. Perhaps she'd stolen someone else's boyfriend, or been in line for a promotion at work. Another girl with her nose put out of joint might have thought she'd teach her a lesson.'

'It's possible, I suppose,' Mum conceded. 'Though I must say I can't see a girl creeping about in the middle of the night with a petrol can and a load of old rags.'

'I'm trying to look at this from every possible angle,' I said. 'And the best way to find out if there's anyone who might have been pushed over the edge into doing such a terrible thing is to talk to the girls themselves, and the people who know them.'

'Oh well, I suppose you know what you're doing.' Mum finished the last of her coffee. 'How are you going to go about it, though? They might not take very kindly to being questioned about their personal lives.'

'No, I know. Oh, by the way, what do you think? Lisa married the baker who rescued her!'

'Well, well!' Mum looked astonished. 'No wonder the café is doing so nicely. A chef and a baker – you couldn't get much better than that.'

'I don't know that he actually works there,' I said. 'He may still be in his old job – probably is. However well the café is doing, I can't imagine it supporting both of them.'

'I'll bet he's responsible for all the fresh rolls and bread for sandwiches, though,' Mum said.

'Probably. Which brings me to how I'm going to approach the girls.' I rested my chin on my steepled fingers, thinking. 'The café's the perfect excuse for meeting Lisa. But the estate agent Dawn worked for is a different matter. I could go in on the pretext of looking for property in the area, but I suppose one of the girls in the office will just give me a load of litera-ture and that'll be it. And she might not even have been there when Dawn was. What I really need is an excuse to get to talk to the boss . . . Ah!' I brightened suddenly as a brainwave struck me. 'Have you got anything that could be put up for sale at auction?' I asked.

Mum gave me a look which suggested she thought I'd taken leave of my senses.

'Compton Properties also run monthly auctions,' I explained. 'Mainly it's the stuff they get from house clearances, but I imagine they'd include anything saleable for a commission. That would almost certainly be run by Lewis Crighton himself. If there was something I could take in − ask for a valuation − I expect I'd have to see him. Then my options would be open if the girls in the office aren't any help.'

'Oh Sally, whatever next!' Mum sighed.

'Do you have anything?' I pressed her. 'Something you don't need any more, but which might sell?'

Mum gave it some thought.

'We've got a couple of hurricane lamps somewhere. Brass, with a glass funnel and a wick. They haven't been used for years. But being as you're on your crutches, you'd have a job to carry them . . .' She broke off, thinking again. 'I know! There's the candle snuffer that belonged to your Great-Aunt Mabel. That would fit in your bag, wouldn't it? And there's a set of apostle spoons, too.'

'Are you sure you don't mind parting with them?' I asked, doubtful suddenly.

'It'll just be a bit less cluttering up the drawer of the dresser. We'd better check with your father, but as far as I'm concerned, you're welcome to them, if they'll be any help to you. And if they don't sell, I suppose we get them back anyway.'

'You can count on it. You never know, though, they might be worth a fortune.'

I was grinning from ear to ear now, and feeling much perkier knowing I had a good excuse for both the calls I intended making tomorrow. And my renewed enthusiasm was making me forget all about Tim and the way he'd cheated on me.

Six

Next morning soon after ten I was ready to leave for Stoke Compton. I'd slipped the case containing the apostle spoons into one capacious pocket of my Berghaus jacket and the candle snuffer into the other – much better than weighing down my bag. Then I drove Dad's car round the farmyard a couple of times, getting used to it before taking it out on to the road. It was a long time since I'd driven, and the Range Rover was much bigger and higher than anything I'd ever handled before. But very soon I was enjoying myself. After being so helpless for so long, the sense of freedom was exhilarating.

When I felt sufficiently confident, I tooted to Mum, who was watching from the porch, gave her a wave and drove off.

I reached Stoke Compton without incident, but as I'd guessed, there were no parking spaces in the High Street, and I headed for a car park on a minor road running parallel to it. There was plenty of room there and I was able to find a space wide enough to fit into easily after considering, and rejecting, one of the disabled bays that was closer to the exit. I was disabled, yes, but I didn't have a permit, and I didn't want to risk coming back to find I had collected a parking ticket.

I locked up the car and set off, ignoring the soreness of my hands and swinging along on my crutches at a reasonable pace. After crossing the road and making my way between blocks of rather dilapidated buildings, I reached the High Street once more and headed in the direction of Lisa Curry's café. As I passed the newspaper offices I glanced in through the plate-glass window and was able to see Tara, the receptionist, sitting behind her desk. But beyond that I could see no one. If Josh Williams and Belinda Jones were in today, they were tucked away, well out of sight. For some inexplicable reason I felt a tad disappointed.

Muffins was just beyond the *Gazette* office. In contrast to

the still smoke-blackened wall above the entrance, the paint-
work was fresh and bright – pristine white and sunshine yellow
– and the windows sparkled, although the traffic in the busy
High Street must produce an awful lot of petrol fumes and
grime every day. I pushed open the door and went inside.

Small tables spread with what looked like proper tablecloths
took up most of the interior, but there was also a counter
where cakes and a selection of breads were on display. Lisa was
obviously into the take-out trade, too. Just inside the door,
two young mothers were enjoying a cup of coffee and a chat
while their offspring gurgled at one another from dinky-looking
white-painted high chairs. A pushchair was obstructing the
gangway; the young mother pulled it closer, out of my way,
and I squeezed past, heading for a table towards the back of
the café, next to one occupied by a middle-aged woman in a
beret and raincoat, whose chair was surrounded by a pile of
shopping bags.

As I dumped my crutches and sat down, a young girl emerged
from a beaded curtain that hung over a doorway behind the
counter. She was wearing a frilly apron and carrying a buttered
teacake and a pot of tea, which she placed on the table of the
woman in the beret.

'Here you go, Brenda. Anything else I can get you?'

'No, that'll do me nicely, thanks,' the woman responded,
and the girl approached me.

'Morning.'

'Morning.' This wasn't going according to plan. I'd expected
Lisa to serve me. But I could hardly say that. 'Could I have a
coffee please?'

'Americano? Espresso? Cappuccino?'

That surprised me. It sounded more like a Starbucks than
a small-town teashop and café.

'I'll have a cappuccino.'

'And a pastry?'

'Oh, no thank you.'

'I can recommend the teacakes.' The woman in the beret
had no qualms about butting in. 'Lisa makes them herself, or
Paul does. You couldn't get fresher or better.'

'I'm sure,' I said politely, 'but I don't think . . .'

'Oh go on! Spoil yourself! You could do with a bit of feeding up!'

I eyed the teacake on her plate. After one of Mum's farmhouse breakfasts, I was far from being in need of sustenance, but it did look tempting, nicely browned and oozing butter, and besides . . . this woman was obviously a regular at the café. If I wasn't going to be able to speak to Lisa, she was the next best thing – or maybe even better. She seemed exactly the sort of person who would know the answers to a lot of my questions, and be only too happy to gossip.

'You've talked me into it,' I said.

The young waitress headed for the kitchen with my order.

'You look as if you've been in the wars, my love,' the woman called Brenda said, shifting her chair around her table so that she was even closer to me. 'What have you been up to?'

'Oh, a skiing accident,' I said, hoping it wouldn't put her off. She didn't look like the sort of person to have ever been on a ski slope, and might dismiss me as a Hooray Henrietta. Not Brenda.

'Well I never!' she said, shaking her head. 'Rather you than me. I slipped down on a patch of ice outside my back door last year and broke my wrist. That's the closest I want to get to skiing – or skating, come to that. So when did this happen?'

By the time I'd told her the story we were chatting like old friends, and I was managing to eat an undeniably delicious teacake.

'So you come in here a lot, do you?' I asked, licking melted butter from my fingers.

'Regular as clockwork.' Brenda poured a second cup of tea from her miniature bone china teapot. 'Have done ever since they opened. We should all support local businesses, I reckon, and Lisa deserved to make a success of it after what she went through.'

'The fire, you mean?' I said disingenuously.

'Oh, a terrible do, that was!' Brenda shook her head and huffed to emphasize her point. 'That wicked, wicked man! Trying to burn those two poor girls in their beds!' She huffed again.

'Brian Jennings, you mean?' I said.

'That's him. I always knew he wasn't right in the head, of course. But to go and do something like that! Well, at least he's locked up now, thank the Lord, where he can't get up to any more mischief. And it all turned out well for Lisa in the end.'

'She married the baker who rescued her, I understand,' I said.

'She did that. And a lovely couple they make too . . . Oh!' she exclaimed suddenly, 'here she is. Hello, Lisa my love.'

A young woman had emerged from behind the beaded curtain and even if Brenda hadn't more or less introduced her, I'd have recognized her from her newspaper photographs. Lisa Curry – or Lisa Holder as she now was – was short, stocky and rather plain, dark hair cut in a short bob that didn't particularly flatter her rather coarse features. She was wearing a red jumper that strained over a hefty bosom, black trousers, and a large blue cook's apron, folded down at the waist.

'Brenda,' she said, not sounding exactly delighted, but it would take more than a lukewarm greeting to put Brenda off.

'I was just saying, Lisa, what a lovely job you've made of this place. That fire was a terrible thing, but it was a blessing in disguise. Just look how it's turned out for you.'

'To be honest, I'd rather not talk about it,' Lisa said shortly.

'Well, that's understandable, my love. But it's true, all the same. Every cloud has a silver lining, you could say. Now.' Brenda reached for her scarf, hanging over the back of her chair, and wound it round her neck. 'I suppose I'd better be seeing about getting home, or Mother will be wondering wherever I've got to. I've got my mother living with me, you see,' she said to me, 'and she gets in a right state if she's left on her own too long.'

'Oh . . . right . . .' I said lamely.

Brenda turned her attention back to Lisa.

'If I could just have my bill, my love . . .'

'Pot of tea and a teacake?' Lisa scribbled on a little notepad and put the tab on the table in front of Brenda, who paid, and gathered her shopping bags together.

The two young mothers had left while Brenda and I had been talking, and the little waitress had disappeared. When

Brenda left too, Lisa and I were alone. This was too good an opportunity to miss, I thought, especially since Brenda had conveniently raised the subject of the fire with Lisa.

'It must have been awful for you . . . the fire, I mean,' I said, trying to sound suitably sympathetic. 'Did you lose everything? All your precious belongings?' It was a pretty crass question, but the sort I thought a nosy stranger might ask. I didn't want to put Lisa on her guard.

'Pretty much,' Lisa said shortly, piling Brenda's plate and cup and saucer together.

'You know I don't think I could bear to stay here, where it happened, if I were in your shoes,' I went on. 'Do you still live upstairs, in the flat?'

'No, we don't,' Lisa said in the same short tone. 'And anyway, there's no danger of it happening again. Brian Jennings is behind bars, where he belongs.' She looked pointedly at my empty cup. 'Can I get you another coffee?'

'No, I'm OK thanks.' I didn't want to risk her going off and leaving her young assistant to serve me. 'So you think the police definitely got the right man?' I persisted.

'Well of course they did!' It was almost a snap.

I risked it. 'His sister doesn't think so.'

Lisa snorted. 'She wouldn't, would she?'

'I suppose not . . . but . . .'

'Brian Jennings was obsessed with Dawn,' Lisa said vehemently. 'Everybody knew that. The nights we looked out of the window and saw him, just standing there, staring up. If Dawn went out, he followed her. She was frightened to death of him. She reported him to the police, but they never did anything about it.'

'But it's what put them on to him, I suppose.'

'I suppose.'

'It must have been really scary for you, too, before they caught him,' I said. 'You must have wondered . . .'

'Wondered what?' Her tone was slightly aggressive now.

'Well . . . it might have been *you* the fire raiser was targeting . . . not Dawn . . .'

'Don't be ridiculous!' Lisa snapped. 'Why would anyone target me?'

'You didn't think somebody might have had it in for you?'

'It never crossed my mind. Dawn was the honeypot. When she was around, she was always the one who was the centre of attention.' There was something that might almost have been resentment in Lisa's voice now.

'But she's not around any more?' I said tentatively.

'No, she's not.' Lisa was whisking away a few odd crumbs from the table where Brenda had been sitting, using an old-fashioned wooden crumb brush and tray.

'Where is she now, then?'

'I haven't the faintest idea. We're not in touch.' Lisa stopped what she was doing and fixed me with a baleful look. 'Look, I don't know what your interest in all this is, but it's pretty morbid. So if there's nothing else you want . . .'

'No, there's nothing else.' And nothing else I was going to learn today, either, I thought. Unless I owned up to the real reason I was asking questions, and possibly not then. But I wasn't ready to come clean yet in any case. I wanted to be able to sniff around a bit more first without people clamming up on me.

'I'll get your bill,' Lisa said, fetching the same pad she'd written out Brenda's bill on. But instead of waiting for me to get out my purse, she carried the used china into the kitchen beyond the curtain, and it was the little waitress who came to take my money.

I didn't see Lisa again. I'd upset her, I knew. But it was more than just that. I was left with a vague but persistent feeling that there was something she had not wanted to tell me.

It took me a good ten minutes to walk down the High Street to the town square where Compton Properties had their office, twice as long as if I hadn't been on crutches. But in any case, I wasn't hurrying. I was busy taking in just how much Stoke Compton had changed in recent years.

I passed the turning to the church hall, where I used to come for ballet classes when I was a little girl – that hadn't lasted long; ballet really wasn't my thing. On the corner was the shop that used to be what Mum called 'the confectioners', a wondrous Aladdin's cave of sweets in rows of jars behind the counter and tiered stands full of chocolate bars. Mum used to take me in to buy 'a treat' after I'd endured my ballet class, and I'd always taken ages choosing between the Cadbury's Roses, the stripy mints, creamy fudge, or a sherbet fountain. The sweet shop was no more – it had been turned into a barber's according to the logo on the window: 'Haircut £8 – No Appointment Necessary'.

A little further on I came to what had used to be Grays' the hardware shop, another place that had always fascinated me. There had always been merchandise spilling out on to the pavement – trays of bulbs and sacks of seed potatoes, baskets full of odd china and even the odd oil heater or stepladder. But it was the smell when you stepped inside that I could remember so clearly even after so many years – a smell like no other, a mixture of all the things Mr Gray sold, I suppose. The hardware shop was gone now, though, and in its place was a pound shop. Their goods were spilling out on to the pavement, too, but weren't nearly as interesting as Mr Gray's had been. Nostalgia tugged at me; the town shouldn't have changed while I wasn't looking!

The post office, at least, was still where I remembered it. I passed it, heading for the Square at the end of the street, and was trying to spot Compton Properties when a voice spoke from just behind my right shoulder.

'Well, hello again!'

I turned my head sharply, almost causing me to lose my balance, to see Josh Williams drawing level with me.

'Hey – careful!' His hand shot out to catch my elbow, steadying me.

'You made me jump,' I said, feeling a little foolish.

'Sorry about that.'

'It's OK. And I must admit I was far away.'

'Anywhere interesting?'

'Not really. I was revisiting my past. Looking at how the Stoke Compton I used to know has changed.'

'*Used* to know?'

'I grew up round here, but I've been away for a long time. I wouldn't be here now if it wasn't for . . .' I nodded my head in the direction of my crutches. 'I came home for a spot of TLC.'

'And you thought you'd do some work on your thesis while you're here.'

'My thesis?' For a moment I couldn't think what he meant, then I remembered – the story I'd invented for the benefit of the receptionist at the Gazette. 'Oh yes . . . my thesis,' I said lamely, and felt myself begin to blush.

We'd reached the corner of the Square.

'Well, good luck with Lewis Crighton,' Josh said, his tone slightly ironic, I thought. 'I take it that's where you're headed.'

'How did you know?' I asked, startled.

'Just guessing. If I was investigating the fire, it would be one of my first ports of call.'

Investigating the fire . . . Not really the way you'd talk about a thesis . . . I had the uncomfortable feeling Josh hadn't been taken in by my story at all. And, in reality, why would he be? I was a good bit older than the average uni student, after all – something I hadn't thought of when I'd come up with my spur-of-the-moment excuse.

'This is me, then.' Josh was now jiggling a set of car keys; there was a sharp click nearby and lights flashed briefly on a blue Peugeot estate standing in one of the few parking spaces in the Square.

'So –' His eyes, dark hazel flecked with gold, met mine – 'how about I take you for a drink this evening and you can tell me how you got on?'

To say I was taken by surprise would be an understatement. More to the point, I was speechless.

'I'm quite harmless, I promise,' he added in an amused tone.

'I'm sure you are,' I managed. 'But . . .'

'But you have other plans.'

'Um . . . yes.' It was a lie, of course – another lie! – but it was a whole lot easier than turning him down flat, or explaining that I had broken up with my long-term boyfriend only yesterday, and was nowhere near ready to date anyone, least of all someone I'd exchanged only a few brief words with.

'Some other time then, maybe?' He didn't look a bit abashed

by the rejection; I guessed it would take a great deal more than that to faze Josh Williams.

'Yes, maybe . . .'

'Take care then.' He gave a wicked nod in the direction of my crutches, opened the door of his car, and got in.

Feeling totally flustered, I made my way across the Square in the direction of Compton Properties.

The estate agent's office was a tall, double-fronted building of the same grey stone as most of the town centre, with a ladies' hairdressing salon on one side and a charity shop on the other. The windows either side of the door were packed with display boards of properties for sale in Stoke Compton and the surrounding area, and there was a model layout showing a small development of new houses out on the bypass. I gave it the briefest of glances, pushed open the door, and went inside.

In the airy, open-plan office two girls were seated at desks. One was on the telephone, the other working on her computer. Both looked like glamour models, or cosmetic consultants in a department store. They were out of exactly the same mould as Dawn, if the photographs of her that I'd seen were anything to go by. Lewis Crighton had certain criteria where his employees were concerned, it seemed.

I didn't think either of them was Dawn, though. The girl on the telephone was a redhead, and a natural one at that, judging by her creamy complexion and light dusting of freckles, whilst the other was very dark – the coffee-coloured skin and glossy black hair that suggested she may be of mixed race. She looked up as I entered the office, flashing me a practised smile.

'Good morning. How may I help you?'

I crossed to her desk, and noticed that an identification brooch pinned to her jacket that read 'Sarah'.

'I understand you run an auction house,' I said.

'We organize auctions once a month, yes,' she corrected me.

'I have a couple of items I'd like to sell,' I said. 'I was wondering if maybe you could help me.'

I balanced one of my crutches against the client's chair, across the desk from where she was sitting, slid the box of apostle spoons out of my pocket and set it down on the desk. The candle snuffer and tray followed.

'It's very old, I think,' I said.

'Yes.' She was eyeing the discoloured pewter doubtfully; though I'd done my best to clean it up, both the tray and the snuffer itself did look a little the worse for wear.

'And you'd like Mr Crighton to include them in the next auction?'

'I think so, yes. Can you give me some idea of what they might fetch?'

Sarah made no attempt to pick up the items. In fact, her disdainful look gave me the impression she wasn't happy to have them on her desk even, and certainly wouldn't want to soil her perfectly manicured hands.

'I can't do that, I'm afraid. You'd need to speak to Mr Crighton.'

This was exactly what I'd hoped for.

'Could I do that, please?' I asked.

'I'll see if he's available.' She lifted a telephone and pressed a single digit. 'Mr Crighton?' There was something quite old-fashioned in the formality – surely it was all Christian names in the workplace nowadays, just as everywhere else? – and something almost reverential in her tone as she spoke to him. 'Would you be able to speak to a lady about a valuation of some items for the auction?'

I couldn't hear his reply, but Sarah nodded as she put down the telephone.

'Mr Crighton will be with you as soon as he's free.'

At least she hadn't used the ubiquitous 'in a meeting'. And it gave me an opportunity to talk to her while I was waiting. I decided to plunge in at the deep end.

'Does Dawn Burridge still work here?' I asked.

'Dawn Burridge?'

'Yes. She used to, didn't she, before the fire at her flat?'

'I really couldn't say. I've only been here a short while,' Sarah replied coolly, but I noticed the other girl, who had finished her telephone call, was listening intently.

'I was here at the same time as Dawn,' she said. 'Were you a friend of hers?'

'Not exactly . . .' I hesitated. 'I do want to talk to her, though. Do you know where she is these days?'

The girl's eyes widened for a moment; she looked startled, shocked even, and on the point of saying something. Then her eyes flicked past me. I turned automatically, following her gaze, and saw a man on the staircase that led upwards from a corner of the office. He was wearing a dark grey suit that looked expensive, a pink striped shirt and a bold tie. His soft suede shoes had made no sound on the staircase, nor did they as he crossed the woodblock floor.

Lewis Crighton. I recognized him at once from his website photograph, though he looked a little older, his dark hair flecked with silver and the lines between his nose and mouth more deeply etched. If anything, though, he was even more handsome in the flesh and he exuded a courtly charm.

'Good morning. Lewis Crighton.' He offered me his hand. My journalist's eye noticed a gold signet ring, studded with a tiny diamond.

'Sally Proctor.' There didn't seem any point concealing my identity as I had at the newspaper office. 'I was hoping you might be able to sell these things for me in your auction, but I'd like some idea of what they might fetch.'

Lewis examined the candle snuffer.

'Interesting. It's had quite a lot of use in its lifetime, by the look of it.'

'I'd think so. I come from a farming family, and they probably didn't have electricity until long after most people.'

'Quite.' He flipped open the box where the apostle spoons nestled in a bed of blue velvet. 'These are quite sought after, too, but I'm afraid I can't possibly guess what they will make at auction. I'm not an antiques expert – just a humble businessman – and so much depends on which dealers come along on the night. If there's interest, then they can drive one another up. Otherwise the price can remain very low. We're not Sotheby's, I'm afraid.' He smiled slightly. 'The best thing would be for you to put on a reserve price – the least amount you'd be willing to accept.'

'And what would you suggest?'

Lewis Crighton gave a small shake of his head.

'That really isn't for me to say. It all depends on how much you want to sell.'

I hesitated. 'I think I should talk to over with my mother. I've brought them in on her behalf. When is your next auction?' I asked.

'In just over a week's time. The second Tuesday of the month.' He replaced the apostle spoons on Sarah's desk, long white fingers with a feathering of dark hairs lingering on the inlaid lid of the box. 'Will you take them away with you while you think it over, or would you like me to keep them here for you?'

'Oh, keep them, if that's not too much trouble.'

The moment the words were out I regretted them. If I took the things away with me it would give me an excuse to come back again. It was too late now, though.

'I'll let you know what she decides,' I added.

'No problem. Sarah will take a few details from you.'

He held out his hand again; the interview was at an end as far as he was concerned, and I couldn't think of any way of prolonging it. But in any case I couldn't see Lewis Crighton telling me anything I wanted to know – he was too much the businessman, all formality and good manners. The girl who'd said she'd worked here at the same time as Dawn was a far better bet.

Sarah opened a file on her computer, entered the details of the items I was leaving in their care, and asked me my name, address, and a contact telephone number.

'I'll just print this off and ask you to sign it . . .' She was all efficiency, something Lewis Crighton demanded, I imagined. Which, in its way, told me something about Dawn. She might have been a glamour girl, but she couldn't have been an empty-headed flibbertigibbet if she'd held down a job here.

The redhead had left her desk now and was rearranging property details on a display board that was positioned just inside the door. When I'd signed the form Sarah had printed off for me I made to leave, but paused beside her.

'You were saying . . . about Dawn . . .' I said, striving to sound casual.

The redhead turned sharply. Her name brooch announced that she was called Alice, I noticed, but it wasn't so much that

that was demanding my attention as the wary look in her eyes. She didn't actually take a step away from me, but it felt almost as if she had.

'It's just that . . . I thought if you knew her, you might be able to tell me where she is . . . how I could get in touch with her,' I went on.

For a moment the girl, Alice, said nothing. She was chewing her lip, her teeth making sharp indentations in her lip-gloss, and she looked scarily as if she might be about to burst into tears.

Sometimes silence is more effective than too much questioning; puzzled, I waited.

Then: 'You don't know, do you?' Alice said.

I shook my head, still waiting, though a shiver of apprehension was prickling over my skin. Alice glanced at Sarah, seeking support, I guessed, and when none was forthcoming, looked back at me. She ran her long, French-polished nails over her lower lip as if to smooth out the indentations her teeth had made, then drew a quick, shuddering breath.

'I'm really sorry . . . if she was a friend of yours . . .'

'What?' I asked urgently.

'I'm really sorry,' she said again, 'but Dawn was in an accident last year. She was killed. So . . . you won't be able to find her, I'm afraid. Dawn Burridge is dead.'

Seven

'Dawn is dead?' I repeated stupidly. Shock and disbelief were washing over me in a great wave that rendered me incapable of coherent thought. 'But when? How?'

'It happened in Dorset, where her parents lived, not long after the trial,' Alice said. She looked genuinely upset.

'And it was an accident, you say?' I was beginning to recover myself. 'What was it – a car crash?'

Alice shook her head.

'She was killed by a hit-and-run driver when she was on her way home from work. I don't know any more than that.' She glanced nervously in the direction of the staircase leading to the upper floor. 'Mr Crighton doesn't like us talking about it. Dawn had been here a long time – he was very fond of her. And besides . . .'

Yes, I could well imagine I wasn't the first reporter to come here asking questions, although presumably they would have simply been looking for a quote. Not the sort of publicity Lewis Crighton would want for his feel-good business.

'Did they ever catch the driver who knocked her down?' I asked.

Alice shook her head, her red hair swinging about her pretty, pale face.

'I don't think so. Look, I'm sorry, but I really must get on with my work . . .'

'Of course.'

I left the office and for a little while I was too busy getting myself back to the car park to think much about what Alice had told me – crossing busy roads on crutches requires a fair degree of concentration. Once I'd made it safely, though, I sat in the driver's seat of Dad's 4 x 4 staring out of the windscreen and giving my thoughts free rein.

What a terrible thing! And how ironic that Dawn should have escaped the fire only to be killed in a road accident!

It was almost as if she was fated – as if her death was meant to be . . .

Meant to be . . . The phrase resonated somehow, and for a moment I couldn't understand why it should, so the thought, when it occurred to me, shocked me all over again.

Supposing Dawn had been meant to die in the blazing flat? Supposing someone wanted her dead so badly that they'd started the fire with exactly that intention, and when it hadn't worked, they'd tried again – and succeeded? It could be, of course, that I was making a leap too far here, too ready to think the worst because I was so eager to find a story that I was inventing one, but it was either a tragic coincidence that Dawn had died so soon after her lucky escape from the fire – or she had been deliberately targeted not once, but twice. And I didn't really believe in coincidences.

If I was right, of course, it would definitely mean that Brian Jennings had been wrongly convicted. He was already behind bars when Dawn was killed. And even if he hadn't been, this wasn't the act of a deranged oddball – it was cold, calculated, carried out by someone with deadly intent. It would mean that Dawn, not Lisa, was always the target. This was all about her, and she was the one I should concentrate on.

I would need to check out the details of the hit-and-run – exactly where and when it had happened, and whether there were any witnesses. Alice had said the driver hadn't been caught, but that didn't mean no one had seen anything. There might have been information that the police hadn't been able to capitalize on – a partial number plate, a vehicle type and colour, a glimpse of the driver – was he male? Female? Young? Old? Black? White? But the vital clues lay here, in Stoke Compton, I felt sure. It was here the whole thing had begun, where, perhaps, Dawn had met someone who had eventually decided she had to die. But who? And why?

Once again I ran over possible motives. Revenge, jealousy, fear. Any of the reasons I'd listed to Mum could be the trigger for murder. And there would be more besides, reasons I hadn't even thought of yet, as to why someone might want Dawn dead. There always were. To find out I needed to talk to people who'd known Dawn. I should speak to Lisa again, obviously, but I had a feeling she was going to be a hard nut to crack. But Dawn must have had other friends – she'd been an outgoing sort of girl from what I knew of her, with a full social life that probably hadn't included Lisa – the amateur dramatics society, to name but one source of possible friends, and I was pretty sure I'd be able to find out where and when they met at the library. Libraries usually kept information on all local activities and the contact details for officials.

I also really wanted to talk again to Alice. They had, after all, worked together, and confidences were often shared between colleagues; all kinds of personal matters were discussed over a cup of coffee and a cream cake. There was no point in going back to Compton Properties here and now though; Alice had made it abundantly clear that Lewis Crighton didn't want Dawn, and what had happened to her, discussed in the office. I needed to get her on her own if I was to elicit any useful information.

I fished in the pocket of my jacket for the paperwork Sarah had given me. She'd clipped a business card to the form, which bore the office telephone number. My mobile phone was in my bag; I got it out and dialled.

The phone was picked up almost immediately, but I didn't know the voices of the two girls well enough to be sure which of them had answered it.

'Would it be possible to speak to Alice?' I asked.

'I'm sorry. Alice is at lunch. This is Sarah. Can I help?'

Damn. Where had the morning gone?

'It really was Alice I wanted to speak to,' I said. 'When will she be back?'

'One fifteen. We take our lunch break in relays. But are you sure I can't . . .?'

'I'll ring again later,' I interrupted her.

'Can I tell her who called?'

Damn again. I didn't want to put Alice on her guard, or blow my excuse for going to the office by drawing attention to my interest in Dawn.

'No, it's all right. Sorry to have bothered you.'

I disconnected, and glanced at my watch. Ten to one. Mum

would be expecting me back; Dad would think I'd crashed his car. But I wasn't ready to leave Stoke Compton just yet.

I punched in my home number. Mum answered, sounding concerned when she heard my voice.

'Is everything all right, Sally?'

'Fine. But I've still got a few things I want to do here. Is it OK with Dad if I don't get back for an hour or so?'

'Hang on, and I'll ask him . . .' Muffled voices, then Mum was back on the line. 'He says that's all right.'

'Thanks. I won't be much longer.'

'Take your time. And just take care.' Mum still sounded slightly anxious.

'I will,' I promised. 'And don't worry, I'm fine.'

In fact, I realized, I was actually feeling rather tired. All that swinging about on crutches had taken it out of me. And I wasn't done yet. But I wasn't going to let a little thing like a pair of sore hands and an aching leg put me off.

I climbed out of the 4 x 4 again and set off back towards the High Street and the library. When I got there, however, it was to find it all locked up. A notice stuck to the inside of the glass-panelled door gave today's opening times as ten a.m. to one p.m., and the next session wasn't until Monday morning. It hadn't occurred to me that the library would be closed on a Friday – when I'd lived at home and used it, it had always been open every day but Wednesday. The reduced hours were, I supposed, a sign of the times.

This was, to put it mildly, something of a blow. I didn't want to have to wait until Monday to gather the information I needed. I stood for a moment, staring balefully at the locked doors, turning over my options. I could go back to the café, have something to eat, and have another crack at Lisa, or I could go to the newspaper office. They'd probably know how I could contact someone from the dramatic society – they must cover their productions. There was a good chance they'd have something on file about Dawn's fatal accident, too, but when I'd been there before no one had mentioned it because they thought it was the fire I was interested in.

A sudden thought struck me – why hadn't Lisa told me about it when I asked about Dawn? She must have known her former flatmate was dead. Very strange. But it confirmed my suspicion I'd get very little out of Lisa, and certainly nothing at all at this time of day, when she was busy with lunches.

I hoped the *Gazette* office didn't close for lunch. The *Western News* offices didn't, but this wasn't a big-city newspaper, but a small-staffed local weekly. Mentally crossing my fingers, I made my way down the High Street.

I was in luck. The lights were all on, and through the plate-glass window I could see the receptionist, Tara, at her desk. I pushed open the door and went inside.

Besides Tara and one girl working on a computer the office was empty. No one in the chief reporter's office where I'd done my research when I was here previously, as far as I could see, and – thank goodness – no Josh. Tara's suspicious look was bad enough; she'd obviously recognized me as the person who'd taken liberties with her boss's files – hardly surprising given my rather conspicuous crutches!

'I was wondering if you could tell me anything about the Compton Players,' I said. Tara looked at me blankly and a little mutinously. 'I'm trying to find out when and where they meet,' I went on, 'and, ideally, a contact number for the secretary.'

Tara shook her head. 'I'm sorry, I can't help you.' Then she thought better of it, her resentment of me losing out to the call of duty. 'Katie!' she called in the direction of the girl at the computer. 'Do you know anything about the Compton Players?'

Katie looked up from what she was doing.

'I've done a couple of reports on them. Why?'

I crossed the office to her desk and repeated my question.

'As far as I know, they meet in the town hall,' Katie said. 'I think their regular night is a Monday, and a couple of other evenings as well when they've got a production coming up. They've only just done their annual pantomime, though, so they may be having a bit of a break.'

'You wouldn't have a contact name or number, I suppose?' I asked.

'Should have, yes.' Katie scribbled on a post-it and handed it to me. 'There you go. And good luck. They're a friendly

bunch, and they put on some excellent shows. Quite professional for a small town.'

Obviously she thought my interest was as a prospective new
member. Well, I wasn't going to disillusion her, though I rather
thought my next question might.

'There was something else . . .'

I never got any further.

'Well, well!' A familiar voice came from behind me. I swung
round to see Josh Williams looking at me with one eyebrow
cocked and a half smile making a deep and unsuspected dimple
play somewhere between his mouth and his ear. 'Twice in one
day! I suppose it's too much to hope you're here to tell me
you've changed your mind about that drink!'

Katie did a double-take, looking from Josh to me with an
exaggerated expression of bewilderment.

'Nothing, nothing, Katie, my love. You need not worry I'm
playing fast and loose with you.'

'I should hope not, since I'm a happily married woman!'
Katie retorted.

'And Steve is one lucky man,' Josh said in a tone of mock
regret. Then, to me: 'So what brings you here if it's not to
make my day?'

'She wants to join the Compton Players, and you'll have no
chance once she's set eyes on the gorgeous George Clancy,'
Katie said tartly, and added to me: 'Half of Compton is in love
with him, and the rest are either too blind, too old, or the
wrong sex.'

I smiled. This was much more like the office banter I was
used to.

'I can assure you he's in no danger from me.'

'Hmm, I don't think it's a leading man you're interested in,
is it, Sally? Josh said enigmatically. 'It's Dawn Burridge on your
agenda, if I'm not much mistaken.'

I pulled a rueful face. I had been rumbled.

'Guilty as charged. And actually that's the other reason I'm
here. She was killed, I understand, in a hit-and-run accident,
and I wondered if . . .'

'You want to raid Belinda's cuttings files again.'

'Well . . . yes . . .'

Josh huffed good-naturedly.

'You'll get me hung, drawn and quartered. Come on.'

He headed off towards the partitioned-off office, I threw a smile and a 'thank you' at Katie, and followed.

'Belinda not here again?' I asked when I caught up with him.

'She's out interviewing a local artist who's running an art trail,' Josh said. 'And guess who's got to go and take pictures of pictures?' He pulled down one of Belinda's files, flipped through it and got out a clear plastic envelope.

'There's not much here, by the look of it. Have a quick shufti and we'll get it packed away again before Belinda comes back and catches you at it.'

This time he clearly had no intention of leaving me alone with the cuttings; instead he lounged against a filing cabinet, hands in his trouser pockets – he was wearing cords today – head on one side, watching me. It was oddly disconcerting.

As he'd said, there was very little in the file, just a brief piece headlined 'Local Girl Dies in Hit-and-Run Accident', and another reporting the inquest. The paper had re-run one of its archive photographs of Dawn, but much smaller than the one that had accompanied the reports of the fire. Neither told me anything I didn't know, beyond that the accident had happened in Wedgeley, the Dorset town Dawn had returned to after the fire. Presumably Alice at the estate agent's had been correct in saying the driver had never been caught, as it was almost certain a report on that would have been included in the file if he had.

What did surprise me a bit was that Belinda hadn't put the accounts of the accident in the same file as those of the fire. But she had her own methods, I supposed, and she hadn't made a connection between the two events. Which may well mean that I was barking up the wrong tree entirely.

I finished reading the cuttings and slipped them back into their sleeve. Josh Williams was still leaning against the filing cabinet; when I handed him the file he slotted it back into the place on the shelf that he'd found it, then turned back fixing me with a direct look.

'There's something that's puzzling me, Sally. Just what is

your interest in Dawn Burridge?' Taken aback by his directness, I floundered, and he went on: 'You're not writing a thesis on the miscarriages of justice at all, are you?'

So – I'd been right. I'd been rumbled.

'What makes you think that?' I asked, stalling.

'Well, for one thing, I can't see why Dawn being killed in a road accident would have anything to do with Brian Jennings' conviction,' he said, watching me narrowly. 'Are you a private investigator?'

'No!' I laughed at the preposterous suggestion, glad at least to be able to answer that one truthfully. 'Absolutely not!'

'What, then? Because you sure as heck are not a mature student.'

I sighed, and decided my only option was to level with him.

'OK – I'm a journalist,' I confessed. 'I work for the *Western News*. But this has nothing to do with them. I'm at home, recuperating . . . well, you can see why . . .' I indicated my crutches, 'I'm bored out of my mind, and I came across this story. I thought I'd find out a bit about it – see if Brian Jennings' sister has any grounds for believing he was wrongly convicted. That's it.'

'And have you discovered anything of interest?'

'I hadn't. Until now. Nobody seems very keen to talk about Dawn, or what happened, and it seemed like an open-and-shut case. But now . . . since I've found out that Dawn is dead . . . I'm not so sure. Killed in a hit-and-run accident, not that long after the fire. By a driver who has never been caught. That's one hell of a coincidence – and I don't believe in coincidences.'

Josh was silent.

'Don't you think it's suspicious?' I asked.

Josh shrugged.

'I wouldn't know. I'm a photographer, not an investigative reporter. Now, if you've finished, we'd better get out of here. Belinda will be back soon.'

'Finished. Thanks for all your help.'

'That's OK.' He treated me to a boyish grin. 'Now, are you sure you won't change your mind about letting me buy you that drink?'

On the point of refusing him again, I had second thoughts.

The newspaper office was a valuable source of information, but I couldn't continue to keep dropping in and asking to see their files. So far I'd been lucky – Josh was a very helpful ally.

Perhaps it would be wise to keep him on side.

And besides . . .

I gave him an appraising glance, taking in his angular face, with its clearly defined jaw, his wicked hazel eyes, his broad shoulders beneath the leather jacket, his long, cord-clad legs. Josh Williams was, I had to admit, rather attractive. I actually quite fancied him, and it was a long time since I'd been on a date, especially one with a man I fancied. Perhaps this would be a good time to mix business with pleasure.

'All right,' I said nonchalantly. 'You're on. As long as you realize you'll have to drive way out into the country to pick me up and take me home again.'

Those hazel eyes twinkled wickedly.

'I'm sure it will be worth it. Shall we say half past seven?'

'A quarter to eight.' I wanted to keep the initiative.

'A quarter to eight it is. So – give me directions . . .'

I did.

I was halfway home when I remembered I had intended to call Alice when she returned from her lunch break. I pulled into a lay-by and left the engine idling while I punched in the number for Compton Properties.

The phone was answered quite quickly, but the voice on the other end of the line sounded very like Sarah, and it occurred to me that she would probably recognize my voice too. People used to dealing with the public had a good ear for things like that, and the fact that I hadn't given my name when I called earlier wouldn't have prevented her from knowing who I was. Well, there was absolutely nothing I could do about that.

'Would it be possible to speak to Alice now?' I said. 'I rang earlier, but she was at lunch.'

'I'm sorry, but she's with a client.' The answer was a little too quick, a little too convenient.

'When will she be free?'

'I really couldn't say. In fact, I think she's taking her client on a viewing. If you leave me a number, I'll ask her to call you back.'

Really, I thought, I didn't have much choice. I couldn't keep ringing the office. They'd quickly realize – if they didn't already – that something was going on. Somewhat reluctantly I dictated my mobile number to Sarah, thinking that at least she wouldn't recognize it as the one I'd given her for the property receipt – Mum and Dad's landline. But somehow I didn't think Alice would be returning my call. It might be true, of course, that she was busy, but I had the feeling that Alice was avoiding me, and her colleague was fending me off.

It really was very odd, I thought, as I set off again. Why was Alice so reluctant to speak to me? Was it just that personal phone calls of any kind were frowned on? Certainly the office had the sort of professional formality that was almost old fashioned. Or was it more than that? When I'd first asked about Dawn, Alice had said as little as possible, making the excuse that Lewis Crighton didn't want her talked about, and I supposed that was understandable – at the time of the fire the office had probably been bombarded by press and even curious members of the public. But the more I thought about it, the more I thought that it was just that – an excuse. Alice wanted to avoid the subject of Dawn Burridge. But why?

I was beginning to get the unavoidable feeling that Dawn was a taboo subject where a lot of people were concerned. And in spite of Joss's warning, it was only making me all the more determined to find out the reason.

Eight

When I turned into the farmyard, a car I didn't recognize was parked beside the barn. Had Dad had to have the vet out again to his sick cow? But this car didn't look as if it belonged to a vet – it was too clean, and too expensive – a top-of-the-range BMW. I parked Dad's 4 x 4 and went in through the front door. I could hear voices coming from the kitchen.

'I'm home!' I called.

'In here, Sally,' Mum called back.

Puzzled, I headed for the kitchen. Mum, Dad, and the owner of the BMW were seated around the table with steaming mugs of tea beside them and a plate of Mum's freshly made drop scones within easy reach.

'Look who turned up on the doorstep!' Mum said, smiling.

'Jeremy! Hello! What a surprise!'

Jeremy Winstanley had been our nearest neighbour and a friend for as long as I could remember. Throughout my growing-up years his family had farmed the land that adjoined ours, and though Jeremy hadn't gone into farming himself – he worked for one of the big financial institutions in the city – whenever he was at home he would drop by to talk to Dad. He was a great horseman, too, riding with the local hunt, and my earliest memories of him were very romantic ones – a big, handsome man in hunting pink, astride a huge grey horse.

It was Jeremy who taught me to ride – Mum and Dad couldn't afford such luxuries as a stable – but the Winstanley family each had a horse of their own, and a pony that had belonged to Jeremy's youngest sister, but which they'd never been able to bring themselves to sell. He was quite old, that pony, by the time I got to ride him, a fat little chap called Mickey, who was quiet and gentle and absolutely perfect for an inexperienced six year old.

I'd spent a lot of time at the Winstanley farm, mucking out stables, hacking on Mickey, and later riding Mrs Winstanley's horse, Duchess, a pretty bay. Mrs Winstanley had developed arthritis, and was no longer able to ride her, so she was glad for me to give her some exercise. Jeremy had once even taken me out with the hunt, but I'd quickly discovered it wasn't for me. I was too worried I might put Duchess at a jump that was too much for her; if she'd fallen and broken a leg I'd never have forgiven myself. I didn't like the kill, either, though of course since the hunting ban that no longer happens. No, I was much happier simply taking Duchess for a leisurely trot around the lanes and the occasional exhilarating canter across the meadows that were almost all Winstanley land or our own.

When Farmer Winstanley and his wife both died, within a year of each other, we'd expected Jeremy to sell the farm. Instead he'd put in a manager, who lived in the farmhouse, and converted one of the outlying barns into a luxury residence for himself. He was no longer working for the city firm, but had set up as some kind of financial adviser, using the new house as a base. But a lot of his business was in the Eurozone and Jeremy spent a lot of time abroad. He'd been away since before I'd come home to recuperate – in Brussels, Dad had said, but judging by the depth of his tan now, I rather thought he'd been somewhere a good deal warmer than Belgium.

'Good to see you, Sally,' he said, getting up and giving me a kiss on both cheeks, continental style.

'You too, Jeremy.'

Besides the tan, he'd put on weight, I thought. He'd always been a big man, but now there was a considerable solidity about him. He wasn't fat – yet! – but there was no doubt that he'd been living the good life. Yet it suited him, somehow adding to his not inconsiderable presence.

'Cup of tea, Sally?' Mum asked.

'Mm, please! And I could do with one of your drop scones, too.'

'Haven't you had any lunch?'

'No, but I'm OK. I had a teacake at Muffins mid-morning.'

I sat down, reached for a drop scone anyway and bit into it. It was still warm.

'You've had a pretty tough time of it, I hear, Sally,' Jeremy said, looking at me sympathetically.

'She was nearly killed,' Mum, setting the kettle to boil, said over her shoulder.

'Sounds nasty.' Jeremy brushed away a crumb that had settled in the thick cable pattern of his Aran sweater. 'No riding for you for a while.'

'I haven't ridden for a long time,' I admitted.

'Pity. Ah well, I suppose you've got other things to interest you these days. Didn't I hear you were engaged?'

'Not engaged, no,' I clarified. 'I was living with someone, but that's over. I'm fancy free and single again, Jeremy. Just like you.'

He snorted, wagging a finger at me.

'Very true.'

'You could do with a good woman to keep you in order,' Dad joked.

'I'm quite happy as I am, thank you, Jack. I've never had time for all that nonsense,' Jeremy retorted.

'When you're old and lonely, with no one to make sure you've got a clean shirt to put on, you'll wish you'd made the time,' Mum chided, setting a mug of tea down in front of me.

We all laughed. The idea of Jeremy old, lonely and in need of a clean shirt was a ludicrous one.

'Seriously, Sally, you must be going quietly mad, stuck out here in the country with nothing to do,' Jeremy said.

'Oh, it hasn't been so bad . . .' I didn't want to hurt Mum and Dad's feelings by admitting that hadn't been far from the truth.

'She's got herself a new project to keep her busy,' Mum said, and Dad added:

'And taken over my computer for all her notes. Nothing changes.'

Jeremy cocked an eyebrow at me. 'And what project is that?'

I was reluctant to go through it all again, but Mum had other ideas.

'You remember that awful fire in Stoke Compton?' she said,

resuming her seat at the table. 'Well, our Sally has got it into her head that the man that went to prison for it was wrongly convicted. She's trying to find out who might really have been responsible. Isn't that right, Sally?'

'Well . . . sort of . . .' I admitted.

'Wouldn't it be a thing?' Mum went on, 'if she were to uncover a whole different story? That that poor man has been sent to prison for something he didn't do? She's been to Compton today, haven't you, Sally? Talking to all the people those girls knew. How did you get on, love?'

'I spoke to Lisa Curry – well, Lisa Holder as she is now. She didn't really tell me anything, but I did find out something awful when I went to Compton Properties. Apparently Dawn Burridge was killed by a hit-and-run driver not long after she went home to Dorset.'

Mum clapped a hand over her mouth, looking shocked.

'Oh my goodness! That poor girl! What an awful thing!'

'Yes, and a bit too much of a coincidence for my liking.'

'For goodness' sake, Sally, surely you don't mean . . .?' Mum said, horrified, and Dad put in:

'You're letting your imagination run away with you, our Sal.'

'Maybe. Just let's say I'm on the case.' Then, in an effort to change the subject, I turned back to Jeremy. 'So when did you get home, Jeremy?'

'Yesterday afternoon.'

'And how long are you planning to stay this time?'

Jeremy shrugged elaborately. 'I really couldn't say. It all depends on the demands of business. But footloose as I might be, it's good to be home. I should think I'll be around long enough to get used to country life again,' he said with a twinkle that included me. He pushed back his chair and got up. 'I really should be going – I've got a lot of things to do. I just wanted to look in and let you know I'm back. And sample some good English cooking and a cup of tea, of course. Anything you need, Jack, just give me a shout and I'll help if I can. You know that, don't you?'

'You're a good chap, Jeremy.' Dad clapped him on the shoulder, but I guessed the offer was really nothing more than polite conversation. Jeremy wasn't really a farmer, and Dad was fiercely independent. I couldn't imagine a situation arising where he would call on Jeremy for help. It was just the way things were between them, and always had been. Which made the relationship familiar and comforting.

'And when that leg's better, come over and take one of the horses out,' Jeremy said to me.

'Will do.'

But it would be a long time before I was fit to be in the saddle again, I thought ruefully.

Mum was surprised, but pleased, when I told her I was going out that evening with Josh, and – typical Mum – wanted to know all about him.

'Mum – I don't really know,' I said, laughing. 'But you'll be able to check him out. He's picking me up at a quarter to eight.'

'I don't need to check him out!' Mum said a little tartly. 'It's been a long time since I've done that. And I don't suppose what I think would make any difference, anyway. Since when have you listened to my opinion on your boyfriends?'

'Since Tim,' I said ruefully. 'You were absolutely right about him.'

'Well, let's hope this one is an improvement.'

'Mum, I'm only going for a drink with him.' I snaffled another drop scone. 'But it would be good if we could have tea a bit early. He's picking me up at a quarter to eight, and you know how long it takes me to get ready these days.'

'I'll see what I can do.' Mum was clearing plates and cups off the table. 'But you'd better not eat any more of those scones, or you'll have no appetite for it, anyway!'

It felt incredibly strange to be getting ready to go on what I supposed could be termed 'a date', and I was actually quite nervous. I'd been with Tim for so long I was totally out of practice and the prospect of having to relearn the protocol of dating was daunting.

I had a shower and washed my hair, leaving it to dry natur- ally into the waves that fell almost to my shoulders when

I didn't tie them up with a hair band, and set about deciding what to wear. This was something of a problem; I'd brought only a few changes of casual things home with me and most of my 'going-out' clothes were still at the flat. I was pulling things out of the wardrobe and discarding them when my phone rang. My first thought was that it was Josh, cancelling, and was surprised at how my heart sank before I realized it couldn't be him – I hadn't given him my mobile number. Alice, then? I hadn't expected her to return my call, but perhaps I'd been wrong about that.

I grabbed my phone from the dressing table.

'Hello?'

No one spoke, though I was fairly sure the line was open.

'Hello?' I said again. 'Sorry – I can't hear you.'

Still nothing.

'This is Sally. Is that you, Alice?'

Still silence. Then the line disconnected. I checked the call log, but whoever had called had ensured that their number stayed hidden. Frustrated, I tossed the phone down on to the bed. Had it been a wrong number? Or was it Alice, and she had changed her mind about speaking to me at the last minute? If it was, I could only hope she'd ring again. And I still had to decide what I was going to wear for my date. Time was getting short, I couldn't waste a minute of it if I was to be ready for Josh.

I went back to pulling clothes out of the wardrobe and eventually found a pair of palazzo pants and a silk tunic that I quite liked. The wide pants really called for high heels, but since they were out of the question I had to settle for pretty pumps. Drop earrings and a narrow silver bangle completed the outfit, and I did a quick make up and sprayed on a squirt of the perfume that Tim had brought me when I was in hospital. I wasn't normally a perfume person, but it did smell rather nice, and very expensive – Tim had picked it up in duty free, I imagined, and with Tim nothing but the best would do.

I was just about ready when I heard a car out in the farm-yard and I hurried downstairs as fast as I safely could. All very well to tell Mum she'd be able to check out Josh, but I didn't actually want her or Dad answering the door as if I were a schoolgirl.

I'd just reached the foot of the stairs as the doorbell rang.

'It's OK, Mum, I've got it,' I called.

Josh was standing on the doorstep, back turned towards me – looking, no doubt, for the source of the frenzied barking that came from the direction of Scrumpy's kennel. As I opened the door he turned towards me, a slightly wary look on his face.

'It's OK – she's on a leash,' I assured him.

'I'm glad to hear it! I thought maybe I was on the menu for supper.'

I laughed.

'She's pretty harmless, anyway.'

'Don't all owners say that? I've met farm dogs before – even been nipped by one.'

'That's not going to happen,' I promised. 'Do you want to come in while I get my coat?'

Josh stepped into the hall. He was wearing his leather jacket over a roll-neck pullover, and looked extremely nice in a very casual way. There was none of Tim's polished grooming – rather it was as though he had no idea how gorgeous he was, hadn't tried too hard, if at all, and I liked it.

Unable to resist, Mum had come into the hall.

'Oh sorry . . .' she said, as if her presence was entirely unintentional.

'This is my mother,' I said, a little apologetically. 'Mum – Josh.'

'Hello, Josh. Nice to meet you.'

'And you. I'll take good care of Sally, I promise.'

I shrugged into my coat, recovered my crutches.

'Let's go then,' I said, thoroughly embarrassed.

Josh helped me into his car, the Peugeot estate he'd been driving this morning, and put my crutches on the back seat.

'Where are we going?' I asked, as he drove down the lane, his headlights cutting a sharp path through the inky blackness.

'I thought the King William at Ulverton,' he said. 'Do you know it?'

'Um . . . yes! I was born and brought up here, remember?'

Ulverton is a tiny village six or seven miles outside Stoke Compton, and the King William an old coaching inn. Josh parked in the narrow street opposite an archway that led to the pub entrance, then seemed to have second thoughts.

'Damn! I forgot. It's all cobbles. Are you going to be able to manage?'

'Oh, I expect so.'

'Sure? We can always go somewhere else.'

'No, this is fine, honestly.'

It wasn't actually that easy, but I managed it with Josh's hand hovering over my elbow ready to catch me should I stumble. He pushed open the door to the bar and held it while I manoeuvred my way through, with some relief, on to the relatively flat flagged floor.

Though I'd sometimes come to the King William with friends in my youth, it was a very long time since I'd been here. Yet it hardly seemed to have changed at all. The bar was cosy and warm, with a log fire burning in an open fireplace, and softly lit, so as not to detract from the candles and tea-lights that were scattered about. Over the bar a string of blue icicles, presumably left over from the Christmas decorations, winked, but strangely did not look out of place.

'What would you like?' Josh asked, and that did feel strange. Tim had known what my tipple was – of course!

'Bacardi and Coke, please.'

'Why don't you sit down and I'll bring it over.'

I picked my way to a vacant table in a nook beside the fireplace, only to find it had a 'Reserved' sign on it. I was about to look for somewhere else, but Josh was signing at me from the bar: 'It's OK – that's ours.'

'You reserved a table?' I asked when he came over with the drinks.

'Thought I should. It can get pretty busy on a Friday night.'

'But – aren't reservations for diners?'

'Probably. But we're having something to eat, aren't we?'

'Oh Josh! You didn't say anything about eating!' I groaned. 'I've already had tea.'

'Oh.' He looked crestfallen. 'Couldn't you manage something?'

My heart sank. I seemed to have been doing nothing but eating all day – apart from the missed lunch. But not only had Josh reserved a table, I was pretty sure that he had been waiting for this meal, and was very hungry.

'Well, something light, perhaps – a starter, maybe,' I said tentatively. 'But don't let that stop you.'

'Don't worry, it won't.' His expression told me he meant it, and I found myself laughing.

What was it about Josh that made him such easy company? Strangely I felt as if I had known him forever and my anxiety over what we'd talk about, and how I should behave, was fast receding.

Josh fetched some menus and I chose a goat's cheese tartlet from the starters menu, whilst he selected a rib-eye steak with all the trimmings.

'So,' he said when we'd placed our order, 'I know next to nothing about you, Sally.'

'And I know next to nothing about you.'

'Then perhaps it's time we introduced ourselves properly.'

'Go on then. You first.'

'Josh Williams. Photographer. Thirty-five years old. Divorced. No children. That's about it.'

'Divorced?'

''Fraid so. Nothing spectacular. It just didn't work out. One of the drawbacks of the job, I expect. Irregular hours.'

'Not that irregular, surely?'

'Oh, you know – evenings, weekends, bank holidays . . . Anyway, it was all pretty amicable. We're still quite good friends. Your turn.'

'Sally Proctor. Recently split from long-term boyfriend, and, as you already know, a journalist by profession.'

'Yes.' He was looking at me thoughtfully. 'An *investigative* journalist.'

'Not really.'

'A *wannabe* investigative journalist, then.'

'Perhaps.' For some reason this was making me a bit uncomfortable. 'How long have you been with the *Gazette*, then?' I asked, trying to change the subject.

'About nine months. So no, I didn't know Dawn Burridge, if that's what you're asking.'

At that moment the food arrived – my tiny plate with a tartlet nestling in a bed of rocket and frisée lettuce, and Josh's huge platter overflowing with steak, chips, mushrooms, tomatoes and peas.

'Let's forget about Dawn Burridge,' I said.

'And enjoy our food,' Josh was unwrapping his cutlery from the napkin it was rolled in.

'Yes – let's.'

But I thought that what I really wanted was not so much to enjoy the food as to enjoy Josh's company.

It was a very long time since I'd felt that way about anyone.

We'd finished eating and were enjoying liqueur coffees when I heard a mobile chiming.

'Oh sorry – that sounds like mine.' I pulled it out of my bag, wondering if it was Alice. 'I'd better get this. I'm half expecting a call.'

'Go ahead.'

I clicked the phone open.

'Hello? Sally Proctor.'

I waited expectantly. But once again, there was nothing but silence at the other end of the line. Well – I say nothing. Actually I could distinctly hear someone breathing.

'Is that Alice?' I asked. No reply. 'Alice, if that is you, please speak to me,' I said. 'Look, all I want to do is ask you a few questions about Dawn. I know you might find it upsetting to talk about her, but I need to know . . .'

I never got any further. The line had gone dead again.

'Damn!' I clicked the phone off, set it down on the table. 'That's twice that's happened!'

Josh was looking at me quizzically, and I explained.

'I'd really like to talk to her, ask her about Dawn's friends . . . and enemies,' I finished. 'She worked with her, she's the perfect one to help me. But when it comes to the point, she just won't speak. It is so frustrating!'

'She hasn't said anything at all?' Josh asked.

'Not a word. All I can hear is breathing.'

'You're sure it is her?'

'Who else would it be? And the very fact that she is so reluctant to speak to me makes me think she must know something. She seems frightened, and I don't know why. Unless, like me, she thinks there's a connection between the fire and Dawn's death. That Brian Jennings was wrongly convicted, and whoever set the fire did it with the intention of getting Dawn out of the way, either by killing her, or by frightening her off. And when that didn't work, they found another way.'

Josh huffed breath over his top lip in a silent whistle.

'You really think that's a possibility?'

'Well, one thing is absolutely certain. The hit-and-run driver couldn't possibly be Brian Jennings. And I think it's highly suspicious that she should be killed like that so soon after she was apparently targeted in the fire.'

For a long moment Josh was silent.

'I'm beginning to be convinced I'm on to something,' I said.

Josh opened his mouth to say something, then simply shook his head and looked down at his coffee.

'What?' I asked.

He looked up at me again, his expression very serious.

'Are you sure this is a good idea, Sally?'

'What do you mean?' I asked, puzzled.

'You could be playing with fire here.' He raised a hand in acknowledgement of the unintended pun. 'I'm not sure you've thought this through. 'Look, suppose you're right, and Brian Jennings was wrongly convicted – that has to mean someone else was responsible, someone who thinks they've got away with it. How do you think they'll react if they find out you're asking awkward questions? If there is anything to find out, and if the real culprit thinks you're getting anywhere near the truth . . . do you really think they wouldn't do whatever was necessary to stop you? And if there really is a link between the fire and the accident that killed Dawn, then that just makes it all the worse.'

His words were chilling, and with a horrible sinking feeling in the pit of my stomach I realized he was right. I'd been so caught up in the excitement of investigating my story I hadn't stopped to consider the implications of what I was doing. But, to be honest, even now it didn't feel real.

'There's probably nothing in it at all,' I said breezily. 'I'm just chasing shadows.'

'If you say so.'

'In any case,' I added defiantly. 'I'm a big girl. I can take care of myself.'

'That may very well be what Dawn thought,' Josh said.

Though we left it there, for a little while that sobering conversation cast a cloud over the evening, and I couldn't help wondering, too, about the two mysterious phone calls. Had it been Alice on the line, and, if so, why didn't she say something? Or was it someone else entirely? Silent phone calls did happen sometimes, I knew – perhaps the first one had been a wrong number, or just a shot in the dark, and when I answered the caller knew they had reached a female, and had rung the number again for the sheer hell of it. I couldn't really believe it was more sinister than that, and yet it was another coincidence that it should have happened today, when I'd been making enquiries about Dawn Burridge. No, on balance it had to be Alice. But I really couldn't understand why she would ring my number twice only to change her mind about speaking to me when I answered.

I had no intention of letting it spoil my evening, though. I was enjoying myself too much. Josh and I had connected in a way I couldn't remember ever connecting with anyone before. I hadn't felt this relaxed with Tim when I'd first met him, rather I'd been in awe of his glamour, and nervous of putting a foot wrong. This was quite different. Besides fancying him, it felt as if we'd known one another for years instead of days. Worrying about the phone calls, and Josh's warning, could wait for another day.

We left the King William soon after ten and were pulling into the farmyard by half past. The security lights came on as we drove in, illuminating Scrumpy racing madly back and forth at the end of her leash and barking like crazy.

'Are you sure that dog is safe?' Josh asked jokingly.

'No, can't you see she's a cross between a pit bull and a Rotty?' I quipped.

'Hmm. Well, I shall make sure I'm wearing my motorcycle leathers when she's not tied up, whatever you say.'

I didn't know which part of that statement surprised me more – the motorcycle leathers or the implication that Josh would be back. I took up the safest option.

'You have a motorbike?'

'My guilty pleasure. I've had motorbikes ever since I was old enough to get a licence. It was one of those that sound like sewing machines, and I practically had to get off and push it up steep hills.'

'You've got something a bit bigger now, I take it.'

'Just a tad. A Ducati.'

'A Ducati!' I was impressed.

'You know them?'

'Of course I do. I can't pretend to know much about motorbikes, but I certainly know the Ducati. Big and powerful with racing-style handlebars.'

'That's the one. I'd offer to take you for a spin, but I don't suppose that's on at the moment.'

'Hardly,' I said ruefully. 'Even if I could get on, there wouldn't be anywhere to stow my crutches.'

'In which case,' Josh said, 'my best offer is another ride in a boring old Peugeot. What about Sunday?'

My heart had given a little skip.

'I don't have any other plans,' I said, trying to conceal my delight.

'Shall we say Sunday afternoon, then? We'll go for a drive somewhere, then stop off for a drink and a bite to eat.'

'Sounds good to me.'

'Right – that's a date.' Josh got out of the car and came around to the passenger side. I already had the door open and was manoeuvring myself to the edge of my seat. He took me by the elbows, easing me out to a standing position. And then, almost before I realized what was happening, he kissed me.

It didn't last long, that kiss, but wow – did it pack a

punch! His mouth was hard on mine, the length of his body pressing me back against the car, with his hands protecting me from the cold rim of the door frame. For a moment I felt nothing but surprise, then, suddenly, I was very aware of him. My hands were on his shoulders; I could feel the well-defined muscles beneath his jacket, and unexpected desire was stirring deep inside me. It was so long since I'd been kissed by anyone but Tim, and that had become so familiar I'd almost forgotten how exciting it had been in the early days. Now, I wanted Josh's kiss to go on forever; I wanted to drown in it.

All too soon, he released me.

'OK?' His eyes met mine, teasing. 'I'll get your crutches.'

I remained leaning against the car. The farmyard seemed to be spinning around me; I looked up, over the barn roof to the inky blackness, and the stars seemed to be spinning too. I must have had one Bacardi and Coke too many, I told myself. Or the liqueur coffee had proved to be the last straw.

Josh came with me to the door.

'Do you want to come in for a coffee?' I asked.

'Better not. I'll see you on Sunday, then? Say about half two?'

I thought – hoped! – that he might kiss me again, but he didn't. He waited until I'd unlocked the door and stepped inside, then he turned with a simple, 'Good night then,' and went back to his car. I watched as he did a quick and competent reverse arc and his tail lights disappeared down the track, then I went in, closed the door, and stood for a moment catching my breath.

I couldn't believe the way I was feeling – exhilarated, happy, still a little wobbly. I couldn't remember a time when I'd felt quite like this, it was so long ago. It *must* be the alcohol that was to blame – mustn't it? But when I got into bed the room didn't spin around me as the farmyard and the stars had. I simply felt good, glowing and warm inside too, and there was a little buzz of something like anticipation of things to come. For the first time since I'd begun my investigation, it wasn't Brian Jennings, Dawn Burridge and Lisa Curry who were on my mind as I drifted towards sleep.

Once – I've no idea what time it was – I stirred, drowsily thinking I heard my phone ringing. But by the time I was awake enough to think clearly there was nothing but silence, and before I knew it I was asleep again.

Nine

Saturday is Farmers Market day in Stoke Compton and Mum always has a stall there selling fresh produce in season, eggs from her flock of hens, and jars of home-made pickles and preserves. For a couple of weeks now I'd been well enough to go with her, though I had to take one of the folding garden chairs with me, as I couldn't stand for too long.

This Saturday was to be no exception. By the time I came downstairs at half seven, Mum had already loaded most of her stock into the boot of her car and was bustling about with a thick coat over her warmest jumper and slacks.

'Are you coming with me today, Sally?' she asked.

'I planned to.'

'That's good. It's a help, having you there to take the money when we get busy. Can you get your own breakfast? I've still got a few things to do. Bread's in the toaster, kettle's on the boil. And you'll need something warm on if you're going to be sitting about it the cold. It really is nippy this morning,' she added.

She didn't ask me how I'd got on last night, but given she was so busy, that wasn't surprising. I knew she'd be giving me the third degree as soon as the opportunity arose, and, sure enough, as soon as we were installed in the car and on our way, it was the first subject she raised.

'You weren't late last night.'

I smirked. 'What does that mean?'

'It doesn't mean anything,' Mum said, affronted. 'I'm just saying, that's all.'

'How do you know what time I got in?'

'I was still awake. I heard the car.'

I had visions of Mum peeking through her bedroom curtains, seeing me pinned against the car, and Josh kissing me, and felt as guilty as if I were a teenager again.

'Well?' she pressed me. 'Are you going to see him again?'

'Yes. Tomorrow, actually.'

'Oh, that's good. Just as long as you don't get too involved too soon, Sally. You've only just broken up with Tim. I don't want to see you hurt again.'

'It'll be fine, Mum,' I said. But for just a moment I did find myself wondering – was she right? Might I be feeling this way about Josh because I was on the rebound from Tim? And was Josh just that little bit too keen for it to last?

For the first couple of hours Mum and I were kept very busy. Invariably the people who came to buy eggs, cheese and vegetables were early birds – they liked to make sure they had the pick of the stock. But towards midday things were quietening down.

'Could you manage without me for a bit if I went down to Compton Properties?' I asked. 'They're sure to be open on a Saturday, and I need to talk to them about the things I took in for the auction.'

I didn't mention that I was anxious to see Alice, and perhaps find out if she'd been trying to phone me. If I told Mum about the silent phone calls it might worry her. But we had talked about the reserve price we should put on the items I'd taken in for auction, and that was my excuse now to return to the estate agent's office.

'I'll be fine,' Mum said. 'Off you go.'

I set out in the direction of the Square, hoping Alice would be in the office. It could be they operated on a skeleton staff on Saturdays, with the girls working alternate weeks. When I pushed open the door, however, I was relieved to find Alice at her desk. She looked up, and the welcoming smile froze on her face when she saw it was me.

'Good morning.' There was hesitancy in her voice too.

'I've come to kill two birds with one stone,' I said cheerfully. 'First – the candle snuffer and the teaspoons. We'd like to put a reserve price of fifteen pounds on each.'

'Let me get the paperwork . . .' Alice rose and crossed to the filing cabinet. I waited while she wrote on the hard copy and pulled up what I presumed was the relevant file on her computer and tapped in an entry.

'Did your colleague pass on my message yesterday?' I asked when she finished.

'Your message?' Alice might be stalling, I thought. But actually she did look genuinely puzzled.

'Yes, I left the number of my mobile with her and asked if you could ring me.'

'You spoke to Sarah?'

'Yes. Didn't she tell you?'

'She didn't say anything to me about it, no. Why did you want me to ring you? Sarah was dealing with your items.'

This was it. *Go for it.*

'I was hoping to talk to you about Dawn. But are you sure . . .?' I broke off. I'd been so certain my mystery caller must have been Alice. But I didn't want to alienate her now by pressing the point.

'Look, I'm sorry, but really there's nothing I can tell you,' Alice said. 'Dawn and I worked together, that's all. She wasn't even here any more when she was killed.'

'But she was here at the time of the fire. Did she ever say . . . did she think Brian Jennings was responsible, or . . .'

I got no further. 'Of course he was responsible!' Alice interrupted sharply. 'Who else could it have been?'

The vehemence of her response struck me as being somehow an overreaction. Or maybe, once again, I was imagining things.

'That's what I'm trying to find out,' I said quietly. 'Whether Dawn or Lisa . . .'

Again she interrupted me before I could finish.

'They'd hardly be likely to start the fire themselves, would they?'

What an odd thing to say!

'Of course they wouldn't,' I said. 'I'm not suggesting that for one moment. I just wondered if there was anyone . . . anything . . .?'

'No, there's not. There was just Brian Jennings. Isn't one stalker enough?'

'But he couldn't have been the hit-and-run driver who killed her.'

'That was an accident!' Alice protested. 'And I already told

you, I don't want to talk about any of this. I'd appreciate it
if you stopped asking all these questions.'

'Is everything all right, Alice?' Lewis Crighton had appeared
on the stairs, obviously alerted by Alice's rising voice.

'Yes, fine, Mr Crighton.' The colour had risen in her face,
turning her pale complexion a rosy pink. I'd get no more from
her, I knew.

'Perhaps you could give me details of where and when the
auction will be,' I said. 'I'd like to come along and see if our
things sell.'

Alice gave me a leaflet. I thanked her, and left. I hadn't
learned a single new thing, but the feeling that I was on the
brink of something sinister was stronger than ever.

As for the silent telephone calls . . . I still couldn't be sure
if Alice was telling the truth when she said Sarah hadn't passed
on my number to her. But if it wasn't Alice, who had it been?
Was it a prank – or something more sinister? I thought again
of Josh's warning that I could be getting myself into something
very dangerous indeed, and shivered. But there was no way
on earth I was going to give this up now. If there was some
kind of cover-up, or worse, I was determined to find out what
it was.

It was almost two by the time we got home from Stoke
Compton. Mum had sold out of eggs and most of the vegetables, and got rid of quite a few pots of freshly made marmalade.
We grabbed some desperately needed lunch – onion soup with
cheese-topped croutons floating on it – and I was hoping to
be able to get on to Dad's computer to update my notes, but
he was using it to pay bills and enter the details into his account
files.

'How the devil Jeremy can work with this rubbish day in,
day out, I don't know,' he said. He looked utterly stressed out.
Dad, who could deal with all kinds of practical crises on the
farm, could be turned into a nervous wreck by his computer.

'D'you want me to help you out?' I offered.

'Oh, go on then.' Dad relinquished his chair and stood over
me issuing instructions while I took over the keyboard and
mouse.

'I really do need a computer of my own,' I said, when I'd finished. 'Trouble is, I suppose I'll have to go into Porton to get one. There's a PC World there, isn't there?'

'Yes, but you'd do better to go to the place I use, on the industrial estate,' Dad said. 'If anything goes wrong you can always call on them to sort you out. We'll give them a call on Monday, see if they've got anything in stock that would suit you.'

'Good plan.' I was really missing my laptop.

I jammed the memory stick Dad had lent me into the computer port and worked for an hour or so on my notes before a dinner of one of Mum's casseroles and an evening spent watching yet another re-run of *Dad's Army, The National Lottery Show* and *Casualty* on the television.

Perhaps because I'd recently been so badly let down by Tim, I couldn't quite shake the irrational fear that Josh would stand me up on Sunday, so when the doorbell rang just after half past two my heart leapt as if I was a teenager on a first date.

'Where would you like to go?' he asked when I was installed in the passenger seat of the Peugeot.

'I really don't mind.' It was true, I didn't. Just being with Josh was enough.

'I was thinking about Longleat Safari Park,' he suggested. 'It shouldn't be too crowded at this time of year, and we could be there in an hour or so.'

'Sounds good to me.'

Josh was right; the long summer queues were missing and we were able to drive straight into the estate, and then through the checkpoint into the safari park.

It was a pleasant afternoon, chilly but fine, with clear patches of blue sky between some heavy clouds that might portend rain later. We stopped to look at the giraffes and zebras and Josh took a load of photographs through the open window of the car.

We bypassed the Monkey Jungle – 'No way am I going through there,' Josh said.

'Oh why not? They're so funny!'

'And very destructive. When I brought my sister's kids

here they pulled every bit of beading off my windows and demolished the wipers and the aerial too. If you want to see the monkeys, you're going to have to get out and walk!'

Since that was not an option even if I hadn't been on crutches, I reconciled myself to missing the monkeys.

'Let's feed the deer instead,' Josh suggested.

The road curved up and round a bend to where a wooden shack stood at the edge of a parking area. A whole herd of deer surrounded the cars that had stopped there, and gambolled eagerly between them. Josh found a pound coin in the well of the car and I used it to buy a cup of food pellets. Immediately the deer honed in on us, jostling the car and poking their heads right through the open windows to take the pellets from the palm of my hand. Some were fully grown and quite tame, others were little more than babies, and more nervous. As I fed them, Josh snapped away with his camera, and at one point I turned to find it trained on me.

'Hey!' I objected. 'It's the deer you're supposed to be photographing!'

He grinned. 'Thought I'd get one of you too. Nose to nose with a deer.'

When the food had all gone we shared the disinfectant wipe the shop girl had given us and set off towards Lion Country.

It was a slightly scary moment as the first set of security gates closed after us and we waited for the second set to open. I've always been a bit claustrophobic, and I didn't much care for being trapped with goodness only knew how many big cats on the loose just the other side of the fence. But the moment the ranger let us through I forgot my fear, sitting forward in my seat and eagerly scanning the woodland for my first sighting.

We were in luck; as we rounded a bend we saw several cars stopped at the roadside, a sure indication that there was some-thing to see. And there was – three females and a male, lounging in the grass. As we watched, one got up and loped off into the trees, and another strolled in front of our car, so close that she brushed against the bonnet. Further on was another pride, gathered around a shelter, and then we were out of the lion enclosure and into the one that was home to the tigers. We must have seen at least half a dozen of the magnificent beasts before we passed through yet another set of security gates and into the domain of the wolves.

'Which do you think are the most dangerous?' I asked.

Josh was driving a little faster now; he'd seen enough wild animals for one day, I guessed.

'Let's say I wouldn't want to meet any of them on a dark night,' he said lightly. 'Time to get out of here before we get locked in, I think, don't you?'

'I suppose.' I was enjoying myself here, but dusk was beginning to fall.

'Plus,' Josh said, 'I could do with a pint.'

We had a drink and a bite to eat in a country pub somewhere between Longleat and home, and for all that I'd eaten a fair helping of Mum's roasted lamb at lunchtime, I still managed a delicious lasagne and garlic bread.

'I seem to be doing nothing but eating these days!' I groaned, mopping up the last of the sauce. And it was true! Where my appetite had come from I hadn't a clue, and didn't much care. All I knew was that I felt better and happier than I had done in a very long time, and that was partly down to having something to occupy me, and partly down to Josh.

Only when he raised the subject of the silent phone calls, asking if I'd had any more, did the niggling discomfort shiver through me.

'No, it hasn't happened again,' I said, neglecting to mention the fact that I'd thought my phone had rung some time during the night. 'I still think it must have been Alice, though she denied it . . .'

I went on to tell him how I'd called in to see her this morning, and once again come up against a brick wall.

'You're still determined to go on with this, then?' Josh said.

'Too true! And I plan to go to a meeting of the Compton Players tomorrow evening, too.'

'Sally, I really wish you'd think again about this . . .'

'Don't start that again!' I warned, and managed to change the subject.

When we finally made it home, Josh once again refused my

invitation to come in for coffee, but he did kiss me very thoroughly whilst sitting in the car, and again when he helped me out. And it felt every bit as good as it had last night – better!

'You fascinate me, Sally Proctor,' he whispered into my ear, and I stretched my neck in what felt to me like a very sensuous way so that he could nuzzle into it.

'Are you going to take me out again then?' I asked cheekily.

'What do you think?'

'I think you might ask . . . and I might just say yes.'

'Oh do you now!' He was nibbling my ear, his tongue flicking. Then he drew back, becoming more serious. 'It won't be until the middle of the week. I've got assignments tomorrow and Tuesday. How would Wednesday suit you?'

Wednesday. One week from the day I first met him. One week! I could hardly believe it. The days had flown by. But at the same time I felt I'd known Josh forever.

'Wednesday? Just let me check my diary,' I joked. 'No, I don't think I've got anything on . . .'

'Good. And in the meantime, just take care of yourself, do you hear?'

'I will.'

'I mean it. Try not to upset any apple carts at Compton Players, do you hear?'

'Honestly, Josh!' I exploded. 'What on earth harm can I come to in the town hall with a bunch of thespians?'

'None, I hope.'

But the grim note was there again in his tone.

'Shut up and kiss me,' I said.

Ten

Monday dragged by almost as slowly, it seemed, as the first days following my accident had done – and that was saying something! There was really nothing I could do at the moment. At some point I would go down to Dorset and speak to Dawn's parents, but that was going to be horribly difficult, and I didn't feel I was quite ready yet to face them, or the long drive. Always provided Dad was agreeable to me taking his car so far!

I wasn't able to do anything about getting myself a laptop either – by the time I came downstairs, Dad had eaten his breakfast and was out and about again on the farm. Mum wasn't sure of the name of the local computer sales firm he dealt with, so that had to go on hold until I was able to ask him for contact details.

I tried several times to ring the membership secretary of the Compton Players, whose number the junior reporter at the *Gazette* had given me, but my calls went straight to voice mail. At the third attempt, I left a message simply leaving my number and saying I was interested in joining. This was the way I was going to play it this time – so far it had seemed that the moment I began asking questions about Dawn, the barricades went up, and I thought a more subtle approach might yield more fruit. If I pretended to be just another new member I'd get to know the others in a more natural way. I could listen to conversations, and, when the opportunity arose, mention Dawn casually. It might take longer, but I reminded myself of the fable of the hare and the tortoise. Rushing in with all guns blazing wasn't always the quickest way to get information – in fact in this case it was proving to be counter-productive.

I had high hopes of the Compton Players, though. In my experience, people who were involved in amateur dramatics – or professionals, come to that – weren't usually reticent types.

Just as long as I didn't put them on their guard they'd probably be quite happy to talk.

It was always possible, too, that one of them was the perpetrator I was looking for. Once again I ran over the list of possible motives for someone wanting to be rid of Dawn, and wondered if any of them would be a fit for a member of the Compton Players. I'd already marked out the man Katie had referred to as 'the gorgeous George Clancy' as being of special interest – he sounded exactly the sort that Dawn might set her cap at, or perhaps have an affair with. But I mustn't let that blind me to everyone else in the society. Besides the other actors there would be the directors – awash with power! – and the backstage crew, the sound and lighting team, the carpenters and electricians who built the sets. Any one of them could have been involved with Dawn, and, if they were married, then all kinds of explosive situations could result.

I couldn't rule out the women, either. A woman could set a fire every bit as easily as a man, or drive a car that could be used as a murder weapon. A cuckolded wife, an ambitious actress, resentful of the fact that Dawn always got the best parts, a girl whose boyfriend she had stolen, or who wanted a boyfriend of Dawn's for herself, any one of them could have been pushed over the edge by powerful emotion.

So far, though, I hadn't even managed to find out if Dawn had a boyfriend at all, never mind an illicit lover. Yet I was convinced the clue to the mystery must lie in a personal relationship and I kept coming back to what Alice had suggested – Dawn made lots of enemies. Unfortunately that was often true of the beautiful or stunningly attractive – people were always resentful of a girl who seemed to have everything. Perhaps Dawn had been a spoiled little madam, but, then again, perhaps she had just been an ordinary, nice girl who happened to have been blessed with good looks, talent, and a vivacious personality.

This was what I hoped to find out from her friends at Compton Players.

It was five o'clock before the membership secretary returned my call, and I'd almost given up on hearing from her. In the event, though, she sounded very friendly, her strong Welsh valleys accent lending warmth. She told me that there was indeed a meeting tonight in the town hall when they would be play-reading in an effort to find something suitable for their spring production, and that I'd be welcome to come along. Then, as I'd expected, she asked if I'd ever done anything on stage before.

I said that I hadn't, and explained I was at home recuperating from a skiing accident, and was at a loose end. I wouldn't be looking to take an acting part, but I'd be happy to help out in any way I could behind the scenes.

Delyth, as the membership secretary was called, told me the meeting time was seven thirty p.m.

'We probably won't get started until nearer eight,' she said, 'but if you get here on time it will give you the chance to get to know a few people before you get thrown in at the deep end.'

Dad, bless him, had agreed that I could borrow his car again, and when we'd had tea I got myself ready and set off in good time. I was hoping I'd find a parking space in the High Street or the Square at this time of day – I really didn't want to have to walk too far if I could help it – and I was in luck. There were a couple of vacant bays in the Square; I reversed into one and sat for a few minutes' waiting time.

The lights were still on in Compton Properties, I noticed – surprising, really, given that it was past seven, and I couldn't imagine they'd have late viewings at this time of year, when it was dark by five, or even earlier if it was overcast. Could be office cleaners, I supposed. But as I watched, the lights in the upstairs windows went off, and then most of the downstairs ones as well, leaving no more than a dull glow that I presumed was from the security lights. Then the door opened, and two figures emerged. One was recognizable as Lewis Crighton, though his back was towards me as he checked that the door was securely locked. The other was Sarah, the girl who had dealt with the items I'd taken in for auction.

Why that surprised me so, I really didn't know. There could, after all, be a perfectly reasonable explanation – that they had both been working late. But there was something in their body language that suggested to me that it was more than that. The angle of her head, as if she was looking up at him adoringly, although of course I wasn't close enough to see if that was the case, the way he put a hand on her back as he turned away from the door and steered her across the Square, looking both ways a couple of times although there was no traffic about – as if he was checking to see if they were being observed, I thought. Lights flicked on a parked car twenty or so yards up the Square from where I was parked, and Sarah got in. Lewis waited until she had pulled away, then walked further up the Square. A few moments later a Range Rover drove past me from the same direction; by the light of the street lamps I could see it was Lewis driving.

I was agog by now. There might be a perfectly innocent explanation for what I had seen, of course, but somehow I didn't think so. Much more likely they had been 'carrying on', as Mum would have called it, in the empty office after hours. Lewis was twice Sarah's age, at the very least, but when had that been a deterrent? He was also distinguished, undeniably handsome, and her boss. A man who liked his staff to look like fashion models, which suggested he had an eye for a pretty girl.

My thoughts were racing now, so fast I could scarcely keep up with them. If Lewis Crighton was having an affair with Sarah, then she might not be the first. Perhaps it was something he made a hobby of, and exactly the same thing had happened with Dawn. I'd suspected her of having an illicit affair – it was one of the things that might well provide the motive for her death. Could it be that Lewis Crighton was the man she'd been involved with? If so, it would explain the brick wall I'd encountered at his office, and why Alice was so reluctant to talk about Dawn.

It would be more than her job was worth to gossip about her employer's liaisons. That could very well be the reason she had shut up like a clam when Lewis had appeared on the stairs on the first occasion when I'd visited and begun asking questions, and why she had failed to return my calls. But for all that Lewis fitted the bill very neatly for an illicit lover, I really couldn't see him as a fire raiser and a hit-and-run driver. He was too suave, too polished. The idea of him creeping about in the middle of the night with a can of petrol was almost laughable.

The clock on the dashboard of Dad's car was showing twenty-two minutes past seven – time for me to get to the meeting of the Compton Players. I locked up the car and headed for the town hall.

As I neared it, however, I realized I might well have a problem. The lights were on in the upper hall, which I knew was reached by a long, curving flight of stone stairs. How stupid of me not to have thought of that before! I'd assumed the Players met in one of the downstairs rooms, but why would they? There was a stage in the upper hall – of course that would be their venue.

The prospect of getting myself up all those stairs was a daunting one, but I couldn't give up at the first hurdle. One of the big double doors appeared to have been left on the latch; I pushed it open and went inside.

I was just preparing to haul myself up the stairs when the door opened again and a girl came in. She was about my own age, with a mop of impossibly curly hair, dark-rimmed spectacles, and she was carrying a large wicker basket.

'Hello! Are you lost?' Her voice was pleasant and friendly; the lilting Welsh accent was unmistakable. Before I could make myself known, though, she went on in almost the same breath: 'Ah, wait a minute. You must be Dawn.'

'Yes. And you must be Delyth.'

'For my sins! Goodness, I didn't realize you were still on crutches! Don't try going up those stairs, whatever you do. There's a lift just by here. Come on, I'll show you.'

A lift. Well, that was new! Installed for disabled access, I imagine. It must have cost a fortune!

'I might as well come up with you,' Delyth said. 'I don't generally bother with it, but seeing as you're here . . .'

She pressed a button, a door slid open and we squashed into the tiny compartment, Delyth's basket sandwiched between us.

'So you thought you'd like to join us then?' she asked as we clattered towards the upper floor.

'Well . . . yes. As you can see, I won't be a lot of use to you,' I said ruefully.

'Nonsense! We can always find something you can do. It's great to get new members. There were about forty of us at one time, but numbers are slipping. People move away, you know, that sort of thing. And you won't be on crutches forever, will you?'

'I sincerely hope not! But . . .' On the point of saying I would no longer be in Stoke Compton when my leg was healed, I broke off. I didn't want to draw attention to the fact that I would be a very temporary member.

The lift came to a stop and we got out. It had deposited us in a corner of the landing between the top of the flight of stairs and the door to the upper hall.

'Come on in then, and you can meet the gang – well, those that turn up on time, anyway,' Delyth said, holding the door open for me to go in.

The hall hadn't changed much since the days when I used to come here as a child for dancing classes. It was still cavernous, with tall arched windows and a low stage at the far end. But it had been decorated fairly recently, from the look of it – the walls were cream emulsion rather than the dirty brown colour I remembered, and the curtains – rich red velvet – at the windows and hiding the stage looked relatively new.

About half a dozen members had already arrived; a little knot were gathered around one of the big old radiators, and a large, balding man was setting out chairs in a circle.

'Come and meet John – he's our chairman.' Delyth laughed. '*Chairman* being a very apt word to describe him by the look of it.'

'Delyth, my angel.' The man unhooked another chair from a stack and positioned it between the others. He was wearing a scarlet sweater that stretched over his impressive paunch and baggy cords. 'Did you get the scripts from the library, darling?' His voice carried across the hall with all the resonance of a trained actor's.

'I did.' Delyth put her basket down on one of the chairs and I could see it contained paperback books divided into sets by rubber bands. '*Blithe Spirit* and *I Remember Mama*. The Ayckbourn was out on loan, I'm afraid.'

'As always. That man is just too popular.' He turned his gaze on me. 'And who are you, my darling?'

'This is Sally, a prospective new member,' Delyth said with a twinge of pride, as if she'd recruited me herself. 'Sally, this is John Hollingsworth. He's our chairman, as I said, but he also directs. And acts sometimes, too.'

'Sometimes!' John rolled his eyes. 'When have I not had to step in to fill a part? Lack of men, you see, that's the trouble. We never have enough men. You haven't a brother who'd be interested in joining us, I suppose?' he asked me.

'Don't you dare scare her off, John!' Delyth warned.

'Can you act, darling?' John looked at me over the top of his rimless spectacles.

'I'm afraid not. I thought perhaps I could do something backstage.'

'Producing, perhaps?'

'Oh, oh no!' I said, horrified. 'And anyway, aren't *you* . . .?'

'I am the *director*, darling.' He laid emphasis on every syllable of the word, giving it due importance. 'I need a *producer* – someone to organize all the routine jobs, liaise with the crew, leave me to get on with the artistic side of things.' He beamed at me. 'We'll see, we'll see.'

With that he returned to the task in hand.

'Don't mind him,' Delyth said, not bothering to lower her voice. 'Now come and say hello to the others, why don't you?'

She led me towards the group around the radiator, but others were drifting in too. A very thin girl in leggings, a fun-fur gilet and towering heels, two elderly ladies, one so fat she rolled as she walked, a gangly lad with a bad case of acne. The group around the radiator were much of an age – mid-to-late twenties – three men, and two girls, one statuesque, with beautiful ebony skin, the other a pony-tailed blonde. All were casually attired in jeans and sweaters. Delyth introduced me – none of the men was 'gorgeous George' and I knew I'd have difficulty remembering their names. All responded with friendly 'hello's, but were clearly more interested in continuing their conversation.

'I'm going to put the kettle on,' Delyth said. 'You'd think one of them would have done it, wouldn't you, seeing as they're here. But no. It's left to Muggins. Come with me, if you like.'

'OK.'

I'd already decided that of the members I'd met so far, Delyth was the one I should concentrate on. Chatty, friendly, she was the one most likely to open up about Dawn. I felt a little guilty at the thought that I was taking advantage of her good nature, but I couldn't afford to have scruples if I was to make any progress with my investigation.

In the kitchen, Delyth set a large kettle to boil, and unlocked a cupboard where mugs were stacked in plastic baskets.

'You can put some of these out,' she said. 'We'll want about twenty, I should think.'

I did as she asked and she spooned coffee powder into them from an outsize jar, chatting as she worked.

A head poked round the kitchen door. 'Do you want any help, Delyth?'

'No, you're all right, Bella. I've already got a helper.'

But Bella came into the kitchen anyway, and a whiff of expensive perfume came with her. She was an older woman, with perfectly coiffed white-blonde hair and was about fifty, I guessed, though she could well have passed for ten years younger. She was wearing the ubiquitous jeans, but with a great deal of style.

'Ah, a new member! How lovely!' She extended a hand, be-ringed fingers topped with scarlet nails. 'I'm Bella Crighton.'

For a second I almost froze.

'Bella *Crighton*?' I echoed before I could stop myself. 'Are you . . .?'

Bella arched a perfectly shaped eyebrow.

'Lewis's wife? Yes, actually, I am. Do you know him? Oh, stupid question. Everyone knows Lewis.'

'I don't know him really,' I said awkwardly. 'I've met him briefly, that's all.'

'Look, can you two talk later?' Delyth interrupted. 'We have to get this show on the road.' She was loading mugs of coffee on to a battered tin tray. 'Take these in for me, will you, Bella? And let me know if we need more. And Sally . . . you go and sit down and make yourself at home.'

She ushered me back into the hall, where John was doing his best to persuade everyone to take a seat in the circle of chairs he'd set out. The two elderly women were already seated; one of them was knitting, her wool in a bag on the floor beside her chair. I took a seat between Delyth and the gangly youth; John was clearly in pole position, with a suitable gap on either side of him to highlight the fact that he was the one in control. He coughed loudly and clapped his hands.

'Shall we make a start? I thought we'd begin with *Mama*. Gillian – will you begin by reading Katrin? And Bella – Mama. We won't worry too much about the Swedish accents at the moment, but if you do feel like attempting it, then so much the better. And of course we'll have to exercise some imagination when it comes to the children's parts . . .'

The play-reading began and I was surprised at just how good they were. Bella, in particular, was amazing, putting on an impressive foreign accent I assumed must be supposed to be Swedish. To my horror, John asked me if I would read one of the children; I couldn't see any way I could get out of it, and struggled through. But there was no danger that I would be cast, I thought ruefully, even if I hadn't been on crutches!

There was still no sign of 'gorgeous George', but I wasn't too bothered. If there had been a mystery man in Dawn's life, I was beginning to doubt that it was him. It seemed to me that Lewis Crighton fitted that role perfectly. And now I'd happened upon yet another link to Dawn – his glamorous, rather hard-faced wife was a member of the same drama group that Dawn had been in.

I cast a sidelong look at her when my nerve-wracking stint of reading was finished. She was so confident, so polished and self-assured. I wondered if some of that poise might slip a little if she knew that her husband and the pretty Sarah had been 'working late' and left the office together. And just how ruthless she could be if she thought her marriage was under threat.

This wasn't the time, though, for turning over the various possibilities. What I needed to do was establish myself as a bone fide would-be thespian so that when I began to ask questions no one would suspect I had any motive other than curiosity.

We broke for another cup of coffee about nine, everyone piling into the kitchen this time, where Delyth was rattling a jam jar and collecting twenty pence in payment. When I went to drop mine in, she covered the jar with her hand.

'Not tonight, Sally. You're a guest. Next time, but not tonight.'

Again I felt a stab of guilt that I was deceiving these people who had accepted me so readily.

'No George again tonight?' one of the girls said as she took her coffee.

'No, don't know where he is.'

'It's strange for him to miss two meetings in a row. Though he's never been as regular as he used to be since we lost Dawn . . .' The speaker moved away, and with the buzz of conversation I was unable to hear any more.

Coffee finished, we all returned to our places and play-reading resumed. Thankfully, John didn't ask me to take a part again, and I was able to study the others and think about the conversation I'd just overheard. Perhaps I was wrong to be so certain Lewis Crighton was the leading man in this mystery – certainly it had sounded as if George and Dawn had been involved in some way. At this stage I really must keep an open mind.

The meeting broke up at about a quarter to ten.

'Some of us go for a drink in the Feathers,' Delyth told me as we were putting on our coats. 'You're welcome to join us if you'd like to.'

The Feathers was a pub in the Square, but tempting as the invitation was, with the opportunity to be a party to more conversation and general chit-chat, I didn't think I should take Delyth up on the invitation tonight. Mum and Dad would be expecting me home and would be worried if I was late. I didn't want to take advantage, either – I couldn't afford for Dad to decide not to let me borrow his car again.

'Thanks, but I think I'd better not. Next time, maybe?'

'I certainly hope so.' Delyth smiled at me. 'There will be a next time, won't there? We haven't completely put you off?'

'Not at all! Next Monday?'

'Oh, we'll be meeting on Wednesday, too. We always meet Mondays and Wednesdays. Can you make it then?'

'Yes, of course. I'll look forward to it.'

Too late I remembered. I had a date with Josh on Wednesday. Well, I'd just have to postpone it. I couldn't miss the opportunity to become part of the scenery here sooner rather than later, and hopefully he'd understand.

People were drifting out now, some saying their goodbyes, some calling: 'See you in the pub' as they went. Delyth left me by the lift, going down the stairs with the lanky youth, who had been waiting to speak to her about something. Only John was left in the hall, going round checking lights and slotting a chair someone had left in the middle of the floor on to an already towering pile.

The lift arrived, I got in, and a few moments later was making my way back to my car. At the corner of the Square I glanced back; the town hall was now in darkness.

A very interesting evening, I thought, unlocking Dad's four-by-four and clambering in. All in all it had given me a lot to think about, and hopefully that was just the beginning.

I pulled away, out of the Square and into the two-way system. Traffic was fairly light, but the traffic lights were red and, as I waited for them to change, another car came up behind me.

Naturally enough, I thought nothing of it. It was only when I'd negotiated two mini-roundabouts, taken a right turn on to the road home, and clocked the fact that the headlights were still behind me that I began to take notice. Even then I still felt quite relaxed about it, expecting the vehicle to peel off into one of the residential roads or the new estate on the outskirts of town. It didn't. As I left the built-up area and headed out into the country, the lights were still behind me, reflecting from the central mirror into my eyes.

I twisted it to one side, but still I could see the following lights in my wing mirror, and for some reason I began to feel uncomfortable. I slowed down, thinking I'd let him overtake me, but he slowed too. I sped up, but still the lights remained exactly the same distance behind me. I took the fork leading to our lane and checked again; the car was still there behind me. My discomfort was fast mutating into full-blown panic now. That car was following me, I was sure of it.

Josh's warning popped into my mind in a very unwelcome

fashion, and I realized just how vulnerable I was. Away from the street lights of Compton, the inky blackness was complete but for the path cut by my headlights on full beam and the following pinpricks, and I was absolutely alone. To meet other traffic on the lane at this time of night was practically unheard of. If my pursuer decided to overtake and box me in there would be no one to come to my aid, and I didn't think I'd be able to reverse to safety in Dad's unfamiliar car – more likely I'd run into the ditch. My heart had begun to beat very fast and I could feel the adrenalin of fear pumping through my veins.

Who the hell was it? And why were they following me? But I wasn't going to hang about to find out. I put my foot down hard and the 4 x 4 shot forward. Not too far to our track now – the trouble was that was even lonelier than the lane – and I couldn't even be sure of being safe when I reached the farmyard. Mum and Dad would probably be in bed – Dad certainly would be. They'd never hear me calling for help. And if my pursuer followed me into the yard he'd catch me easily before I could find my keys, get the front door unlocked and be safely inside.

I was practically sobbing now, my hands moist with perspiration on the steering wheel as I rocketed along the narrow lane between the high hedges, fighting to keep the 4 x 4 on the road around the bends. The entrance to our track was coming up – should I turn into it, or just keep going?

At the last moment the pull of home was too strong. I stood on the brakes and veered wildly to the left. The tyres screeched, mounted the bank, and for a horrible moment I thought I would lose control. But the 4 x 4 was equal to the challenge. With a jolt and a slither I was back on the track.

It struck me suddenly that the darkness was more complete than ever – no reflected lights hurting my eyes. Shaking with terror I checked – nothing. Just the inky blackness. At first, unable to accept I was no longer being followed, I kept my foot down, jolting over the rough ridges and gulleys made by the tractor. Then, as I made it into the farmyard, I slowed and stopped right beside the door, my hand poised over the horn, ready to blare hard enough to wake the dead if the following car appeared again. It didn't, and when I switched off the engine and opened the door, the silence was as complete as the darkness.

For a moment I sat there, waiting for my breathing to steady and my heart to stop thumping, and as it did I began to wonder if I'd blown up this whole thing out of proportion.

The car hadn't followed me into the track – perhaps it hadn't been following me at all. Why would it? Who would do such a thing? But there was no denying that it *had* been there, all the way from Stoke Compton. It *had* adjusted its speed to mine.

Could it simply have been a couple of lads on a night out, having a bit of fun? They'd seen a lone woman in a car, guessed from my reactions that I was rattled, and decided it would be a lark to carry on with the game, and really frighten me.

Well, if that was the explanation, they'd certainly succeeded!

Calmer now, I found my keys, locked up Dad's car and got myself into the house. But the unpleasant feeling lingered.

Was I stirring up a hornet's nest with my investigations? Was I putting myself in danger – the same sort of danger that Dawn had been in? Even now it seemed preposterous. But if I was being targeted, it could mean only one thing – there was something sinister waiting to be uncovered, and I was getting too close to whatever it was for the perpetrator's comfort.

It was all the incentive I needed. I was going on with this if it killed me!

Eleven

In spite of my fright of the previous evening, I was more determined than ever to pursue my story. Dad, bless him, phoned his local computer man, and as luck would have it, he had a laptop in stock that suited my needs and my pocket. He'd get it all set up for me, he promised, and I could pick it up any time after four.

'This is getting to be a bit of a habit, Sally,' Dad said, putting his car keys where I would be able to find them if he was out on the farm when I needed them. 'I reckon you should buy yourself a car while you're at it.'

'Ha ha!' I'd got rid of my little run-around when it had become clear it would be a very long time before I could drive it – I didn't want it sitting around gathering rust. But there was no way I could afford to go out and buy myself something suitable just at the moment.

Something else I needed to do was to get in touch with Josh and tell him I'd have to postpone our Wednesday date. The trouble was I didn't have the number of his mobile; the only way I could contact him was at the *Gazette* office.

The phone was answered by the receptionist, Tara. Josh was not in the office, she told me, and she didn't know when he'd be back. Naturally enough, she wouldn't give me a contact number, but she offered to ask him to call me. I dictated my name and the number of my mobile, which she read back to me, very slowly and deliberately.

'You will be sure to pass on the message, won't you?' I said, all too well aware of how chaotic a newspaper office could be.

'I'll see he gets it . . .' She broke off, and I could hear a woman's voice in the background. I was about to hang up when she said: 'Could you hold on a moment? Belinda would like to speak to you.'

My heart sank. The redoubtable chief reporter, whom I had

not yet met. It had got back to her that I'd been making use of her cuttings, and I was about to be torn off a strip.

There was a hiatus in which I could hear footsteps – the clacking of high heels – and I guessed Belinda was heading back to her office to speak to me on her own extension. Then a couple of clicks were followed by a voice that carried all the authority of the woman who was queen bee at the *Gazette*.

'This is Belinda Jones. You are the Sally who's called in here a couple of times recently, I take it?'

'I am, yes,' I confessed.

'I thought so. Tara and Katie have filled me in, though Josh has been remarkably reticent,' she said dryly. 'You're interested in the fire in the High Street a couple of years ago, I understand. And Dawn Burridge's death. As a mature student writing a thesis, rumour has it.' Again her voice was heavy with irony.

'Um . . . yes . . .'

'Let's not go there, shall we?' she said crisply, and I thought: *Oh, here it comes.* So I was completely taken by surprise when she went on: 'I'm going to suggest you pop in and see me sometime, and I can fill you in on a few things I gleaned at the time that never made my reports. I'm busy this morning, but I should be free for a short while this afternoon. If you'd like to, that is.'

'That would be great!' I managed.

'Right. Shall we say about three?'

I thought quickly. Actually that would fit quite nicely with my plans. I could go to see Belinda before picking up my new laptop, making one journey instead of two. Besides which, I might get to see Josh.

'I'll be there.'

I rang off, scarcely able to believe my luck. At last someone was actually willing to talk to me about what had happened! Someone who, if she was any good at her job – and I was pretty sure she was – wouldn't have missed a trick.

Hardly had I put the phone down than it rang again and I answered it quickly, hoping it might be Josh. It wasn't. It was Rachel.

'Hi there, Sally! How are you doing?'

'Rach. Fine, actually. You're not going to believe this . . .'

I told her about the two dates I'd had with Josh – she was delighted for me, saying she was really glad I'd met someone to help me forget Tim once and for all – and I filled her in on the progress of my investigation.

'I'm really beginning to think I'm on to something,' I enthused. 'Wouldn't it be marvellous if I could prove that Brian Jennings was innocent all along? I'm going to see the chief reporter at the *Gazette* this afternoon, and to another meeting of the Compton Players tomorrow, and then I think I'm ready to go to Dorset and talk to Dawn's parents.'

'How are you going to get there?' Rachel asked.

'Borrow Dad's car, I suppose. He's being really good about letting me use it.'

'It's a long way for you to drive, though. Listen, why don't I take you? I was going to suggest we went out somewhere. If we left early enough one morning we should be able to be sure to be back in time for me to pick the children up from school.'

'Oh, Rach, are you sure?'

'I'd quite enjoy it. When do you want to go? What about Thursday? Or one day early next week?'

'I've got to find out exactly where they live,' I said. 'Let me give you a ring when I'm ready.'

I was less than enthusiastic about the thought of being driven by Rachel all the way to Dorset, but if she was willing, it did seem to be the answer. It was quite a way for me to drive, and in any case it would save me having to ask Dad to borrow his car yet again. Besides which it would be quite nice to be able to chat over my findings on the way home.

Things really were beginning to look up!

I was lucky enough to be able to find a parking space in the High Street quite close to the *Gazette* offices. I'd allowed myself plenty of time, and was actually a good twenty minutes early for my appointment with Belinda Jones, so I decided I'd pop into Muffins and try for another quick word with Lisa. It was possible the café would be less busy at this time of the afternoon, and she might be more ready to talk to me. At the very least, I was hoping to get an address for Dawn's parents. At the moment I only knew that the accident had happened in Wedgeley, but Wedgeley is a fairly sizeable town, and in any case Dawn's family might live anywhere within, say, a ten-mile radius.

I'd been right in thinking there would be a lull in business in the café. The tables were all vacant, and there was just one woman at the counter buying cream cakes. As I waited for Lisa to serve her, I feigned interest in the iced buns, doughnuts and cup cakes, but the trays were seriously depleted, and I guessed that Lisa had done brisk trade earlier in the day.

When my turn came, I chose a lardy cake, which looked delicious with its sticky glaze, and would, I thought, be something Mum and Dad would enjoy. I'd intended to wait until Lisa had served me before trying to open a conversation about Dawn, but she had other ideas. As she slipped the lardy cake into a paper bag she looked up at me suspiciously.

'You were in here the other day, weren't you?'

'I was, yes.'

'You're not from round here though, are you?' Her beady little eyes were sharp in her rather doughy face.

'Actually I am,' I said. 'I think we went to the same school, though I was a couple of years above you. Sally Proctor.'

'Sally Proctor,' she repeated. 'Yeah, I do remember you.' She was still staring at me, trying to reconcile my thirty-something face with the girl I'd been then, I supposed, but it was rather disconcerting all the same. 'You were good at sport.'

'Not so good now,' I said ruefully, trying to establish a rapport.

'Weren't you friends with Becky Auden's sister?'

'Rachel. That's right. We're still friends.'

I held out my hand for my lardy cake, but Lisa didn't pass it to me.

'Dawn wasn't at our school, though,' she said.

'No, I know.'

'So what's your interest in her?'

That took me by surprise. Though I had asked where Dawn was now on my previous visit, I'd done it quite casually, and thought it would have sounded like nothing more than idle curiosity. But for all that she looked a bit of a country bumpkin, there were clearly no flies on Lisa. On the spur of the moment I decided the best thing would be to level with her.

'Truthfully?' I said. 'I'm a journalist these days, with too much time on my hands, and I've been following up the story of the fire. I'm not convinced Brian Jennings was the perpetrator, and if he didn't start the fire, I'd like to find out who did.'

'Oh, for goodness sake!' It was the same impatient response as before, but as she thrust the lardy cake at me, I noticed Lisa's hand was shaking.

'I know you think they got the right person,' I went on, 'but just suppose there was a miscarriage of justice? Brian Jennings could be rotting in jail for something he didn't do, and the real culprit walking free – to do it again, perhaps.'

'Brian Jennings did it all right,' Lisa said fiercely, but the little tremble was there in her voice now, too. 'He was stalking Dawn – I told you that before. He was a horrible creep.'

'I'm sure he was. But that doesn't mean he should have to spend his life behind bars if he wasn't responsible for starting the fire,' I argued. 'And it's not as if he can bother Dawn any more, is it? She was killed, I understand, in a road accident.'

Lisa said nothing, simply passed me the lardy cake.

'That'll be one pound fifty.'

She was feeling guilty for not having mentioned it when I'd asked about Dawn before, I guessed.

I fished the money out of my purse.

'Where exactly do her parents live?' I asked, handing her two pound coins. Lisa shrugged. 'You must know, surely,' I went on. 'You were her flatmate, after all?'

'Wedgeley.'

'That's quite a big place. Can't you be a bit more exact?'

'Wedgeley Down. It's a village.' Lisa opened the till, got out a fifty-pence piece and put it on the counter. 'Now, if you don't mind, I'm waiting to close.'

'Oh, sorry.'

But I wasn't, really. I'd narrowed down the area where I might find Dawn's parents. And I'd confirmed the impression

I'd gained when I last spoke to Lisa. She really did not want to talk about the fire, or Dawn, and not, I thought, just because it brought back traumatic memories. It was almost as if she was afraid. Lisa knew something, I was certain of it, but getting her to tell me what it was would be like getting blood out of the proverbial stone. She was even closing the café in the middle of the afternoon to avoid talking to me, if I was not much mistaken.

Clutching the paper bag, through which a film of grease from the cake was already spreading, I left the café. Behind me, the bolts were shot, and when I glanced around the sign on the door had been turned over to 'Closed'.

I glanced at my watch. Time to make my way to the *Gazette* office for my appointment with Belinda Jones.

Tara was, as usual, sitting behind the reception desk, and before I could say a word she was reassuring me that she had left a message on Josh's mobile for him to contact me. He hadn't picked up when she called him, it seemed. That concerned me a bit – I hated that I hadn't yet been able to tell him I needed to change our date – but Belinda Jones was at the door of her little partitioned-off domain beckoning to me, and there was no time to worry about that now.

The chief reporter was a slightly built woman in her mid-forties, I judged, smartly but not ostentatiously dressed in the perennial uniform of a journalist – well-cut slacks and a sweater. A matching jacket was draped across the back of her chair. Her hair, dark with a few silver streaks, was cut into a sharp bob, and her eyes, also dark, flicked over me, summing me up.

'So you're Sally,' she said.

'Yes. And as you so rightly guessed, I'm not actually a mature student writing a thesis,' I felt obliged to admit.

'We all do what we have to do sometimes.' She smiled, a little tightly, but the connection had been made. Belinda and I understood one another.

'So, you are interested in the fire, and in Dawn Burridge,' she said briskly, gesturing for me to take a seat on one of the two chairs. 'How much do you actually know about it?'

'Really, just the basic facts. Nobody seems to want to talk about what happened.'

She nodded, eyes narrowing in what might have been agreement.

'And what about Dawn herself?'

'Again – nothing beyond that she was very attractive, and possibly not very well liked. I haven't been able to find out anything about any relationships she might have had, and that's something I'm especially interested in.'

'OK, let's start with Dawn then . . . Oh, would you like a tea, or coffee? Sorry, I should have asked before.'

'No, I'm fine, thanks. Unless you're having one.'

'I drink far too much coffee. Let's just crack on. I have to go out for an appointment at four . . .' She rescued a stray paper-clip that I hadn't even noticed lying beside the stack of wire trays, and dropped it into a desk tidy. 'As you so rightly say, Dawn Burridge was a very attractive young lady. As for not being liked, I really couldn't say. I always found her perfectly pleasant, but then, perhaps I only saw her best side. She wouldn't have wanted to alienate me for fear I'd write something less than flattering about her. But in my experience, when you look as good as Dawn did, it's bound to invite jealousy of the 'who does she think she is' kind. She was talented, too, she had a great stage presence and a nice singing voice. I think she put a few noses out of joint at the dramatic society when she arrived on the scene, especially Amanda Fricker's. Amanda had been principal girl in their panto since she was about fourteen or fifteen, and thought she had a divine right to the part. Then along comes Dawn and snatches it from under her nose.'

Amanda Fricker. I didn't remember anyone of that name from the meeting, but then again, I had been pretty overwhelmed by all the unfamiliar faces. I made a mental note to look out for her next time.

'So how long ago was that?' I asked.

'Maybe . . . the year before the fire? I'd have to check. But Dawn wasn't here that long.'

'Do you know why she chose to come here?' I asked. 'It's not the sort of place I'd expect to attract a girl who's looking to move away from home. Surely she could have got something in her line of work somewhere with a lot more life than Stoke Compton.'

'I can answer that,' Belinda said. 'She came because of a boyfriend. He was another thespian and they met at some drama festival or other.'

'George Clancy,' I said.

Belinda's eyebrows lifted a shade.

'You know George?'

'No, but your colleague, Katie, described him as the Players' leading man, and 'a heart-throb'. He sounds exactly the sort of chap a girl might up sticks for.'

'I think Katie has a soft spot for him.' Belinda smiled wryly. 'But yes, you're right, he's a sort of male equivalent of Dawn.'

'They weren't living together, though. Obviously.'

'Oh no, it hadn't got that far, and never did, of course. Dawn had got a job at Compton Properties, and Lewis Crighton fixed her up with accommodation. He was the letting agent for what was the electrical shop and the flat above, and he knew Lisa was looking for someone to share – her previous flatmate had just got married, and Lisa was finding it difficult to meet the rent.'

'Well, well! Lewis Crighton was the letting agent?' Here was yet another link with the man who was my prime suspect for an illicit involvement with Dawn.

'He was – still is, for all I know.'

'So Lisa and her husband don't own the property, then?'

'I don't think so. They just took over the whole of the building after whoever owns it had it refurbished.'

'Lucky for them, then. The café seems to be doing really well.'

'It would seem so. I don't think it's done a lot for their relationship, though. Word on the block is that they're at one another's throats half the time.'

'Interesting.' That could explain why Lisa was so sullen and resentful, I thought. 'So.' I changed tack. 'Was Dawn still seeing George at the time of the fire?'

'I don't think so. They broke up not so long after she

came here. I suppose what had seemed like the perfect romance at a distance lost its sparkle when they were able to see each other every day.' She smiled wryly. 'Much the same as Lisa and Paul, I suppose.'

'Was it an amicable break-up?' I asked.

Belinda shook her head, her lips pursed.

'I really couldn't say. All I know is that it was over, and Dawn, at least, was playing the field. And who could blame her? When you're young and have the world at your feet, why shouldn't you have your fun?'

I smiled. 'Why not indeed? And George?'

'Again, I couldn't say. I have better things to do than track the love lives of the young folk of Compton,' Belinda said crisply.

'Point taken.' I didn't want to alienate her by pressing the point. 'You said there were things that you never put in your reports. What did you mean by that?'

Belinda reached for a pen from the desk tidy, twirling it between her fingers, though I didn't suppose she had any intention of writing anything.

'This is where it gets tricky,' she said. 'I'm not going to be talking facts here, just impressions.'

'Fair enough.' From my own personal experience I knew just how important gut feelings could be.

'Number one. Neither Dawn nor Lisa wanted to talk about the fire. Now, in some ways I suppose you could say that was understandable. But I usually find people are only too eager to talk. It's cathartic for them, somehow, to let it all out to someone willing to listen. But not those two. Neither of them would open up. It was almost as if they were hiding something. Or were scared out of their wits that they might say the wrong thing. Don't ask me what – I haven't a clue. I can only tell you it's what I thought at the time.'

I mulled this over.

'You're talking about the immediate aftermath of the fire, I presume.' She nodded. 'What about when Brian Jennings was arrested and tried? Did you interview them again then?'

Belinda's lips twisted into a crooked grin.

'I tried, of course. But neither of them was ever available

for an interview, not even after it was no longer sub-judice. I had the devil's own job to drag so much as a sound bite out of them. And to me, that's . . . strange. Or certainly unusual.'

'It is,' I said thoughtfully. In my experience too, generally speaking, people, and victims especially, wanted to have their say. To demand justice, to express relief or dissatisfaction with a verdict. Not to want to say anything at all was certainly unusual, but something I was beginning to grow used to in this investigation. Nobody, but nobody, wanted to say anything.

'You never wondered about that, pursued it?' I asked.

Belinda shrugged. 'Not my job. I did wonder, of course, but I'm a local hack, not an investigative reporter, and in any case, I'm kept too busy to look into things too deeply. The flower show has to be covered, and the swimming-club galas, and the main problem is finding a good lead story for the front page each week. Sometimes they come looking for you – parents of sick children raising funds to take them for treatment abroad, or whatever, the occasional bit of excitement like a shooting or a drowning, or plans for a new supermarket causing an upset, but sometimes I'm struggling, and it all eats into my time.'

Movement in the main office on the other side of the window attracted my attention – a tall figure in a leather jacket had come in and was walking up the aisle between the desks. Josh! My heart skipped a beat.

A moment later the door opened.

'Oh, sorry Belinda, I didn't realize you had someone with you . . . Sally! What a surprise!'

'Hello, Josh,' I said, thinking: *That was a tall one!* Surely Josh had seen us through the window – the slatted blinds were open and he'd been heading straight for us.

'Just filling her in on a few details, Josh. Things that aren't in my cuttings files that you so generously made available to her,' Belinda said, her tone heavily overlaid with sarcasm.

'In that case I'll leave you to it.'

'It's OK – I've got to go out now in any case.' Belinda got up, reaching for her jacket and slipping it on.

I got up too. 'Thanks very much, Belinda.'

'No problem. Though I'm not sure I've been much help.'

'You have, actually.'

'Good.' She grabbed her bag, slid a shorthand notebook and a pencil into it, and left.

'So what's she been telling you?' Josh asked when we were alone.

'Background stuff about Dawn, mostly,' I said.

'Oh come on, it must have been a bit more than that.'

'Background stuff is very useful. I'm looking for someone who might have wanted rid of Dawn – permanently – remember. And she also said the girls were very reticent about the fire. I think I should try to talk to Lisa Curry again – for all the good it will do.'

Josh sighed. 'Oh Sally, is there no way I can talk you out of going on with this?'

'None,' I said flatly. 'And by the way, I've been trying to get hold of you. Tara said she'd left a message on your mobile.'

'Oh, I haven't picked them up lately,' Josh said blithely. 'And I try to avoid Tara's as long as possible, anyway. They usually mean more work. Now if I'd known it was you . . . I must give you my number. I don't know why I haven't. So why were you trying to get hold of me? Something nice, I hope.'

'Actually I wanted to rearrange for tomorrow. I went to the meeting of Compton Players last night, and there's another on Wednesday. I'd really like to make it.'

'That's me put in my place then,' Josh said ruefully.

'Oh no, it's not like that! It's just that . . .'

'I know. Your investigation comes first.'

'Couldn't we make it another time?'

'What about tonight then?'

'I thought you said you were busy tonight.'

'Things change,' Josh said breezily. 'If you turn me down, I'll know you really are trying to avoid me.'

Though I was a bit puzzled as to why he was now suddenly free tonight, a little shiver of warmth tickled deep inside me.

'You've talked me into it.'

'I'll pick you up at about eight.'

'Fine. And now I have to go and collect my new laptop. Exciting or what?'

'Sally, you are incorrigible.'

I grinned. 'I know.'

Twelve

Next day I spent a good long while transferring all my notes to my new laptop, and drinking plenty of strong coffee. Goodness knows, I needed it!

Josh and I had spent another very pleasant evening together, checking out the merits of yet another country pub. I filled him in on my visit to the Compton Players, though I didn't, of course, mention the fright I'd had when I thought I was being followed on the way home, and Josh regaled me with some amusing stories of situations he'd encountered in his line of work – the nonagenarian who couldn't find her false teeth and refused to be photographed without them, the time he'd been trying to capture scenes of heavy snowfall, slipped and ended up in a deep drift.

When he drove me home we spent a good quarter of an hour getting to know one another more intimately in the privacy of his car, parked well out of the sight-lines from Mum's bedroom window, and Josh suggested that our next date should be him cooking a meal for me at the cottage he was renting on the outskirts of Stoke Compton.

'You can *cook*?' I teased. 'This I must sample!'

Josh grinned. 'Bit of an exaggeration,' he admitted. 'But I'm very good at ordering tasty takeaways.'

'That's more like it . . .' I began, but he silenced me with another kiss, and I thought that it really was not Josh's culinary talents I was interested in!

Now, as I tried to concentrate on making some sense out of the tangled bits of information I'd gleaned so far, it occurred to me how things had changed. Not much more than a week ago I'd been trapped in a moribund relationship that was in even worse shape than I'd realized at the time, and bored out of my mind by enforced inactivity. Now I was fully occupied, but actually having to force myself to concentrate on Dawn Burridge's romantic involvements because my mind was wandering to my own very promising budding relationship!

That evening I set out in Dad's car for Stoke Compton, and once again I was lucky enough to find a parking space close to the town hall. I wondered if I'd spot Lewis Crighton and Sarah again, but tonight the upper windows of Compton Properties were all in darkness.

I made my way via the lift to the upper room in the town hall where the players met, and some of them greeted me like an old friend while others ignored me. John, the director, was quite cool – he'd realized I was no budding Emma Thompson, I supposed. Once again 'gorgeous George' failed to put in an appearance, and Bella Crighton was missing too. The meeting took much the same form as before, though tonight we were reading *Blithe Spirit*. And when proceedings drew to a close, Delyth once again invited me to join some of the members for a drink at the Feathers, and this time I accepted, having warned Mum I might be a bit late home.

The Feathers had none of the cosy comfort of the inns I'd been visiting with Josh. It was a typical town-centre pub, rather shabby, with ring-marked tables, tatty cardboard beer mats and a large screen television mounted on the wall that was, mercifully, not turned on tonight. The walls were hung with faded, ancient prints and discoloured by years of cigarette smoke in the days before the ban, the chairs were slightly wonky and the floor covered in a threadbare carpet. The members of the group didn't seem unduly bothered, though – as their local, they probably no longer noticed how run down the place was, and they took all the liberties of regulars, pushing tables together so that we could sit in one big circle.

Everyone seemed to be buying and paying for their own drinks – a long-established ritual to avoid big rounds, I imagined – but I insisted on buying one for Delyth. She really had been very nice to me. I sat between her and the girl whose perpetual uniform seemed to be a fun fur and leggings and who, I discovered, was Amanda Fricker, the girl whom Dawn had usurped as principal girl in the annual pantomime.

At first the conversation was dominated by discussion about

the relative values of the plays we'd been reading, and how they might be cast. George's name came up. 'He's not here, though, is he?' someone said.

'He'll come out of the woodwork if there's a good part on offer,' someone else remarked.

'I've heard a lot about George,' I ventured. 'He's very good, isn't he?'

Delyth nodded. 'He won best actor in the one-act festival a couple of years ago.'

'And brought Dawn back as well as the cup.' Amanda's tone was unpleasant. 'It didn't last long, though, did it? Dawn was never going to be satisfied with someone who couldn't afford to keep her in the manner she thought she deserved.'

There was a small embarrassed silence. Then: 'Don't let's go into all that again,' Delyth said. 'Especially not now poor Dawn's not here to defend herself.'

Amanda snorted. 'What's to defend? No man was safe with her around. She even worked her wiles on John, getting him to cast her in all the best parts. And the trouble she caused between Bella and Lewis . . .'

'I don't think Lewis was entirely blameless,' Delyth said. Her cheeks had turned a little pink. 'And John cast her because she was good.'

'That's a matter of opinion.'

'She was good! And honestly, Amanda, this is the sort of talk that's driving George away. You know how much he thought of Dawn, even after . . .' She broke off. 'Anyway, I don't like to hear you speak ill of the dead.'

'Let's change the subject,' one of the others said. 'Or George isn't the only one we'll be driving away.' She winked at me, and I smiled back, but my mind was busy.

Dawn certainly had made enemies, just as Alice had inferred. And it had just been confirmed to me that she did have a fling with Lewis Crighton, and probably others too, both married and single. But I was still a long way from discovering who she might have upset so badly that they could have wanted her dead.

Not George, it would seem – it sounded as if he still carried a torch for her. Or was it guilt that was keeping him away

from the Compton Players? I didn't know, and short of continuing to insinuate myself into their group, I couldn't see how
I was going to find out.

It was gone half past ten by the time people began getting
up to leave, and I took my cue to do the same.

As I got into my car, the memory of the last time I'd made
this journey hit me, and a sensation of unease fluttered in my
tummy. Since some of the others had left the pub at the same
time as me, there was a flurry of cars pulling out of the Square
as I did, and there were headlights behind me through the
traffic lights and the first junction. I kept checking nervously
as one by one they peeled off and by the time I was out of
the built-up area, my mirror reflected only the last street lamps
and an empty road behind me. A little way out into the country
and headlights glared in my mirror again; I put my foot down
hard, but still the lights closed in on me and I saw the car was
pulling out to overtake. My stomach muscles tightened and I
felt the beginnings of the same panic I'd experienced the other
night – was he going to box me in? But hardly had the thought
formed in my mind than he was roaring past me, going like
a bat out of hell. Normally I'd have been worried that I might
come upon him around the next bend, having either lost
control or collided with an oncoming vehicle; tonight I felt
nothing but relief that at least he wasn't following me.

Apart from a few cars going in the opposite direction, I saw
no one else. But I was very glad, all the same, when I reached
the farm yard.

'You see? There was nothing to worry about, was there?'
I said aloud. And the only reply was Scrumpy's obligatory
greeting.

Thursday dawned wet and windy; with a leaden sky making
everything dark and gloomy, the onset of spring, which had
seemed imminent only yesterday, now seemed as far away as
ever. Definitely a day for staying indoors to work rather than
going out to investigate!

I booted up my new laptop, organized the files I'd transferred
from my memory stick, and was staring at the screen, deep in
thought, when the phone rang. Mum was out seeing to the

hens, I knew – I didn't envy her in this weather! – so I answered
it and was surprised to hear Rachel's voice.

'Sally? That is you, isn't it?'

'Oh yes, it's me. Hi, Rach.'

'Are you in this morning? I've got a couple of hours free,
and I was thinking of popping over.'

'I'm not going anywhere. I'd love to see you.'

'I'll be over in about half an hour, then. And we can talk
about going down to Dorset.'

That reminded me – I hadn't done any more about finding
an address for Dawn's parents. Whilst waiting for Rachel, I went
on line and searched for a family named Burridge in the Wedgeley
Down area. There were two, a C.T. Burridge, and an Andrew,
and I hadn't a clue which was Dawn's father. But Burridge wasn't
exactly a common name, and the chances were they were both
related – a brother or an uncle, perhaps. I checked the addresses
– Ivy Cottage, Parsonage Lane, and forty-nine Keats Road.
Chances were, I thought, that Keats Road was a new estate, and
Ivy Cottage an older property. But I really didn't have time to
try either of them now. Rachel would be arriving at any minute.

Or was I just making excuses? I wasn't looking forward to
approaching Dawn's family, and I knew it was just another sign
that I was definitely going soft. Contacting the bereaved was
never something I enjoyed, but I'd never shrunk from doing
it where necessary. Now the thought of trying to elicit information from the parents of a dead girl, and possibly informing
them I didn't believe her death had been accidental at all, was
making me shudder inwardly.

I was going to have to toughen up again, not a doubt of
it, when I went back to work if not now, so it might as well
be now. My hand hovered over the telephone.

'Sally! Hello! Are you there?' Rachel's voice from the hall.
She'd obviously let herself in. I felt guilty relief at the welcome
reprieve.

For the next hour Rachel and I sat chatting over coffee and
custard cream biscuits at the kitchen table. Mum had come in,
rivulets of rain that had dripped from the hood of her Barbour
running down her face, and her trousers creased from where
they'd been jammed into her wellington boots.

'It's a quagmire out there,' she said, cheerfully enough. Mum had never been one to let bad weather get her down; just as well, since a farm has to be run whatever the elements throw at you – the animals fed, the cows brought in for milking, the eggs collected.

'Steve's not going to be happy with me,' Rachel said anxiously. 'There was no way I could avoid the puddles in the lane, and he only took the car to the car wash on Sunday.'

I couldn't help but smile.

'You worry too much, Rach. Muddy splashes, scraped wing mirrors – you need to get a run-around of your own or you're heading for a nervous breakdown.'

'And how could we afford to run two cars?' Rachel demanded. 'It's not going to happen, unless we come up on the lottery, or I get a full-time job.'

'So what do you think about Sally's new boyfriend, then, Rachel?' Mum asked.

'I think it's great.' But Rachel sounded somehow a bit hesitant. I'd noticed she'd gone quiet earlier when I'd been talking about Josh, and thought I was imagining things, but now there was no mistaking it.

'Come on, Rach, show a bit of enthusiasm!' I urged her. 'You were the one who wanted me to ditch Tim and find somebody new.'

'I know, I know! And I'm really pleased if he's all you say he is,' Rachel said.

'He is!'

'You don't really *know* him, though, do you?' Rachel said cautiously.

'Well, you never know anyone if you don't give yourself the chance,' I argued.

'That's true. But you shouldn't let yourself get carried away – get involved too heavily too soon. It sounds to me as if you've fallen head over heels for this chap, Sally, and I don't want to see you hurt.'

It was almost an echo of what Mum had said to me, and I began to feel as if they were ganging up on me.

'Oh for goodness sake!' I exploded.

'Just be careful, Sally.' Rachel had her serious face on, which, to be honest was the one she wore most often. 'There are a lot of rotters out there, who'll tell you whatever they think you want to hear. You're sure he's not married, for starters?'

'Unlikely. He's invited me to his cottage for our next date.'

That took the wind out of her sails for a minute. Then she recovered herself.

'OK, so he's not living with anyone. But I still think you should be careful. He could be telling you a whole pack of lies about himself, and you'd be swallowing all of them. He could have a violent streak, or be some kind of pervert with all kinds of porn downloaded on his computer. It's no good you making that face – I'm just saying. Don't get carried away until you know him better.'

'She's right, Sally. He might seem nice, but you never know . . .' Mum cautioned.

I raised my eyes heavenward.

'Honestly, just listen to the pair of you! Nobody would think I decamped to the big city when I was eighteen years old, and I've managed to live there without getting myself raped or murdered ever since. I'm a big girl, OK?'

'Just saying,' Rachel repeated in a conciliatory tone.

'Shall we change the subject?' I suggested.

We did, going back instead to tentative arrangements for Rachel to drive me down to Dorset. But for all my insouciance, I couldn't help a tiny niggle of unease. I really liked Josh. More than liked, if I was being honest. And really, I couldn't imagine him being any of the things Rachel was implying he might be. A liar, a wife-beater, a pervert – or even just a heel. It didn't tie in with the Josh I'd been dating – was, possibly, even falling in love with.

But the truth of the matter was I really knew nothing whatever about him beyond that he was a newspaper photographer, and very attractive to boot. I didn't have a clue as to what he'd been doing before he came to Stoke Compton, his family, or where he called home. Somehow we'd never got around to talking about any of those things – or if we had been close, the conversation had always slipped away in another direction. When Josh had mentioned taking his sister's children to Longleat, it was the closest we'd ever got to his background, and even then he hadn't expanded on the bare remark.

I didn't actually know a single thing about him. But what the heck? Surely I could rely on my instincts to warn me off if there was anything dodgy about the man who was beginning to loom large in my life?

'How about one day next week then?' Rachel was saying.

'Sounds good to me,' I said, and let my anxiety about meeting Dawn's parents supersede the niggling doubts I was suddenly having about my whirlwind romance with Josh.

Late afternoon, and the rain was still falling, a thick drizzle now, with a gusting wind tossing it in flurries against the windows. I'd spent the last couple of hours on my computer, and sitting around, I'd got chilled to the marrow without even realizing it. I dragged myself upstairs to find a thick sweater, and sat down again, staring thoughtfully at the two telephone numbers I'd unearthed, one of which I felt sure must be for Dawn Burridge's parents.

It was quite possible, of course, that there wouldn't be anyone at home at this time of day, but if I didn't try, I wouldn't know. And if I didn't at least attempt to make the call now, I wasn't sure I'd ever do it at all.

I decided on one of the two numbers, and before I could change my mind, dialled it. After just a couple of rings, an answering machine kicked in, and I killed the call. This wasn't something I could leave a message about. Without much hope I tried the second number. It rang interminably and I was just about to hang up when it was answered. A man's voice, abrupt, as if he was less than pleased to have been interrupted in whatever he had been doing when the telephone rang. But my nervousness had melted away as if by magic; it was like riding a bicycle, I thought – once you were back in the saddle it just came naturally.

'Do I have the right number for the parents of Dawn Burridge?' I asked smoothly.

The man answered my question with one of his own.

'Who is this?'

'My name is Sally Proctor,' I said. 'You won't know me, but I'm trying to get in touch with them.'

'Were you a friend of Dawn's?'

'Yes,' I lied. 'I live in Stoke Compton. Are you Dawn's father?'

'Her brother.'

Ah. So I was on the right track.

'Would it be possible to speak to either her mother or father?'

'You'll have a job to speak to Dad,' the man said tersely. 'I'm afraid he passed away just before Christmas.'

I was, I have to confess, a bit shocked.

'Oh, I'm really sorry to hear that . . .' I said awkwardly.

'I'm not sure whether Mum is up to talking to anyone,' the man went on. 'Losing first Dawn, and then Dad . . . she's not in a good place just now.'

'No, I can imagine . . .' I broke off as I heard a woman's voice in the background.

'Who is it, Andrew?'

A few moments' silence ensued; Dawn's brother had covered the receiver with his hand, I imagined. And then, to my surprise, the line opened up again and the same voice I'd heard in the background, oddly sharp, yet with a Dorset burr, was speaking in my ear.

'This is Grace Burridge.'

'Mrs Burridge.' My nervousness had returned, but I was, thankfully, able to control it. 'This is Sally Proctor.'

'So my son said. You were a friend of Dawn's, I understand.'

'Yes.' This time I felt really guilty for the lie. 'Can I say how sorry I am for your loss?'

'You can say it, but it won't bring them back, will it?' she said flatly.

'No, I realize that. Mrs Burridge, the reason I'm ringing is that I was wondering if I could come and see you.'

'What for?'

'I want to talk to you about Dawn . . .' I was expecting her to ask me why I wanted to talk to her, and I really hadn't made up my mind what I was going to say. Instead, to my surprise, there was complete silence at the other end of the line. 'Mrs Burridge?' I ventured.

I heard what sounded like a muffled sob, followed by another silence. I waited. Sometimes it was better to say nothing at all.

After a moment when Grace Burridge must have been collecting herself, she spoke just two words.

'All right.'

'You don't mind talking to me?' I wanted to be sure I'd understood her correctly.

'I expect I'll upset myself. But it's nice to talk to someone who knew her . . . not many people want to talk about her at all. They cross the street, you know, rather than have to think of what to say to me. Yes, my dear, if you want to talk about Dawn, you're most welcome.'

I really did feel guilty now, dreadfully, horribly guilty. But it was too late to tell her the truth now. And besides, if I was able to get justice for Dawn, surely that wasn't such a bad thing?

'When do you want to come?' Grace Burridge asked.

'Would one morning next week suit you? I won't take up too much of your time.'

Grace Burridge snorted. 'Huh! I've enough of that on my hands now. I'm on my own here most days, except for when Andrew pops in, like now. No, you come whenever you like. Just give me a ring and let me know when to expect you.'

'Thank you, Mrs Burridge. I'll do that.'

I put down the phone and sat for a moment massaging my temples with my fingertips. That conversation had been horrible, and there would be worse to come.

Time, I reckoned, for a cup of tea!

I headed for the kitchen. The delicious aroma of frying onions wafted out to greet me.

'Something smells good!' I enthused.

'Just a casserole for tomorrow.' Mum was at the Aga, wearing a dark cook's apron and stirring meat and vegetables in a cast iron pot. 'It's going to be a busy day, and a casserole always tastes better when the flavour's had a chance to develop.'

'You must give me the recipe so I can make one for myself when I go home,' I said, checking the kettle for water and putting it on.

Mum laughed. 'And when will you have time to cook, Sally? You're always on the go.'

'You never know.' The way I was coming to feel about Josh

was actually making me yearn to do the simple, homely things I'd never bothered about in the past. Things I'd certainly never wanted to do for Tim. The niggling doubts that had assailed me when Rachel had pointed out that I knew nothing whatever about Josh had subsided now as if they'd never been. I only knew that when I was with him it felt so right, and the thought of cooking for him was just one of the things that gave me a warm, rosy glow of anticipation.

'You want a cuppa?' I asked Mum.

'Do you know, I wouldn't say no,' Mum said. 'Have you had a good afternoon?'

'I've spoken to Dawn Burridge's mother.' I went on to tell her about the conversation, setting out mugs, milk and sugar on the worktop as I did so.

'Poor soul! What she must be going through.' Mum shook her head sympathetically. 'If I was to lose you and your dad, I don't know what I'd do. You will be careful, won't you, Sally, what you say to her? You don't want to go making things even worse than they are for her.'

'I'll be careful,' I promised. But truth to tell I was worried about the forthcoming interview, very aware that there really was no easy way to tell Dawn's mother of my suspicions, and wondering if I'd done the right thing in contacting her. Talking to her would have been bad enough under any circumstances, but with Dawn's father having died so recently it really was a minefield. Perhaps I should make further enquiries before going to see her. I really needed to be a good deal surer of my ground than I was at the moment. Yet who would know better than Dawn's mother if she'd been worried about something in those last weeks of her life, frightened even?

The kettle was boiling; I propped my crutches against the edge of the table so as to have two hands to make the tea.

'Careful, Sally!' Mum warned.

'It's OK, I'm fine . . .'

Just at that moment the kitchen door burst open, making me jump, and I banged the kettle down quickly so that I could regain my balance. But if any boiling water splashed out, I didn't notice.

'Oh – Mrs . . . Mrs . . . come quick . . .' Sam Groves, Dad's farmhand was in the doorway, breathing heavily as if he'd been running. His face was red, too, but it was his anguished expression that made my heart almost stop beating, the near panic in his voice.

'Sam − what ever . . .?' Mum, still clutching her wooden spoon, was like a frozen statue.

'Quick, quick, phone for an ambulance . . .'

'Why? What's happened?'

'Oh my lord, it's the boss . . . the cows . . . they stampeded in the lane . . . oh, for the love of God get an ambulance . . . he's been trampled. Jack's been trampled by the herd!'

Thirteen

In that first startled moment my heart seemed to stop beating. All the blood left my body in a rush and I was as chilled and shocked as when I was caught in the avalanche, and my legs as weak and helpless as when the snow whipped the ground from under me.

This couldn't be happening, Dad trampled by his beloved, docile herd of cows? It made no sense. But there was no denying it; Sam, the farmhand who was normally stolid and imperturbable was in a state of utter panic.

'Oh my lord . . . !' Mum's usually ruddy face was drained of colour. She made a dive for the phone; I took it from her.

'I'll do it. Go on, Mum, go to Dad.'

I stabbed in 999, realized I had no line, and managed to lose what I'd dialled as I fumbled stupidly with the button that would give me one. By the time I'd redialled, Mum was shoving her feet into her wellington boots with no care for the chunks of wet mud that were falling from them and miring the kitchen.

'Emergency. Which service?'

'Ambulance.' My throat was so dry I could scarcely speak.

Mum grabbed her coat and ran out the door, pulling it on over her cook's apron. Sam followed her, so there was no chance for me to ask him any more details, but as far as my emergency call was concerned it hardly mattered. I knew the stretch of lane along which the cows were driven for milking; the routine was always the same, and had been for as long as I could remember. As for Dad's condition, that was something I was going to have to find out for myself.

When I'd finished speaking to the ambulance control room I grabbed my walking boots and struggled into them, my hands shaking so much it was all I could do to tie the laces. My Berghaus was hanging on a hook in the hall; I flung it on. As I swung into the farmyard as fast I was able, I saw Scrumpy standing shivering beside her kennel, tail down, head hung low.

She took a couple of steps towards me, then retreated, the picture of a dog in disgrace. Scrumpy always went with Dad when he was out and about on the farm; when the herd stampeded she must have fled, and now was feeling as guilty as if the catastrophe was somehow her fault.

I was halfway across the farmyard when I remembered – Mum had been in the middle of cooking when Sam came bursting in. Had she left something on the ring of the Aga? The onions I'd smelled frying, perhaps? If so, the pan could catch fire and the whole kitchen go up in flames. I struggled back inside, sick with fear. With the present pervading aura of nightmare, no disaster seemed beyond the realms of possibility.

The cast-iron casserole was still on the ring, but safe enough – Mum had reached the stage of adding stock, which was now bubbling furiously. I lifted it off and set it down on the nearest worktop, not caring whether or not it would damage the wood work surface. The dish was so heavy I couldn't manage to limp any further with it, and a scorched work top was the least of my worries just now.

One of my crutches had fallen on to the floor; I rescued it, and hopped outside.

It was still raining, a horrible thick drizzle. By the time I reached the track my hood had come down and my hair was clinging damply round my face. I ignored it. I didn't have a free hand, and I didn't want to stop to pull my hood up again. I could see the cows milling about outside the milking shed; they'd obviously made their way to their usual destination, and seemed quiet enough now, apart from some jostling and the occasional plaintive 'moo!' Up ahead, about a hundred yards away, I could see Mum on her knees on the lane, Sam beside her. And though they were blocking my view, an outstretched leg told me it was Dad they were kneeling beside.

The sick feeling pulsed now in my throat as I swung on along the track, stumbling sometimes as my crutch hit a muddy rut, but somehow managing to recover myself. Then I slowed, my breath coming in shaky gasps.

Dad was lying across the verge, his head cradled in Mum's lap. There was blood everywhere, streaking his paper-white face, clotting in his hair and pooling in the mud. His arm was at an impossibly crazy angle, his eyes were closed. For a heart-stopping moment I thought he was dead.

'Dad?' I sobbed.

'He's breathing,' Mum said. She sounded unbelievably calm now, as if from somewhere she had found reserves of strength.

I bent low, wishing that, like Mum, I could get down on my knees, but since I wasn't able to bend my leg, I couldn't do that. I could see now that the blood was coming from a huge gash on the side of Dad's head, but it looked to me as if he'd taken a blow from a flying hoof rather than been trodden on. I wished desperately that I'd thought to bring towels or even a sheet or pillow case, anything with which to stem the bleeding, and a blanket to cover Dad with, but I hadn't. Just getting to him had been all that had mattered.

'I've called the ambulance,' I said. 'They'll be here soon.'

I wasn't too confident of that actually; way out in the country we were too far from the ambulance station to be favoured with the fastest of response times. But to my surprise and relief it could only have been a matter of minutes before I heard the sound of a siren, distant, admittedly, but getting louder. Once or twice it faded, as the ambulance negotiated the winding road, I supposed, but then grew louder again, and then it appeared at the end of the lane, blue lights flashing, the most welcome sight I'd ever seen in my life.

It came to a halt just a few feet from us, and two paramedics in green overalls jumped out and ran towards us.

'OK, my love, just stand back and leave this to us,' one of them, a slight, balding man, said, and his partner, a comfortably large woman, knelt beside Dad.

'Hello there, can you hear me? Can you tell me your name, dear?'

Dad made no response. His eyes remained closed, and he gave no sign whatsoever that he had heard her.

Mum answered for him.

'Jack. Jack Proctor.' Then the terrified tremble returned to her voice as she asked: 'He is going to be all right, isn't he? Please tell me he's going to be all right!'

* * *

They couldn't, of course. 'He's in good hands now,' was the best they could do. I stood to one side looking on anxiously as they went about their business, and at one point I heard the air ambulance mentioned. In the end, though, that didn't come to anything. They got Dad on to a back board and into the ambulance, fixing up drips and heaven only knows what else – I really couldn't see, except that there was a lot of activity.

'Are you coming to hospital with him, sweetheart?' the female paramedic asked Mum.

'Oh yes – yes, of course . . . Will you be all right, Sally?'

'Yes. Just go, Mum.'

'And the cows . . .?' She turned to Sam. 'You'll see to the cows?'

'We'll see to everything here, don't worry.'

'I'll ring you, Sally.'

'*Go!*'

The female paramedic got into the back of the ambulance with Mum and Dad, her partner went around to climb into the cab. And then they were reversing back along the lane, the blue lights strobing in the gathering dusk, and Sam and I were alone.

'Oh, t'is terrible! Terrible!' Sam was in shock, I could see, his hands twitching, his ruddy face pale.

'You'd better come back to the house and have a cup of tea,' I said.

'No, no, I've got to see to them cows . . .'

'All right. I'll help you.'

Between us we got the cows into the milking parlour and set about what had to be done, both of us on autopilot.

'Now we'll have that cup of tea,' I said when we'd finished and the cows were safely locked up. 'No arguments, Sam. You look terrible. And besides, I want to know what happened.'

The milking parlour had been no place to talk, with the clatter of machinery, and getting the details out of Sam was never going to be easy – he was such a taciturn man. In any case, it had been all I could manage to carry out the necessary tasks with my emotions in turmoil and my head spinning, not to mention my need for the crutches. Now, though, I was desperate for answers.

I set the kettle to boil, experiencing a weird nightmarish sense of déjà vu. Was it really less than an hour ago that I'd been making tea for Mum and myself? In that short space of time the whole of our worlds had been turned upside down.

Sam was standing awkwardly in the doorway, clutching his cap between both hands as if it were a lifeline he didn't want to part with.

'Sit down, for goodness sake, Sam!' I instructed him.

He sat reluctantly on one of the heavy old dining chairs; in all the years he'd worked for Dad I couldn't ever remember him taking a seat in our kitchen before. I set a mug of scalding tea in front of him and added three generous spoonfuls of sugar. I had no idea how sweet he liked it normally, but right now he needed the lift – and so did I. In fact, I thought we could both do with something stronger. I found a half bottle of brandy in the cabinet and poured two generous measures.

'Here – this might help too.'

Sam didn't argue. He emptied his glass in one swallow. I sipped mine more judiciously, then asked the question that was burning on my lips.

'What on earth made the cows stampede, Sam?'

Sam shook his head, the mug of hot sweet tea cradled now between his weather-beaten hands.

'Well, t'were that bloody motorbike, weren't it?'

'A *motorbike*?' I was startled. 'In our lane?'

'A motorbike,' Sam repeated. 'Damn great powerful thing. Bloody fool came roaring down the track, blaring his horn like a bloody madman. Frightened me to death, never mind the cows. Course they got in a panic. They were off before I could do a bloody thing. I was behind them, see, moving on the stragglers like I al'us do, with your dad on up ahead, going on to see 'em in through the gate. He couldn't get out of the way, I don't s'pose.'

His voice trailed away and he relapsed into silence. It was probably the longest speech Sam had ever made in his life. But I couldn't let him stop there.

'So what did the motorcyclist do when the herd stampeded?' I asked. I was totally puzzled as well as angry that anyone could have been so stupid. A motorbike in our lane was unheard of, especially one whose rider was so impatient he'd terrified a herd of docile cows.

Sam scratched his head.

'Well, he must've turned round and gone back the way he came. I were in such a state I never noticed.'

That was understandable, I supposed. Sam would have set off after the cows, and the motorcyclist, realizing what he'd done, had hightailed it. But why had he been in our lane in the first place? And in such a hurry? The lane led nowhere except to our farm. He must have taken a wrong turning. Or perhaps it had been a crazy hot-rod kid looking for somewhere he could go off-road and indulge in a spot of scrambling. Off-road bikes didn't usually have engines you'd describe as powerful, as Sam had, but then Sam wasn't the most articulate of men, and he was in such a state it was possible he wasn't remembering what had happened as accurately as he might.

'We're going to have to report this to the police, Sam,' I said. 'Do you want to phone your wife and tell her you're going to be late home?'

'I s'pose I'd better, ah.'

While Sam was speaking to Mary, his wife, I looked up the number for the police station. I couldn't tie up the 999 line again – traumatic though this was for us, it was no longer an emergency. But in the event I didn't need to make the call. There was a knock at the door, and when I answered it, it was to find two uniformed police officers on the doorstep, one a man in his forties, the other a fresh-faced girl who hadn't been long in the job, I guessed.

'PC Alan Bicknell and PC Claire James,' the man said by way of introduction. 'We're here about the incident in the lane.'

'Oh, right.' The emergency-services control room had been in touch with the police, then. Of course, I should have realized they would, but I wasn't thinking very straight. 'You'd better come in.'

The two police officers followed me into the kitchen.

'I was just going to phone you,' I said. 'This is Sam Groves. He works for my father.'

Sam was shifting uneasily in his seat, but for the moment the policeman merely nodded at him, speaking instead to me.

'And you are . . .?'

'Sally Proctor. Jack Proctor's daughter. I'm the one who made the nine-nine-nine call.'

'And your father has been taken to hospital, I understand?'

I nodded. 'Yes. He was unconscious. I don't know how he is now – I'm waiting for my mother to call when there's any news.' A feeling of utter helplessness overwhelmed me, and suddenly tears were pricking behind my eyes.

'No news is good news,' the young policewoman said chirpily, and the older officer shot her a warning look.

'So can you tell us what happened?' he asked, then indicated a chair. 'All right if we sit down?'

'Yes – yes, of course. Would you like a cup of tea?'

'We wouldn't say no to that.' He laid a clipboard, notebook and phone on the table and sat down, easing open his jacket to reveal a stab vest, something that always struck me as incongruous out here in the sticks. But health and safety rules, I suppose, and you never know when or where violence may occur. Or a horrible accident . . . I felt the tears pricking again and busied myself making the tea.

'So what can you tell us about what happened, Miss Proctor?' PC Bicknell was asking.

I half turned towards him.

'It's Sam you need to talk to. He was helping my father get the cows in.'

'Right. Go ahead then, Mr . . . Grove, is it?'

'Ah, Mr Groves,' Sam said, and fell silent again. This was going to be a long and laborious process, I knew.

By the time I'd made the tea and placed the mugs in front of the two police officers they had dragged from Sam the same story he'd told me.

'Can you tell us anything about this motorcycle?' PC Bicknell was asking, and Sam was huffing and puffing in confusion and shaking his head.

'Can't say. All I know is t'were a motorbike.'

'Big? Small?'

'Oh, a big 'un.'

'Colour?'

'Don't know. Didn't see.'

'What about the rider?'

'Didn't see him really, either. He had one o' them girt big crash helmets on . . .' Sam was obviously making a huge effort to remember what he could. 'It were black,' he announced triumphantly. 'An' he were all in black, too. Black leather, I reckon.'

Great, I thought. Black leathers and a full-face crash helmet. That really narrowed the field. But what did it matter? What did any of it matter? The only thing of any importance was Dad . . . how was he? What was happening? I should be at the hospital with Mum, not sitting here drinking tea. I'd get over there the minute the police officers had gone, either call a taxi or drive Dad's car . . . The hospital. It struck me suddenly I wasn't even sure where Dad had been taken. Porton was our nearest A & E, but with his head injury maybe they'd take him straight to Frenchay, the specialist unit in Bristol . . .

The phone was ringing. I snatched it up.

'Hello?'

'Sally – it's me. Mum.'

'Mum!' I hobbled across the kitchen and into the hall where I'd have more privacy. 'What's happening? How's Dad?'

'There's no change really. He still hasn't come round. They're doing all sorts of tests, scans – oh, I don't know what they called them. His shoulder was out and they've got that back in. But they're worried about internal injuries as well. I don't understand half of what they're saying, so I can't tell you much, but I thought I ought to give you a ring. I knew you'd be worried.'

'Yes, thanks, Mum. Look, the police are here at the moment, but . . .'

'The police?'

'Yes. It seems it was a motorcycle that caused the cows to stampede, and they're talking to Sam. But as soon as they've gone, I'll drive over. You are at Porton General, I presume?'

'Yes, but . . . there's nothing you can do here, love.'

'I can be there for you and Dad.'

'I know that. And there's nothing I'd like better than to have some company, but . . .'

'But nothing! I'll be there.'

'No, Sally, listen to me. The farm won't run itself. Somebody's got to be there to see to it.'

I felt a surge of panic. She was right, of course, the farm wouldn't run itself. But I couldn't do it! I wouldn't know where to start! Born and brought up here I might have been, but I hadn't lived here now for years, and even when I did, the nitty-gritties had been way outside my domain. Besides which, still partially disabled, I was not physically up to doing all the things that needed to be done.

'Look, you've got Sam,' Mum said, trying to reassure me.

'But he can't manage on his own.'

'No, but he knows what needs to be done. Now listen, Sally, I think the best thing would be for you to try and get hold of one of the casuals your dad uses in the summer. There's Bill Turnbull and his boy Mark, and the Greenings. All their numbers are in the book – you know the one – it's by the phone in the hall. Ring them now, see if any of them can come and help out.'

'Yes, I know the book . . .' I could see it from where I was standing, a quarto-sized yellow book with a floral design on the cover. 'But what if they can't help?'

'We'll cross that bridge when we come to it.' Mum was her usual pragmatic self – the self that had kicked in, I supposed, when she'd conquered the effects of the first shock of what had happened to Dad.

'Don't worry, Mum. Leave it to me.' I was trying very hard to match her no-nonsense attitude and failing miserably. Inside I was a quaking jelly.

'I don't know when I'll be home,' Mum went on, 'but I'll ring you again as soon as there's any news.'

'If you're going to be staying, there are things you'll need.' I was thinking on my feet now. 'I'll pack a bag for you, and one for Dad too, and bring them in as soon as I've sorted out things here.'

'Perhaps that would be a good idea,' Mum agreed. 'There's clean pyjamas in the airing cupboard, and his shaving kit is in the bathroom cabinet, and . . .'

'Don't worry, I'll find it. What about you? Is there anything you want especially?'

'No, just a toothbrush and comb and a change of clothes. Oh, and my handbag so that I've got some money for a cup of tea, and my mobile phone. I'm on the hospital one at the moment.'

Mum asking for her mobile phone really was a turn-up for the books. I'd bought it for her two Christmases ago, and it was something of a sore point with me that she never so much as switched it on, let alone used it. 'I've got it for emergencies,' she always said, typically stubborn. Well, this was certainly an emergency, albeit not the sort she had in mind.

'I'll be there as soon as I can,' I promised.

Back in the kitchen the police seemed to have more or less finished interviewing Sam, and when I'd given them all the other details they required they got up to go.

'We'll keep you informed if we make any progress with our enquiries,' PC Bicknell said, packing his paperwork together. 'I wouldn't hold your breath, though. We haven't got a lot to go on, and unless the culprit's got a conscience and decides to own up, there's not going to be a lot we can do.'

'I realize that.' I just wanted them to go, so that I could get on with all I had to do, and drive into Porton to be with Mum.

With one last request to Sam to let them know if he remembered anything else that might help to identify the motorcyclist, they left, and after I'd phoned Bill Turnbull and got his promise of his son Mark's help with the morning milking, Sam left too. Bill himself was busy with a job he'd been contracted to, and he couldn't speak for Mark's commitments in the coming days, but at least I had the immediate problem sorted. Further arrangements could wait until later. For now, my priority was getting to the hospital with some things for Mum and Dad.

I was upstairs packing a couple of bags when I heard someone at the door. I struggled back down the stairs, wondering if it might be the police again, but when I opened the door it was Jeremy who was standing there.

'I've just heard your dad has been involved in an accident, Sally,' he said anxiously. 'Is it true?'

Once again I could feel the tears welling.

'Yes, Jeremy, I'm afraid it is,' I said.

'So what's happened? It was the cows, I heard . . .?'

'Yes, they stampeded and Dad was trampled.'

'Is he all right?' Jeremy clapped a hand to his forehead. 'Stupid question. But you know what I mean . . .'

'He's been taken to hospital in Porton, and Mum's with him. The last I heard, he still hadn't regained consciousness. I'm on my way there now, so I won't stop to talk, if you don't mind.'

'Oh Sally, I'm very sorry to hear that.' Jeremy looked truly shocked. 'But how are you going to get to Porton?' he asked.

'I'm going to take Dad's car. Then at least we'll have transport on hand.'

'Are you sure that's a good idea?' He was looking down at my crutches.

'I've been driving it for the last week or so,' I said. 'I'll be OK.'

'I'm not so sure,' Jeremy said doubtfully. 'You're upset, Sally, as well as incapacitated. We don't want you having an accident too.'

I shrugged. 'I don't have much choice, Jeremy. Apart from taking a taxi, and that's going to cost an arm and a leg.'

'Hmm.' Jeremy consulted his watch. 'Tell you what, Sally. Give me half an hour to do a few things I need to do, and I'll take you.'

'Oh, Jeremy, no! I couldn't put you to that trouble!' I protested.

'No trouble,' he said gruffly. 'I'd never forgive myself if anything happened to you, Sally. Get whatever it is you need together, and I'll be back shortly. And I don't want to find you've taken matters into your own hands and gone already.'

'OK,' I said meekly. 'I'll take you up on that. To be honest, I don't really feel much like driving all the way to Porton and back again.'

'I'm sure you don't. See you in a bit.'

I closed the door and felt the tears pricking at my ⌐ brought on this time, I felt sure, by Jeremy's kir something like this happened, you certainly fo. your friends were.

But, apart from the medical team at the hospital, there was nothing anyone could do to help Dad. I felt sick all over again as an image of him lying in the lane, unconscious and covered with blood, rose before my eyes.

'Please, oh please, let him be all right,' I prayed.

Then, pulling myself together, I struggled back upstairs to finish packing the necessaries into bags for Mum and Dad.

I honestly don't know how I'd have managed without Jeremy that night. We'd scarcely set out in his BMW than my mobile rang – Mum, saying that Dad was being transferred to Frenchay Hospital, in Bristol, where they specialized in serious head injuries. When I relayed this information to Jeremy, he took it in his stride, immediately changing direction, and although I felt horribly guilty that his kindness had landed him with a much longer journey than he'd bargained for, I was also relieved that I didn't have to drive all that way on my own in a car that I was still not completely familiar with.

When we reached Frenchay, he came in with me – with my crutches, I'd really have struggled to carry two bags – and then accompanied me to the wing where Dad had been taken.

'I'll wait for you in the car, Sally,' he said when we reached the nurses' station. 'You'll be all right now, won't you?'

'Don't you want to see Dad?' I asked.

'I'd only be in the way, and your mum will want to talk to you alone, I'm sure.'

He was right, of course, but for all that I didn't want him to go. The company of someone just one step removed from total involvement in this nightmare was somehow comforting.

'I don't know how long I'll be,' I said tentatively.

'Take as long as you like.' Jeremy squeezed my arm. 'You know where the car's parked, and I'm not going anywhere.'

It soon became clear that Jeremy might be waiting a very long time. Dad had been whisked off for more scans, and Mum and I sat tensely waiting in the relatives' room, drinking disgusting-tasting coffee from paper cups and alternating talking out what had happened with bouts of anxious silence.

Eventually a doctor came to see us; his serious expression and the tone of his voice as he introduced himself did not bode well.

Apparently they had discovered Dad had something called a subdural haematoma – a clot between the brain and skull – and they were going to perform an emergency operation to relieve the pressure.

'There's no point you staying, Sally,' Mum said, doing her best to sound calm and in control. 'You can't keep Jeremy waiting half the night, and in any case you've got to get home to look after things on the farm in the morning.'

She was right on both counts, of course, but I really didn't want to leave her here alone, and I wanted to stay at least until Dad came out of surgery. I was wishing fervently now that I'd driven myself to the hospital – at least that way I'd have had freedom and flexibility. As things were, the best option, as I could see it, was to tell Jeremy to go home, and I'd get a taxi when I knew that Dad had come through his operation safely.

Leaving Mum in the relatives' room, I made my way out to the car park. Jeremy was sitting in the BMW just as he'd said he would be, and I could hear Classic FM playing softly on the radio. He'd reclined the seat and his eyes were closed; I thought at first that he might be asleep. But when I tapped tentatively on the window, he sat up immediately and opened the door.

'What's happening? How is he?'

I explained about the operation, and that it would be a couple of hours at the very least before I was able to leave the hospital, and suggested it would be best if he didn't wait for me any longer, but Jeremy would have none of it.

'I'll wait, Sally. The last thing you're going to want to be doing is trying to get a taxi in the middle of the night.'

'It should be easy enough here,' I argued. 'We're not out in the sticks now.' But Jeremy, bless him, was insistent.

'I'm not going to abandon you, Sally, so you might as well give up trying to make me. I will stretch my legs, though, and I could use a cup of coffee.'

'It's pretty rubbish,' I said, 'but it's better than nothing.'

'Tell you what,' Jeremy suggested. 'I'll go for a drive around and find a Pizza Hut or a McDonalds. I can get a takeaway and bring it back here. I don't suppose you or your mum have had anything to eat since lunchtime.'

'We haven't, but I'm not at all sure I could eat anything . . .'

'You can at least try,' Jeremy said. 'You go back to your mum, and I'll come and find you when I've done my late-night shop.'

And so it was back to the relatives' room, back to the endless anxious waiting, albeit this time with Jeremy and the pizza he brought back with him, which Mum didn't touch and I could only nibble at.

It was the wee small hours before the doctor came to tell us that Dad was out of theatre. The operation to remove the clot had gone according to plan, but the doctor was still cautious about giving us a positive prognosis. Dad was still in a critical condition and it was too early to know if any lasting damage had been done. We were allowed to go and see him, but it was dreadfully upsetting to see him lying there, unresponsive and on a ventilator, and the thought that he might remain in this state for days, weeks, months, even perhaps forever, made me feel sick. My lovely dad, my rock, reduced to this! I wanted to kill the motorcyclist who had been the cause of it with my bare hands.

Mum was insistent I should go home now.

'There's nothing you can do, Sally. There's nothing any of us can do but wait. I'll stay here, of course, but you need to be around on the farm to keep an eye on things. It's what your dad would want. You can always come back tomorrow when you've got everything sorted out.'

I didn't tell her I was very worried about getting the help we would need in the weeks ahead; tomorrow morning was covered, and that would have to suffice for now. But I did say as much to Jeremy when we were driving home through the pitch black of a wet February night, and I could hardly believe it when he offered his help in that direction too.

'I'm sure we can spare one of our hands until you can find a more permanent solution,' he said. 'Rod, my manager, was telling me only the other day that he thought we were overstaffed, but they've all been with us so long I'm reluctant to get rid of any of them.'

Relief flooded my weary, stressed-out body.

'Oh Jeremy, that is so kind! We'll pay for the labour, of course.'

'Let's not worry about that now. You've got enough on your plate.'

That much was certainly true, but I knew Dad would want it sorted as soon as possible. He was old school, paying bills the minute they came due, not holding off to the last possible moment. He hated owing anyone a penny. Jeremy might be well off, but that was no reason to take advantage of his generosity.

'We'll talk about it tomorrow,' I said.

Jeremy dropped me in the farmyard and waited until I reached the front door before driving away. There was no sign of Scrumpy; she must be asleep, I supposed, but it was very unusual for her not to emerge, barking, from her kennel at the sound of an unfamiliar vehicle entering her territory.

I fitted my key into the lock and attempted to turn it, but couldn't. Puzzled, but too tired to think straight, I tried again without success before it dawned on me – the door wasn't locked. In my haste to get to the hospital I must have forgotten to lock up properly.

I opened the door and went inside, switching on the hall light, and was totally taken by surprise to see Scrumpy in the kitchen doorway. Her tail was down and she looked thoroughly wretched.

'Scrumpy? What on earth are you doing in here?' I asked, puzzled. Scrumpy rarely, if ever, came into the house; when she wasn't out on the farm with Dad, she lived in her kennel, and the last time I remembered seeing her was cowering in the yard when I rushed out to go to Dad after his accident.

She must have slipped in unnoticed during all the subsequent comings and goings, I supposed, and unknowingly I'd shut her in.

'It's all right, Scrumpy,' I said. 'I'm not cross with you. You've got to go outside now though.'

Scrumpy slunk towards me, then put on speed, running out

of the door and heading for her kennel. I followed her out and clipped her to her leash. She was obviously very upset, and I didn't want her running off again, perhaps in search of Dad.

Back inside, I locked the door after me and eased my feet out of my boots. The answering machine was blinking, indicating messages, and I was half tempted to leave picking them up until morning. But I couldn't bring myself to do that. Though common sense told me that if Mum wanted me she'd have called me on my mobile, I couldn't take the risk.

None of the messages were from Mum, of course.

The first was Josh.

'Sally – I've just heard from Belinda about your dad. I've tried to get you on your mobile, but it's switched off, so I assume you're at the hospital. I just wanted to say if there's anything I can do, just let me know.'

A little spark of warmth flared in the cold place inside me. Josh sounded worried. Josh cared. He was there for me.

There were a couple of other messages in the same vein from friends of Mum and Dad – bad news travels fast, I thought. The last one was Rachel.

'Steve just came in from playing skittles and says he heard Jack has had an accident and is in hospital. Is he all right? I'm really worried. Big hugs to you all. I'll ring again tomorrow.'

Good old Rach. Another real friend. The concern everyone was expressing made me feel less alone, though of course it did nothing to alleviate my awful anxiety. I went into the kitchen, intending to make myself a hot drink, decided I couldn't be bothered, and poured myself the last of the brandy from the half bottle that was still on the table. Then, somehow managing not to spill it, I hauled myself upstairs, got undressed, and collapsed into bed.

Predictably, I slept badly, horrible dreams interspersed with periods of wakefulness when I tossed and turned and worried. I couldn't get the picture of Dad lying in the lane out of my head, nor the one of the last glimpse I'd had of him in hospital, hooked up to drips and the ventilator. By six thirty I was wide awake again, feeling as if the weight of the world was pressing down on my chest, and my mouth dry with the horrible aftertaste of the brandy. There was a dull throb behind my left temple too; I hoped it wouldn't develop into a full-blown headache.

I got up, got dressed, and went out into the cold, grey dawn to make sure Mark Turnbull had turned up to help Sam with the milking. He had, and he promised to come back again this afternoon – no need to call on Jeremy's farmhand today at least then.

I returned to the farmhouse to make myself some breakfast. I wasn't at all hungry, but I thought I really must force something down – goodness only knew what the day would bring. It was too early yet to ring the hospital, anxious though I was for news, and too early to return the calls of the people who'd left messages on the answering machine.

I set the kettle to boil, and a pan of water for a boiled egg, then went to switch on the radio, more for company than because I wanted to listen to it. But it wasn't in its usual place on the window ledge. Mum must have moved it, I supposed – sometimes, if there was a programme she was particularly interested in, she carried it around with her. It was very unusual for her not to have brought it back to the kitchen, though.

I went through to the sitting room to see if it was there, but as I pushed the door – which was ajar – fully open, I froze, confused and alarmed. The sitting room was in disarray, drawers in the dresser open, their contents spilled over the floor, and the television had been removed from its stand and propped up against the fireplace. What on earth . . .? In disbelief I glanced around, and saw that the mantelpiece was bare but for a couple of framed family photographs, and one of them appeared to have been knocked over. The anniversary clock that was Mum's pride and joy was missing.

We'd been burgled! Somebody had been in here ransacking the house while Mum and I had been at the hospital! I could scarcely believe it, but now the things that had puzzled me last night were making sense – the front door unlocked,

Scrumpy in the house, looking guilty – when someone who had no business to be here had either broken in or walked in through the open door if I'd forgotten to lock it, she must have tried to warn them off. Maybe she'd succeeded and that was why they'd left the television behind, making off with just the small items they could carry easily – the radio, the anniversary clock, and maybe a few other bits and pieces that I hadn't yet missed.

The phone was ringing. Leaving the drawing room I hurried as fast as I could manage into the hall. My heart had begun to hammer so hard it was making me feel sick. For the moment I forgot all about the burglary – what did a few stolen possessions matter? The only thing of any importance was news of Dad.

I grabbed the phone. 'Hello?'

'Sally. It's me. Mum.'

'Yes? How are things?' I could scarcely breathe.

'Better. You'll be glad to hear, Sally, your dad has regained consciousness.'

My knees went weak from relief. 'Oh, thank God!'

'I know. It's wonderful, isn't it? I can't tell you, Sally, when I saw his eyelids flutter . . . and when he squeezed my hand . . .' She broke off, emotion overcoming her. 'He's not out of the woods yet, of course,' she went on after a moment. 'He's still very drowsy, and I don't think he can remember anything about what happened, but at least he's come round. And there doesn't seem to be any serious internal damage either. He's badly bruised, of course, but nothing is broken. I think he must have flung himself out of the way when the cows stampeded, but got kicked as they went by. And he would have dislocated his shoulder when he fell.'

'Yes, that makes sense.'

'How are things there?' Mum asked.

No way was I going to tell her we'd been burgled. She had quite enough on her plate just now. There would be plenty of time to break that to her later.

'Fine,' I lied. 'Mark Turnbull came to help Sam with the milking, and he's coming again this afternoon. And Jeremy has promised us one of his hands for as long as we need him. So everything is under control.'

'Oh, that's good. Your dad will be relieved.'

I couldn't help but smile. The idea of Dad being relieved was almost amusing, given the state he'd been in the last time I'd seen him. But it was also amazingly cheering.

'Do thank Jeremy for me,' Mum went on. 'He's been a brick, hasn't he?'

There was no denying that. The last thing he'd said to me when he dropped me off last night was that he'd take me to Frenchay again today if I wanted to go and didn't feel up to driving myself.

'I'll be in later, Mum,' I said. 'I've got a few things to do here first though.' *Understatement of the year,* I thought grimly.

'All right, love. No rush.'

'Give Dad my love. And Mum . . . I am so glad he's back with us.'

'You and me both,' Mum said.

I hung up, and wondered if I should ring the police now, while I had the phone in my hand. But perhaps it would make sense to check again what was missing before I did that. I could still scarcely believe that we really had been burgled. Could it be that Mum had been doing some spring cleaning yesterday and not got around to clearing up after herself? But why would she take the TV off its stand? In all honesty, I doubted she could even manage it, even if she'd wanted to. It wasn't a huge set – Mum and Dad were not the home-cinema types – but it must be at least two feet in width, a flat screen that sat in a groove on its stand. And where was the anniversary clock and the DAB radio? And why had the dresser drawers been pulled out and rifled through?

No, unlikely as it seemed, a burglary was the only explanation. I looked around the living room to see if anything else was missing, but couldn't spot anything obvious, and what Mum kept in the drawers of the dresser I hadn't a clue, beyond the tablecloth and napkins that came out on special occasions, mail-order catalogues and the Yellow Pages and local telephone directories, all of which were scattered about the floor. Perhaps the burglar had been looking for money – but he'd be lucky! Apart from a jar of loose change on the kitchen shelf and the cash in her purse, Mum never kept money in the house, and more often than not Dad's wallet was empty. He didn't go anywhere to need cash, he always joked; he left that to Mum.

Had the burglar been upstairs? If he had, he'd have found little of value. Apart from her wedding and engagement rings, Mum didn't go in for jewellery. But I'd better check, I supposed.

First, though, I'd have a good look around downstairs. I went to Dad's office, and the minute I went in the door, my heart sank. The computer monitor, keyboard and mouse were still sitting on his desk, but the tower was missing, and the external hard drive too.

I swore softly. This was terrible. All Dad's records were on that computer, meticulously backed up to the external hard drive in case something went wrong – correspondence, accounts, details of his suppliers and customers, everything to do with the day to day running of the farm. He was going to be utterly lost without all that, and if he was going to be incapacitated for long it would make it almost impossible for anyone else to take over the clerical side.

If I hadn't had my new laptop and the memory stick Dad had lent me, I'd have lost all my notes for my investigation, too. Though it was as nothing compared to what Dad had lost, it would have been a big setback for me. Thank goodness for my laptop . . .

Or had that been taken too? I hadn't noticed anything out of place in my room, but to be honest, the state I'd been in last night, everything but the bed could have been missing and I'd never have noticed, and this morning I'd been in a hurry to get out and make sure Mark had turned up to help Sam.

I struggled up the stairs and into my room, but everything seemed to be in place, and, to my relief, my laptop bag, still zipped up, was where I'd left it, tucked under the little upright chair behind the door.

I checked Mum and Dad's room, but everything there seemed

to be in order too, no drawers pulled out, and everything on the dressing table as it should be. It didn't look as though the burglar had been upstairs, then. Perhaps Scrumpy, bless her, had frightened him off, and he'd decided to escape with the few things he had.

I was on my way back downstairs to call the police when the phone began to ring, and I hopped the last couple of stairs to answer it.

It was Rachel.

'Sally! Are you all right? What's going on?'

I lowered myself to sit on the stairs.

'Oh Rach, you may well ask . . .'

I went through everything that had happened, glad that at least I was now able to tell her that Dad had regained consciousness.

'You think he's going to be all right, then?' she said anxiously.

'I certainly hope so. Things are looking a lot better than they were yesterday.'

'It's a terrible thing to have happened, though. Just terrible! I can't believe it.'

'That's not all you won't believe,' I said grimly. 'While we were at the hospital we were burgled.'

'Burgled!' Rachel repeated, gobsmacked.

'Yep.' I went on to tell her about it, what had been taken, and what hadn't. 'Would you believe they had the tele all ready to carry out as well, then just left it!'

'Druggies,' Rachel said. 'Bet you – it was druggies, wanting something to sell so they could get their next fix.'

'Perhaps. But out here . . . in the country? And if it had been any other night, they'd have found themselves looking down the barrel of Dad's twelve-bore.'

'Perhaps it's just as well he wasn't there when they broke in then,' Rachel said wryly. 'Have you called the police?'

'Not yet. I was just about to ring them when you called. Not that I imagine they'll be able to do much. The stuff that's been stolen has already been fenced, I expect.'

'There might be fingerprints . . .'

'There might, I suppose. But . . . oh, sugar, I suppose I'm

going to have to wait in until their scenes-of-crime people
have been, and I wanted to go and see Dad.'

'Tell you what,' Rachel suggested, 'why don't I come over?
I could stay until it's time for me to pick the kids up from
school. I was going to offer to drive you to the hospital, but
perhaps I'd be more use fielding the fingerprint bods.'

'Oh Rachel, that would be such a help. I can give you a
list of what's missing, tell you where the burglar went . . .
then, once I've made the initial report . . . oh, and fed the
hens . . . I can be on my way.'

'I can do that too,' Rachel said. 'Feed the hens, I mean. I
used to love doing it, do you remember? But are you sure
you'll be all right, driving all the way to Bristol?'

'I'll be fine – though Jeremy did offer.'

'Well, if he's up for it, I think you should let him.'

'Oh, I don't know. I'd rather be independent. And I can't
impose any more. He's been so good.'

'Hmm. Yes. Very good, I'd say.' There was heavy innuendo
in her tone.

'What do you mean?' I asked.

'Are you sure he hasn't got an ulterior motive? I reckon he
fancies you, Sally.'

'*Jeremy?*' I laughed. 'Of course he doesn't!'

'Why not? He's single, isn't he?'

'Well, yes, but in his own words, a confirmed bachelor. And
he's at least ten years older than me.'

'So what? It might have been a lot when you were seven
and he was seventeen. But now, it's nothing.'

'Honestly, Rachel, you do talk rubbish! Look, I must go
and get this call in to the police. They'll think I'm stalking
them, I shouldn't wonder! Twice in two days!'

'OK, I'll be over in . . . what . . . say an hour?'

'You're a star, Rach.'

I put down the phone, thinking that actually everyone was
turning up trumps. Rachel, I'd expect. We'd been mates for
so long. But for someone I hadn't seen in years, Jeremy was
being extremely kind. Was he just being neighbourly? He was,
after all, a good friend of Dad's. Or was it possible Rachel
was right and he had a soft spot for me? Oh, surely not!

In any case, I didn't have time to think about that now. I had far too much to do, and too many other things on my mind.

Sighing, I dialled the number for the police, and prepared myself for a long wait.

Fourteen

Would the phone never stop ringing? I began to feel as if it was actually attached to my ear. Many of Mum and Dad's friends who had left messages last night were ringing again, and I felt duty bound to return the calls of those who didn't. All were deeply concerned, and those who had tried to phone again this morning whilst I was waiting to get through to the police about the burglary were fearing the worst when they found the line engaged for so long.

Rachel arrived, bless her, and Jeremy too. The knowing look Rachel gave me when he arrived at the door made the colour rush to my cheeks. Was it really possible he fancied me? If so, I wasn't sure it was a good idea for him to drive me to Bristol again, as he was offering to do, but between them, he and Rachel bullied me into it.

The one person who hadn't called again was Josh, and the omission hurt me. But perhaps he was waiting for me to ring him. I grabbed a moment to try his mobile, but it went straight to voicemail. I left a message saying I was just heading off to Bristol, and updated him briefly about Dad's condition. Then I got my coat and bag and Jeremy and I set off, leaving Rachel to wait for the police, who might not arrive for hours. Rachel would be able to show them where the burglars had been; if they wanted a statement from me, it would have to wait, but I somehow doubted they'd bother unless they were able to collar an offender, and Jeremy agreed with me.

'All they'll do is give you a crime number for insurance purposes,' he said. 'To be honest, I sometimes wonder what the police force in this country is coming to.'

There was a huge cellophane-wrapped bouquet of flowers on the back seat of his car – he must have visited a florist in Stoke Compton early this morning, I guessed, and realized guiltily that I hadn't got a single thing to take Mum and Dad beyond the bare necessities.

'We could stop off on the way if you'd like to buy flowers or grapes,' Jeremy offered.

'It's OK, I'll take something next time,' I said. I wasn't sure whether flowers would be allowed in the ICU, and besides, anything I could buy in a garage shop or supermarket would look horribly cheap up against Jeremy's sumptuous offering. As for grapes, Dad didn't care for them at the best of times, and as things were I couldn't see that he'd be up eating them before they shrivelled to sultanas.

This time Jeremy came into the hospital with me, and I was glad of his solid presence beside me as we walked along the endless corridors. My heart was in my mouth in spite of Mum's reassuring phone call earlier. I've always hated hospitals, and I don't suppose all the time I had to spend in one after my accident helped. There's something about the smell that is universally horrible – antiseptic and linoleum, food trolleys and sickness – that gets right inside me, and the purposeful bustle, the false cheerfulness of the nurses and visitors grates on my nerves. Oh yes, I was really glad Jeremy was with me, even though I wasn't casting so much as a glance in his direction, just ploughing purposefully on and trying to hide the appre-hension I was feeling.

At the door to Dad's room I paused, peeping in through the small window. Dad looked much as he had last night, immobile, his head swathed in bandages; Mum was in the chair beside him. Her chin was resting on her chest and she looked as if she might be asleep. When I opened the door softly, though, she jerked upright.

'Sally! Jeremy!'

'Hi, Mum.' I nodded in Dad's direction. 'How is he?'

'Resting. But oh, Sally . . .'

Dad's eyes flickered.

'Sal . . .' It was just a whisper, but it was music to my ears. I leaned over the bed and took his hand in mine.

'Oh Dad.' And then: 'You old rascal, fancy frightening us like that!'

We stayed with Dad for about an hour. Anything more would have been too much for him, and in any case Mum was anxious for me to get back and see to things at home. She'd taken the news of the burglary well though.

'It's only possessions, Sally. They're not important. It's a good thing you managed to transfer all your notes on to your new laptop, though, or you'd have lost all your hard work.'

'Oh, shucks to that . . .'

'Exactly,' Mum said. 'Your dad is getting through this, and that's the only thing that matters.'

When we left the hospital and I switched my mobile on again it showed two messages waiting. The first, to my delight, was Josh, enquiring how things were and asking me to give him a call when I was able.

The second . . . I didn't know who the second one was. There was nothing but a moment of silence before it cut out. I went cold, remembering the silent calls of a few days ago. But this time there was no breathing to be heard, and it was only a few seconds before the phone went down at the other end and the line went dead. A wrong number, perhaps? Someone who realized they'd made a mistake in dialling and hung up immediately?

Jeremy glanced at me. 'Something wrong?'

'No . . . it's nothing.' I didn't want to go into all that now. 'I must ring Josh though.'

'Josh?'

'My . . .' I hesitated. How to describe Josh? Boyfriend? That sounded stupidly juvenile. Lover? Hardly – not yet, anyway. 'A friend,' I said. 'You don't mind, do you?'

'No, go ahead.' But he did look a bit put out, I thought, but I rang Josh anyway.

He answered more or less straightaway and I filled him in on the situation and told him about the burglary.

'You're on your way home now?' he said. 'Look, I'll try to pop in between jobs. It sounds to me as if you could do with some moral support.'

'That would be great,' I said. 'Hope to see you later, then.'

I'd scarcely disconnected when my phone rang again. I answered it, and was completely taken by surprise when the voice at the other end said: 'Is that Sally Proctor? This is Alice Benson.'

'Alice – hello!' My astonishment was echoed in my voice.
'What . . .?'

'Look, I can't talk now,' Alice said softly and rather hurriedly.
'But there's something I should tell you. Could we meet
sometime?'

I was staggered. I'd scarcely given a thought to my investigation since Dad's awful accident. Now, suddenly, here it was,
rearing up to bite me.

'Yes, yes, of course,' I said. 'When . . .?'

Voices in the background.

'I'll ring you again.' Same soft whisper. And then, louder:
'Yes, that's right. Next Tuesday at the warehouse. The auction
begins at eight sharp, but there's viewing from ten until twelve
and again from four p.m. Thank you for your enquiry.'

The line went dead.

'Well!' I said. I was puzzled now, as well as startled. Had
Alice been saying she'd see me at the auction house, or was
that just a way of covering up the fact that she'd been caught
on the telephone?

Jeremy cast me an enquiring glance.

'That is very odd,' I said. 'The girl at Compton Properties
– Alice, the one who knew Dawn – wants to talk to me. She
wouldn't say a word before. And she sounds scared now.'

Jeremy laughed.

'Lewis Crighton runs that office with a rod of iron, from
what I've heard.'

'Maybe. But it's more than that . . .' A little twist of excite-
ment shivered in the pit of my stomach. 'I'm on to something,
I'm sure of it. And everything seems to be pointing to Lewis
Crighton as being behind whatever it is.'

'Wishful thinking, Sally,' Jeremy said lightly. 'Ever the news
hound, eh?'

'Well, yes,' I admitted. 'But I knew Alice was hiding something. And so is Lisa Curry, though I've as much chance of
getting anything out of her as I have of walking on the moon.
Well, I'll just have to wait and see if Alice phones me again
– she said she would. Otherwise I'll go to the auction on
Tuesday and hope to see her there.'

★   ★   ★

Back at the farm everything seemed to be running smoothly. The scenes-of-crime bods had been to dust for fingerprints and the local police had simply phoned with a crime number, as Jeremy had said they would. Rachel had fed the hens and picked up the eggs, and Mark Turnbull had stayed on after milking to help Sam with the various jobs that had to be done.

Rachel was just leaving as Josh arrived, and I knew she'd be annoyed that she had little more than a fleeting glimpse of him – she was dying to meet him and give him the once over, I knew.

'I can't stay long,' Josh said apologetically, 'but I'm free this evening if you'd like to meet up. I did promise to cook for you,' he said with a rueful grin.

'Why don't *I* cook for *you*?' I suggested. 'I think Mum will be staying for at least one more night with Dad, and I really don't think I want to leave the house unoccupied after what happened last night, though I still don't understand it. I mean, who on earth would come all the way out here to steal just a few bits and pieces? Farms get targeted for equipment – tractors, for instance, often get nicked, and I've even heard of livestock going missing. But a computer, an anniversary clock and a couple of brass candlesticks? It's crazy.'

'The computer,' Josh said. He was looking very serious. 'Is that the computer you've been using for all your notes about the fire and Dawn Burridge's death?'

'*Was* using, yes. I've got my laptop now.'

'You've got a laptop?' Josh asked, surprised, and I realized I hadn't mentioned buying it.

'Yes – I got it a couple of days ago. But . . . I'm not following you, Josh. What has that got to do with . . .?'

Josh shrugged. 'Nothing probably. I was just wondering . . . Well, you know what I think about you pursuing this investigation of yours. I think you're playing with fire. And it just occurred to me there might be some connection. That it was the computer the intruder was after, and the other bits and pieces were taken to make it look like a run-of-the-mill burglary.'

'Oh, that's ridiculous!' I retorted. 'Why would anyone . . .?'

'Perhaps someone wanted to know what you've found out.

Or put a spoke in your investigation. I've said it before and I'll say it again: if there is anything in all this, Sally, you could be dealing with very dangerous people.'

'I can't believe that anyone would stage a burglary to get their hands on my notes,' I said forcefully. 'And anyway, how would they know the house was going to be unoccupied?'

'News of your dad's accident spread pretty fast . . .'

'And got picked up by some local low-life who grabbed the opportunity to break in and take anything they could sell to get the money for their next fix,' I said. 'That's why I don't want to leave the house empty tonight. If word gets round we're spending time at the hospital, some other druggie might decide to try his luck.'

'If you say so,' Josh said wearily. 'Anyway, it's all the more reason for you not to be here alone. So OK, I will take you up on your offer to cook for me. If only so I can make sure you're safe.'

I rolled my eyes. But there was no denying the feeling of warmth deep inside me.

My phone was ringing.

It was late afternoon and I was assembling the ingredients I'd managed to find in the fridge, freezer and store cupboards to cook an evening meal without going into town. The best I could come up with was a lasagne with garlic bread and salad. The mince was defrosting in the microwave and I was chopping an onion, tears streaming down my cheeks. As I heard the ringtone of my phone, I wiped my hands on Mum's cook's apron, which I'd borrowed, and scooped it up.

Could it be Alice?

It was.

'Sorry I had to go in a hurry this morning,' she said.

'No problem. You said you wanted to talk to me?' I was trying to keep the excitement out of my voice, and failing miserably.

'Yes.'

'About Dawn?'

There was a brief silence. Then: 'I'd rather not go into it over the phone,' Alice said. She still sounded nervous, though I guessed she was no longer in the office. 'Could we meet?'

'Of course. Where? When?'

'How about Sunday morning? I'm working all day tomorrow. And I suggest the children's play park at the sports centre. Say eleven o'clock, somewhere near the swings? Do you know it?'

'Yes.' She'd chosen a spot that was likely to be busy on a Sunday morning, I guessed – always provided it was fine. 'What if it's pouring with rain?' I asked.

'In that case, inside, in the sports centre coffee shop. But the forecast is good.'

'I'll be there,' I said.

And I felt a spiral of jubilation.

Dad was recovering, Josh was coming to dinner, and Alice Benson wanted to talk to me. Perhaps, at last, things were actually moving in the right direction!

And they continued to do so. A phone call from Mum was upbeat – Dad was still making good progress – and Josh and I spent a lovely evening together. In fact, he ended up staying the night.

He was still worried about me, I knew, but neither of us mentioned that as we climbed the stairs to my room, and certainly not as we lay together in my bed. Josh was a wonderful lover, gentle and considerate – well, with my injured leg he would have had to be a sadist not to be – and I thought that Mum and Rachel couldn't have been more wrong when they warned me against getting too involved too soon.

This was right – so right – and I'd never been happier. Why delay when my heart was telling me that Josh was the one I'd been waiting for all my life?

Falling asleep in his arms, I felt rosy and content and cherished. If nothing came of my investigations, at least I'd met someone very special.

It was a good place to be.

Next morning I woke to find myself alone. I hadn't so much as stirred when Josh got up, but now I could hear the clatter of china in the kitchen, and when I padded downstairs I found him fully dressed and busy with mugs and tea bags.

'Hey, what are you doing up?' he greeted me. 'I was going to bring you a cup of tea in bed.'

'Nice thought, but too late,' I laughed.

Today, Saturday, was market day, but Mum's pitch would have to remain empty today. There was no way I could cope with running it, and I was anxious to get to Bristol to see Dad again.

This time it was Josh who took me. On the way we stopped off to update Jeremy and leave him a spare door key in case of any emergency occurring. I was delighted to find Dad was still steadily improving – the fact that he was insisting there was no need whatever for Mum to keep a bedside vigil clear evidence that he was beginning to think like his old self. It was Dad all over – he hates fuss – and in any case, he was worried about the farm. All very well to assure him that with Jeremy's help I had everything under control – he still wanted Mum back in the saddle, so to speak.

She was torn, I knew, but after some discussion it was agreed that she would come home with me and Josh today, and drive back tomorrow, after I'd had my meeting with Alice. Should there be any crisis – which, please God, there wouldn't be – then obviously I'd have to cancel my appointment.

Apart from that brief encounter in the hall when he called for me on our first date, this was the first time Mum had met Josh. But from the outset they seemed to get on really well. He'd earned brownie points for bringing me to the hospital, of course, but he was also a very easy person to like, with his laid-back, friendly manner, I thought, feeling pleased and rather proud. Mum gave me a furtive nod of approval when his back was turned. 'A great improvement on Tim' that look seemed to say.

'So you're still managing to go on with your investigation in spite of what's happened?' Mum said as we were driving home.

'More's the pity,' Josh muttered.

'Actually Alice came to me,' I said, ignoring him, but Mum picked up on it.

'What do you mean, Josh?' she asked.

'I keep warning her – she could be disturbing a hornet's nest,' Josh said. 'She won't listen to me, though. Perhaps you can talk some sense into her before she ends up like Dawn Burridge.'

'Oh for heaven's sake!' I exploded. But I could see he'd got Mum worried.

'Oh my goodness – surely you don't think . . .?' she said anxiously.

'Sally knows exactly what I think.' Josh's tone was grim. 'I think she should leave well alone.'

'You are *so* melodramatic!' I said crossly. The last thing I wanted was for him to alarm Mum. If she thought I might be playing with fire she'd be reluctant to let me use Dad's car again. 'If there's anything at all to discover, it's all to do with emotional entanglements, not some kind of gang war between Mafia godfathers. This is Stoke Compton, not New York, or even London. And I'm going to talk to a girl who works in an estate agent's office, not Mata Hari.'

I didn't add that I was beginning to be more and more certain that Lewis Crighton was behind what had happened to Dawn, and that Alice was frightened to death of him. If I wanted to continue following my story, the less said the better.

But Mum's thoughts had returned to Dad.

'I wonder if I should have stayed another night? I don't like leaving him . . .'

'He's in good hands, Mum,' I said, grateful for the change of subject.

At home everything appeared to be under control. Mum asked Josh if he would like to stay for supper – her way of thanking him for providing a taxi service, I guessed, but Josh had a better idea.

'I'll treat you both to a pub meal,' he offered.

Eating out isn't really Mum's thing, but when I added my weight to the argument – I hadn't been able to get to the shops to buy food, and, in any case, the last thing she needed was to have to cook a meal – she agreed.

Though there could be no intimacy between Josh and me

tonight, I really enjoyed the fact that Mum was with us. It
had the comfortable feel of family, a sort of warm stability to
anchor all the euphoria of the attraction that existed between
us. Something else I'd never experienced in all the time I'd
been with Tim. And when Josh kissed me goodnight, although
I'd have liked more, I felt truly content. There would be other
nights for us to be together. For starters we'd decided that
tomorrow evening we'd go to the cinema to see *The Best
Marigold Hotel*, and grab a bite to eat afterwards.

For now, I was perfectly happy that things were progressing
exactly as they should.

Sunday morning. Mum said she'd wait for me to get back
from my meeting with Alice so that we could go to the hospital
together. I helped her with the various chores until it was time
to get ready to go, and then set out for Stoke Compton.

The weather today was quite pleasant, with the promise of
spring. Already the hedgerows were beginning to sprout green
against the bare brown of winter, and clusters of daffodil spears
had erupted in the banks along the stretch of main road on
the approach to town. Soon, given some warm sunshine, they'd
open into a sea of golden yellow.

This was a new development. I didn't remember daffodils
at the roadside when I was young. Someone must have planted
bulbs there at some time, and they'd grown and spread with
each passing year.

The sports centre was at 'our' end of town. I drove into the
car park and found a space, surprised at just how full it was.
Judging by the number of parents and children going in and
out carrying sports bags there were probably swimming lessons
this morning, and I imagined the gym and squash courts were
well patronized too.

I waited in the car until just before eleven, then made my
way to the children's play area. This was also already busy, boys
and girls of all ages rushing about between the swings, slides
and roundabouts, whilst their parents sat on benches or stood
beside the low perimeter fence watching them. One lone
woman wearing a parka with the hood up was standing at the
far end with her back to me, and I wondered if it might be

Alice. But as I neared her I saw her drop a cigarette butt on the grass, tread on it and call to a boy who was on the climbing frame. Not Alice, then.

I walked all the way around the play park, but there was no sign of her. I stood watching the cars that were coming in, and the people emerging from them and walking towards the sports centre; Alice was not among them. I was beginning to get a bad feeling here. Had she changed her mind and decided not to meet me? Or was it possible there had been a misunderstanding and she was waiting for me in the cafeteria?

I headed for the sports centre. The main doors led directly into an open-plan area where there were tables, chairs and vending machines. This, too, was busy, most of the tables occupied and children rushing about between them. But I could see at a glance that Alice wasn't here. The clock above the viewing window for the swimming pool showed eleven fifteen. It might, of course, be a few minutes fast, but the fact remained – Alice was late – if she was coming at all.

I went back outside, did another circuit of the playground, and waited by the path from the car park, my frustration growing with every passing minute.

She wasn't going to come.

I waited until half past, and a bit beyond, just in case she'd thought she'd said eleven thirty, but without much hope, and at a twenty to twelve I eventually gave up.

I was cold – for all that the sun was shining, there was a definite nip in the air – and I was utterly fed up. To have had this carrot dangled in front of me and then snatched away was disappointing to say the least.

Alice knew something; she'd been on the point of sharing it with me. But – perhaps out of fear of losing her job – she'd changed her mind, and I had no way of knowing what it was she had been going to tell me.

But once again, everything was pointing to Compton Properties and Lewis Crighton. The answer to everything lay with him, I felt sure. And somehow I was going to find out what it was that he – and everyone around him – was hiding.

★   ★   ★

'So you had a wasted journey,' Mum said sympathetically when I got home, but I had the feeling she was actually secretly relieved. Josh and his warnings of doom had worried her, I knew.

We headed off to Bristol, Mum driving, and spent a few hours with Dad, who was still making slow but steady progress.

When we got home again, I thought I'd have a session on my computer. I left Mum watching television and went up to my room.

I'd tucked my laptop in its case under the small upright chair behind the door, and I bent to pull it out. But the moment I went to lift it I knew something was wrong. Though the case was still zipped, as I'd left it, there was practically no weight to it at all. I put the case on to the bed and opened it.

It was empty. My laptop had gone.

For a moment I stared at the empty case scarcely able to believe the evidence of my own eyes.

So the burglar had been upstairs after all – had stolen my laptop as well as Dad's computer. I hadn't realized it was missing before because the case had been zipped up again and replaced where I'd left it. Naturally I'd assumed it hadn't been touched.

Naturally! The mess downstairs, the emptied drawers, the overturned photograph, even the TV removed from its stand and stacked by the fireplace, was typical burglar behaviour, especially if, as I suspected, the culprit was some young thug looking for something to sell for drug money. But a leather case zipped up and replaced in its original position after the laptop had been removed? I'd never have suspected that in a million years. And why hadn't he taken case and all? It made no sense whatever.

But there was no getting away from the fact: it *had been* stolen. Unless I was going quietly mad and had left it in Dad's office after I last used it. That must surely be the explanation. The burglar hadn't come upstairs at all, but had taken it at the same time as taking Dad's computer.

'My laptop's gone as well,' I said to Mum, going back downstairs.

'Oh no! Oh Sally, all your work!'

'Well, I've still got it on a memory stick, thank goodness,' I said, 'but much good will that do me with no computer to run it on.'

'You'll just have to get another,' Mum said. 'And we'll have to replace Dad's, too. There's no way we can manage without it. We'll get on to the insurance company first thing in the morning, and they'll tell us what to do.'

I nodded.

'They'll say we can go ahead, I'm sure,' I said.

But the bad feeling I'd had ever since Alice failed to keep her appointment with me this morning had intensified. Since I'd begun this investigation everything seemed to be going pear-shaped. Could it be that Josh was right to warn me I was playing with fire? Was there something going on that was more than sheer bad luck?

I shivered. Perhaps it would be wise to give up on my enquiries. Perhaps if I did all the bad things that were happening would stop. But that was nothing but foolish conjecture, surely. No way could there be any connection.

Could there?

Fifteen

It didn't take me long, of course, to put all such thoughts out of my head. I'd never have had them at all if my nerves hadn't been so on edge, I felt sure.

The afternoon flew past. By the time I'd spent what seemed like hours on the telephone talking to the insurance company, it was time to get ready to meet Josh, and I'd barely had a moment to so much as think about my investigation, let alone do anything to further it.

Whilst I was waiting for Josh, however, Rachel rang to ask after Dad, and when we'd covered that, she mentioned our proposed trip to see Dawn's mother.

'I don't suppose you'll want to go to Dorset this week with your dad in hospital.'

Instantly all my enthusiasm for my project returned with a vengeance. Dad was out of danger now, and if I didn't take Grace Burridge up on her offer to talk soon, she might change her mind.

'Actually, I don't think Dad would mind if I missed visiting just one day,' I said. 'In fact, it would give some of his friends a chance to go and see him – loads of them have been asking, but the hospital aren't keen on him having more than two or three at his bedside at any one time, and so far that's been me and Mum.'

'OK,' Rachel said. 'In that case, I could make Thursday, if that suits you and Mrs Burridge. Steve's working from home that day, so he'd be on hand to pick up the children if we should get delayed.'

'It would be fine by me. I'll ring Mrs Burridge tomorrow and let you know what she says . . .' I could hear a car outside; Josh had arrived and there would be no time for me to make the call now.

And I wasn't going to tell him about it either, I decided.

I didn't want another argument about what I was planning
to do.

The film was excellent – very different – and I thoroughly
enjoyed it, though I couldn't help feeling it wasn't Josh's usual
fare and that he'd suggested it because he thought I'd like it.
Afterwards, we went to the TGIF next door to the cinema
and ordered fajitas and drinks – wine for me, a beer for Josh.

'I'll cook that meal for you on Saturday,' he said as we licked
our sticky fingers.

'Promises, promises!' I joked.

'No – a definite plan. I'm afraid I won't be able to see you
again until then, though. I've got a few days off, and a pal and
I are planning to walk part of the Cotswold Way.'

My heart sank. Five whole days when I wouldn't see Josh
seemed like an eternity.

'I know – sorry,' he said, as if reading my thoughts. 'But
this was arranged weeks ago. And let's be fair, you've got
enough going on at the moment not to miss me.'

'What makes you think I'd miss you anyway?' I teased, and
his hand closed over mine on the table top.

'You'd better!' he said, mock threateningly. 'And I don't want
to come back and discover you've been getting off with
someone else in my absence, either.'

I laughed. 'Chance would be a fine thing!'

'That's all right, then.'

The warmth was beginning inside me again, and with it the
desire. I could feel it, electric in the air between us, and when
Josh made a detour on the way home I wasn't in the least
surprised. He didn't say where he was going and I didn't ask,
but as we bypassed Stoke Compton and pulled in through the
gateway of a small, isolated cottage, I could hazard a pretty
accurate guess.

'My place,' Josh said nonchalantly. 'Are you coming in?'

I didn't need asking twice.

I have to admit I noticed very little about Josh's cottage at first
beyond the fact that the tiny lobby opened directly into a long
low room with rough wood beams and an open fireplace. I
was rather too focused on the staircase, leading up from the

corner opposite the door, and the magnetism sparking between Josh and me as he helped me climb it. Later, though, I thought what a charming little place it was, all sloping floors and uneven walls and funny little nooks and crannies. The fact that he had chosen to live here rather than a modern house or flat showed another side to Josh, one that I liked a lot. But then, to be honest, what was there I *didn't* like about Josh?

When he took me home – I had to go home, of course, much as I would have liked to stay – I thought again how I would miss him in the next few days. I could hardly believe that just two short weeks ago I hadn't even met him. Perhaps Mum and Rachel had been right, and I should have taken more time before falling head over heels in love like this. But then again, maybe this was the way a once-in-a-lifetime love struck – like a bolt of lightning. If so, the way I was feeling made perfect sense.

Next morning, after I'd fed the hens and collected the eggs, I phoned Grace Burridge and asked if it would be convenient if I came to see her on Thursday, and she said it would. Once again I felt dreadfully guilty at the way I was deceiving her, but I told myself that if I could find out who had been responsible for her daughter's death, then maybe that would help. At present the hit-and-run driver was still unidentified; even if the circumstances that had led up to the accident proved to be upsetting, at least it would mean that Grace had some sort of closure.

When I returned to the kitchen, it was to find Mum washing the eggs I'd just collected and putting a dozen into a cardboard tray.

'For Jeremy,' she explained. 'He said he'd pop by later, go through your dad's accounts files, and try to set up some sort of system on his own computer so we can keep things up to date. We're so lucky he was back home when all this happened. He's been a brick, and I thought he might appreciate a nice fresh egg as a thank you. He won't take any payment, that I do know.'

'I'm sure he'll be really pleased,' I said. Jeremy didn't keep hens – it wasn't that kind of farm. It was much more highly mechanized than ours, and without the homely touches, though there did used to be a flock of geese strutting about in the days when his mother had been alive – I remembered being terrified of them.

'Will you be here this morning?' Mum asked.

'Actually I'm popping over to Dad's computer man to pick up a new laptop,' I said. 'I gave him a ring yesterday after I'd spoken to the insurance company, and he's got one in stock that's pretty much the same model as the one I had stolen. So if Jeremy can build some sort of database I can install it, and we won't have to keep bothering him.'

'I haven't got a clue what you're talking about, Sally,' Mum said blithely, 'but I'll tell Jeremy. I'm sure he'll know what you mean.'

'Trust me, he will. Computers for accounting purposes are definitely Jeremy's territory.' I fetched my coat and the car keys. 'It is all right if I take Dad's car, is it?'

'You know it is,' Mum replied.

I drove first to Dad's friendly computer supplier and picked up my replacement laptop, which he had ready and waiting for me. Then, on the way home, I decided to make a little detour and see if I could locate the warehouse where the auction would be held the following evening. I was determined to go along, partly because I was hoping Alice might be there, and partly because I wanted the opportunity to see Lewis Crighton again, but I wasn't entirely sure exactly where the warehouse was situated, and I thought it would be a good idea to check it out in the daylight, rather than looking for it in the dark.

In the event, I found the industrial estate more easily than I'd expected. It was on the outskirts of Stoke Compton, in a lane that followed a river valley which had once been quite a beauty spot, but was now marred by sprawling industrial development. Vast, ugly, prefabricated buildings sat behind yards where plant and machinery sprouted like ungainly carbuncles, and the revoltingly sweet smell of animal foodstuff from one of the units mingled with the odour from the nearby sewerage works and was drawn into my car through the air conditioning system. I drove on along the rutted lane, past an engineering works and what appeared to be the parking area and garage of a local coach firm, wondering if I'd got the right industrial estate. Then I saw a board at the roadside bearing the legend 'Compton Auctions – Antiques and Collectibles' and a large white arrow pointing straight ahead.

The lane curved over a river bridge and as I rounded the bend I saw it – just another big, faceless edifice fronted by a large parking area. Like the other buildings I'd passed, the plot was surrounded by a high wire fence, but there were overgrown hedges too behind the wire, masking the warehouse from the road. A sign, identical to the one I'd spotted further up the lane, was mounted on a post at the entrance.

OK, I could definitely find this again tomorrow. The lane was too narrow at this point for me to be able to turn, and the sensible thing seemed to be to reverse into the yard. I positioned myself close to the offside bank and swung carefully round until my bonnet was facing back the way I had come. Then, just before moving off, I glanced around – and did a double take as I saw the car drawn up in a corner of the yard, close to the building.

It was hardly surprising, I supposed, that someone would be here today, the day before the auction. It wasn't that that had made my eyes widen, but the fact that for a moment I thought it was Josh's car – it looked exactly the same. Then common sense kicked in. Why on earth would it be Josh? There must be dozens of blue Peugeot estate cars in and around Stoke Compton. Besides which, Josh would be on his way now to start his Cotswold Way walk.

I stuck the gear lever into 'drive' and headed for home.

Monday night, of course, was one of the nights the Compton Players met, and I had wondered if I would go along. But I rather thought I'd gleaned all the information I could from them, and after spending the afternoon visiting Dad, I was actually feeling very tired. In any case, I didn't want to leave Mum alone too much and I'd be out tomorrow night at the auction. So I spent a quiet evening transferring my notes from my memory stick to my new laptop, and then sitting down with Mum to watch some television. But I didn't know the characters or the storylines in the soap Mum followed, and soon my mind was wandering, running over all the details I'd just scanned through again, and wondering if I was ever going to get to the truth.

Was I chasing the impossible? Maybe I'd been wrong all along. Brian Jennings had started the fire, and Dawn's death was just an unhappy coincidence. And if it wasn't, did Josh have a point when he said I could end up like her? For the first time, the doubts crowded in around me.

With a huge effort I pushed them aside. I wasn't a quitter. I was going to keep on going with this until I was sure whether or not Brian Jennings had been wrongly convicted. Whether Dawn's death had been an accident, or whether there was a murderer walking free. This was more than just a diversion for me now, more than simply another story. I was on a mission.

Next morning I was in the bathroom washing my hair when I heard voices downstairs – Mum and a man. Anxious that it might be Sam with some problem on the farm, I wound a towel round my head and went to investigate. Halfway down the stairs, though, I recognized the voice – Jeremy – and was turning to go back up when Mum called to me.

'Sally? Is that you?'

'Who else would it be?' I called back, laughing.

'Come and see what Jeremy's done!'

It was too late now to retreat. I struggled down the last few stairs and went into the kitchen, where Jeremy was bending over a laptop, open on the table. With a padded gilet over his Aran sweater, he looked more like a big bear than ever.

'He's an absolute marvel!' Mum said wonderingly.

'I wouldn't put it quite like that.' Jeremy looked up and smiled at me. 'Morning, Sally.'

'Morning.' I felt a bit self-conscious, still in my dressing gown and with the towel wound into a turban over my wet hair. 'What have you done, then, to earn such high praise?'

'Saved our bacon, that's what!' Mum enthused. 'He's been through all Dad's paperwork and put in on here – he's going to lend us this laptop until Dad gets a new computer. I don't understand it, of course, but you will. Show her, Jeremy.'

'Well, basically, I've just set up a couple of simple spreadsheets for the accounts, and a directory of customers and suppliers,' Jeremy said, flicking the cursor over the screen. 'I don't suppose it's complete by any means but it's the best I could do from Jack's paperwork. It's a good thing he kept hard copies, otherwise it would all have been lost for good.'

'And to think I used to tell him he ought to be worrying about saving the rain forests when I heard his printer going,' Mum said, shaking her head. 'He always said he liked to be able to look at things in black and white, though.'

'Well, there you are anyway.' Jeremy straightened, switched off the laptop and closed it. 'The best I can do. Jack will be able to fill in the blanks, I expect, when he's home again.'

'Let's hope so,' Mum said fervently. 'Are you going to stop for a cup of coffee, Jeremy?'

He glanced at his watch.

'I shouldn't . . . but seeing as you're offering . . .'

His eyes, with the hint of a smile, turned to me, and suddenly I was horribly conscious of my state of undress.

'I really must dry my hair and get some clothes on,' I said, and for the first time Mum seemed to notice and share my embarrassment.

'She's not normally in her dressing gown at this time of day . . .'

'And why shouldn't she be?' Jeremy said easily, but I made my escape anyway.

By the time I came back down, hair dried, and fully dressed, Jeremy had gone.

'He had to meet a client,' Mum explained. 'But what a good friend! Fancy doing all that work for your dad, and all out of the goodness of his heart! Oh – and he's offered to take you to the auction tonight, too. I told him you were going and he was worried about you driving Dad's car in the dark.'

'Oh, for goodness sake!' I was a little annoyed at my ability being questioned. 'I've done it before.'

'I did tell him that,' Mum said defensively, 'but he said he'd be quite interested to see what went on, and how much our bits and pieces fetched and, to be honest,' she added, 'I'd feel happier for you to have someone with you. I expect they get all sorts at a do like that.'

'Oh Mum, it'll just be the dealers and a few curious locals,' I scoffed.

But actually, though I didn't much care for being treated like a helpless little woman, a part of me was quite glad that I wouldn't be alone. Too many bad things had happened lately, and I was feeling a little vulnerable. If I was with Jeremy I wouldn't have to worry about strange cars following me in the dark lanes, and if Lewis Crighton had become aware that I was rather too interested in him, there would be no opportunity for him to see that I ended up like Dawn, tonight at least!

Whereas yesterday morning the parking area outside the Compton Properties warehouse had been deserted but for that one blue car, tonight it was already half full. Jeremy found a space between a couple of transit vans – obviously the dealers were here in force – and we crossed to the main door of the warehouse, which was standing ajar.

The first thing that struck me as we went in – apart from the smell of mustiness and portable gas fires – was the clutter. I'd never been to an auction before, and somehow the only image in my mind was the likes of Christie's or Sotheby's, seen on TV when some piece had gone for an amazing price – all rows of plush chairs and the auctioneer behind a lectern on a platform, and well-suited men gabbling into their mobile phones as they placed bids for absent buyers.

Compton Auctions was nothing like that. Pieces of furniture were banked along the bare walls of the cavernous room – worn easy chairs and ring-marked tables, a sixties-style sideboard, long and low, next to a little dressing table with triptych mirrors and carved legs that must have been at least a hundred years old. The smaller items were arranged along trestle tables at the rear of the warehouse, all marked with stickers showing their lot numbers. Prospective buyers were examining the various items and making notes, not on programmes, but in notebooks or even on the backs of envelopes, and chatting in groups in the open space in the middle of the warehouse. There wasn't a single chair – apart from those in the sale – in sight. My heart sank at the prospect of having to stand for the next couple of hours.

I looked around for Alice, but couldn't see her. Sarah was there, though, leafing through a pile of paperwork at a table from which I imagined Lewis Crighton would be conducting the auction, and the man himself was moving between the groups of customers, stopping to speak to a heavily made-up woman in a tatty fur coat here, a weaselly looking man in an anorak there.

When he spotted Jeremy, however, he made a beeline for us, extending his hand.

'Jeremy, my friend! We don't often see you here!'

Jeremy shook the proffered hand, but he was smirking.

'You don't really have anything here that would interest me, Lewis. I've chauffeured this young lady, who wants to make sure the items she's selling go to a good home. And that you're not doing her out of what's due to her, of course. Sally Proctor. I expect you know her father, Jack.'

Lewis nodded in my direction, but there was a certain frostiness in his manner – whether because he was annoyed at the suggestion that he might be cheating clients out of the true proceeds of the items they were selling, or because he recognized me as the girl who was asking too many questions about Dawn, I didn't know. Certainly he gave no indication of having ever seen me before, though he'd spoken to me in the office on my first visit to Compton Properties, but that didn't mean a thing. It was always possible he didn't want me – or Jeremy – to know that he'd taken notice of me.

'Right, old chap, must get on,' he said to Jeremy. 'I've got a busy night ahead, and I'm an assistant down. One of my young ladies has gone AWOL. Simply hasn't turned up for work this week. Probably sunning herself in Ibiza. You just can't get the staff these days, you know.'

'Which is why I prefer to operate solo,' Jeremy said easily.

But I was all ears. 'One of my young ladies' was undoubtedly Alice – she and Sarah were his only employees, as far as I was aware. She'd missed her appointment with me, and now Lewis was saying she hadn't turned up for work this week . . .

Alarm prickled on my skin like tiny electric shocks. Alice

had been afraid of something – or someone. But she'd plucked up the courage to speak to me and arrange a meeting anyway. Now, it would seem, she was missing. Was this yet another coincidence? Or had something happened to her?

I'd lost all interest in the auction now – I could think of nothing but Alice and what the implications of her disappearance might be. But at the same time I was registering everything about Lewis – his immaculate appearance, his smooth demeanour, the competent way he handled his duties as auctioneer – and the intimate little glances that passed between him and Sarah, which I might never have noticed had I not seen them leaving the office together after hours. Was it possible that this suave man was a murderer who coldbloodedly disposed of anyone who threatened to expose him? It seemed utterly preposterous, and yet the evidence against him was stacking up. Once I'd talked to Dawn's mother, I thought I would really have no alternative to going to the police with my suspicions. Otherwise, as Josh had predicted, I might well be the next to disappear, or be run down by a hit-and-run driver.

Preoccupied as I was, I almost missed the moment when the apostle spoons and the candle snuffer came under the hammer until Jeremy nudged me, beaming. Both items had been snapped up by the dealers – they hadn't made a fortune, but they'd exceeded their reserves.

'At least it will buy a decent bottle of champagne to welcome Jack home,' Jeremy said with a smile. 'I hope you'll invite me over to share it with you.'

'Dad would rather have a pint of bitter, if I know anything about it,' I retorted.

At last the auction was over and people began to drift away. A beefy-looking youth with the bulging muscles of a weight lifter, tattooed arms and an earring was helping one dealer to carry out his acquisitions, which included the sixties-style sideboard, and he managed to back into me as he passed.

'Careful!' Jeremy warned sharply. 'You're going to injure someone if you don't watch what you're doing!'

The lad, wearing only jeans and short-sleeved T-shirt in spite of the chill in the warehouse, muttered something under his breath and continued backing towards the door.

'Jason Barlow,' Jeremy said dismissively. 'He came to my farm manager for a job once, but was given short shrift. Lewis must have been desperate to give *him* a job.'

Jason Barlow. The name sounded vaguely familiar to me, though I couldn't for the life of my think why. It was only as we were driving home that it came to me where I'd heard it before, and even then I couldn't be sure I wasn't imagining things.

The minute I'd filled Mum in on what had happened with regard to the items we'd sold, I went up to my room, switched on my laptop, and pulled up my notes on Brian Jennings' trial. And as I scanned quickly through them, I realized I'd been right.

Jason Barlow. A Jason Barlow had been one of the witnesses who'd claimed to have seen Brian Jennings hanging about outside Dawn's flat on the night of the fire. And now here he was, working for Lewis Crighton.

Sixteen

Really the whole of the next day – Wednesday – is a blur to me. I went through the motions, but my thoughts were spinning around and around. Everything kept coming back to Lewis Crighton and my suspicion that he was a cold-blooded killer.

He'd been having an affair with Dawn, I felt sure, just as he was having one with Sarah, and for some reason he'd wanted rid of her, not just an end to their relationship, but something far more permanent. But it couldn't be, as I'd first thought, simply that he was afraid she'd spill the beans about their affair – that had already been common knowledge. Mention had been made at Compton Players of the trouble that Dawn had caused between Lewis and Bella, his wife. There had to be more to it than that, perhaps some kind of shady goings on at Compton Properties: tax evasion, false accounting, offshore bank accounts. Certainly Lewis wasn't short of a penny or two, and the property business had been very flat these last few years.

Had Dawn wanted the affair to continue when Lewis wanted it to end, and threatened him with what she knew? Had he set the fire – or got someone else to do it – and when that didn't work, arranged for her to be mown down by an unidentified vehicle? Whatever he'd been hiding, it must have been something pretty big to go to such lengths. Or, then again, perhaps not – just something that *seemed* very important to him.

And now Alice was missing. She hardly seemed to me to be the sort of girl to play hookey from work and jet off to the sun, as Lewis had suggested, and I felt very sure that her disappearance was actually connected to her decision to talk to me about what she knew. It could be, of course, that she'd been so frightened that she'd gone to ground of her own volition – I certainly hoped it was that. I'd never forgive myself if something dreadful had happened to her; I wouldn't be able to help feeling it was my fault for asking questions and, perhaps, stirring her conscience. But whatever the reason for her disappearance, it pointed once again to something big – something Lewis was determined to keep hidden.

'You're very quiet today, Sally,' Mum said, but I simply made the excuse that I was tired. No way was I going to worry her by telling her the turn my investigations had taken.

Josh telephoned me in the evening, and I didn't tell him either. It wasn't a long call – he and his friend had landed up in a B & B somewhere along the Cotswold Way, and dinner was going to be served shortly. He was tired, footsore, and in need of a bath, he said, but he was enjoying himself, and there was a cold beer waiting for him downstairs. I didn't mention that I was going to Dorset tomorrow – time enough to tell him when I saw him at the weekend. Perhaps by then I would have some answers. For now I absolutely did not want to face his disapproval of what I was doing.

To be honest, I was beginning to wonder just what I'd got myself into, but until I could gather enough evidence to take to the police, I couldn't see that I could give up.

But I was going to be very careful indeed. I didn't want to end up another victim.

Rachel arrived to pick me up as soon as she'd taken the children to school. She loaded Grace Burridge's address into the satnav, and we set off.

To begin with the journey was far from pleasant. Thick fog hung in the valleys, making driving slow and difficult, and Rachel's incessant chatter was wearing on my nerves. I wished she'd be quiet and concentrate on what she was doing, and I really didn't feel like talking myself – I was too strung up at the prospect of having to talk to Dawn's mother and try to elicit what information I could without upsetting her unduly.

As we neared the Dorset border the fog lifted and the sky brightened to a hazy blue. The satnav was doing a good job, and soon articulating: 'You have reached your destination'.

Grace's house – Dawn's home, I reminded myself – was a whitewashed bungalow in a small close of similar residences.

The front garden had been laid to gravel, dotted with shrubs and planters. They were empty now, but I guessed that in summer they would be bright with geraniums or petunias. I rang the bell beside the door, holly green, and recently painted, by the look of it, and heard the Westminster chime ringing in the house.

The woman who opened the door was much younger than I'd expected, not about Mum's age as I had supposed. Slim, with short blonde hair and wearing leggings and a tunic, she was probably in her late forties. But there was a haunted look about her. Grace Burridge was still a very attractive woman – had been stunning, no doubt, in her youth – but the tragedies that had touched her life in the last year were etched in her face.

'Sally?' she said.

'Yes. And this is my friend, Rachel. I hope you don't mind . . .?'

'No, of course not. Do come in.'

She showed us into a pleasant, open-plan room and indicated a cream leather sofa and matching chair.

'Sit down. Can I get you a coffee?'

'That would be nice. Thank you.'

She disappeared into the kitchen, and I looked around. There were photographs everywhere, lined up along the mantelpiece and, on top of a bookcase, some of family, including one of herself and her husband on a black-tie occasion, but mostly of Dawn. Her beautiful, photogenic face seemed to light up the room. It was a sobering thought that she would never again smile engagingly for a camera.

'So,' Grace said, returning with a pot of coffee and elegant little cups and saucers set out on a tray, 'you were a friend of Dawn's.'

I took a deep breath. I really didn't want to lie any more to Grace Burridge, so I avoided the direct question.

'What happened to her was shocking,' I said. 'I'm going to be honest with you, Mrs Burridge, I can't help wondering if what happened to her was really an accident. It seems really strange that she was killed so soon after the fire, and I . . .'

I broke off. Grace Burridge had gone very still, the coffee

pot suspended over one of the little cups, and she was staring at me, those sad eyes narrowed in a face that, I felt sure, would have been very pale if not for her make-up.

'You think so too,' she said.

This wasn't at all the reaction I'd expected. I'd thought I'd meet with astonishment, denial even.

I nodded slowly, and Grace Burridge gave up trying to pour the coffee and set the jug down on the tray.

'You have no idea what a relief it is to have somebody actually agree with me,' she said, her voice shaking with emotion. 'My late husband always told me I was imagining things, and Andrew, my son, thinks I'm just desperate for someone to blame. They may be right, of course. But they didn't talk to Dawn as I did when she came home after the fire, and it was only after the accident that I started putting two and two together. She was frightened, Sally. Really frightened, not like my Dawn at all. Something was very wrong. And you saw that too, did you?'

'Not exactly,' I said carefully. 'I don't live in Stoke Compton any more, and I didn't actually see Dawn after the fire.' I was treading on eggshells here, and I wondered if Grace Burridge would realize that if I wasn't living in Stoke Compton, I couldn't actually have known Dawn at all. But she was too caught up in the moment, too relieved to find someone who actually agreed with her, to think of that.

'It just wasn't Dawn,' she repeated. 'She was always such a happy girl – his little ray of sunshine, her Daddy used to call her. And so beautiful! She had the sort of looks that made people turn round and stare at her in the street. She was so talented, too. She loved her acting, and she was so good at it. She could have made a career of it if she'd gone to drama school – would have done, I expect, if she hadn't met George and wanted to be with him. The girl who left home was bright and happy, all her future before her. The one who came back . . .' She shook her head and her chin wobbled with the effort of holding back the tears. 'Oh, I'm sorry . . .'

'That's OK, Mrs Burridge,' I said.

'Grace. Please call me Grace.' She picked up the coffee pot again, poured coffee and pushed the cups across the low table to Rachel and me, and the simple, everyday task seemed to restore her equilibrium a little.

'Of course, I didn't really think anything of it to start with,' she went on, sitting down on the edge of one of the leather chairs opposite us. 'Being trapped in a terrible fire like that would be enough to upset anyone. She must have been so frightened, and she lost everything, all her lovely clothes, everything. But she seemed to be taking it in her stride, trying to get on with her life. She even got her old job back, the one she left when she went to Stoke Compton. They were only too happy to take her back – that's the sort of girl she was.'

Another pause; she bit her lip.

'Yes,' I agreed, but said nothing more. Grace seemed eager to talk, to just let all of it come pouring out, and I was anxious not to interrupt the flow.

Once again Grace recovered herself, and sighed.

'Oh, if only she'd never gone to Stoke Compton! It didn't even work out, you know, between her and George. But by the time they broke up she'd settled there, had her flat and her job and new friends – she'd even met someone else, I think.'

Yes, Lewis Crighton, I thought, but I said nothing.

'She seemed so happy,' Grace went on, 'even though, of course, Brian Jennings was making a nuisance of himself. Had been from the moment she went to work at Compton Properties.'

I frowned. What did Compton Properties have to do with Brian Jennings and his obsession with Dawn? For the moment I was afraid to ask, but Rachel couldn't resist jumping in.

'Brian Jennings worked at Compton Properties?'

'Well, yes – I thought you knew that . . .' Grace looked a little puzzled.

'Sorry, it's just me . . .' Rachel put in quickly.

'Brian Jennings worked as a sort of odd-job man,' Grace said, addressing Rachel. 'Mostly he helped out with the house clearances and auctions, shifting the heavy furniture, and so on – just manual labour. He wasn't bright enough to be trusted with anything else.'

The job Jason Barlow had been doing last night. Jason Barlow, who had been a witness for the prosecution at Brian Jennings' trial . . .

'Lewis got rid of him, of course, when he developed this fixation on Dawn,' Grace went on. 'It didn't stop him, though. He still went on pestering her. Lisa, her flatmate, persuaded her to report him to the police, but what could they do? There's no law against walking up and down a public street, and they didn't think he was in any way dangerous.'

'Until the fire,' I said.

'Exactly. They went after him then, all right, and when witnesses came forward to say they'd seen him hanging about, and all the photographs of Dawn and so on were found in his flat, they were convinced they had their man. Then, of course, traces of petrol were found in his jacket pocket, and that was it. He never stood a chance after that . . . well, really he probably never stood a chance at all, someone like him . . .'

'But even after he was convicted and locked up, Dawn was still frightened,' I prompted her.

She nodded. 'I don't think Dawn ever really believed Brian Jennings was guilty. She said he was annoying, scary, even, but she didn't think he'd ever do anything to harm her. And there was something else about the fire that was worrying her, too, something to do with Lisa, her flatmate . . .'

At once I was remembering the feeling I'd had when talking to Lisa Curry that she was hiding something.

'What do you mean?' I asked.

'Dawn said that that evening – the evening before the fire – Lisa was really jumpy and strange. "Perhaps she's psychic" she said, "Perhaps she knew something bad was going to happen". That was her way of explaining it. Lisa was her friend, after all. But I'm not sure whether she really believed that. It was Lisa who realized the shop was on fire, too, and woke Dawn – she saved her life, not a doubt of it. If they'd both been fast asleep and overcome by smoke, they'd never have been able to get out of the window when the baker fetched the ladder. And I can tell you, too, that it was after Dawn went back to Stoke Compton to see Lisa that she came back really upset. And I've often wondered if it was something Lisa told her that got her into the state she was in.'

I could feel prickles of excitement beginning in the pit of my stomach. A scenario was suggesting itself to me. Was it just a little bit too convenient that the baker had been passing at exactly the right moment? Not to mention that a ladder just happened to be at hand? A baker who was now married to Lisa, with her successful business established in the refurbished shop that had been the seat of the fire? Had it all been an elaborate ploy to get their hands on a prime High Street location?

But if so, why had Dawn been *frightened* when it was all over? She might have had her suspicions about who was really responsible; she might have felt guilt that Brian Jennings had been wrongly accused. But Lisa was her friend, and she and Paul were just an ordinary couple. They might have set a fire to get what they wanted, but I couldn't see them as murderers.

Perhaps after all the two events were unconnected. But that brought me back to my very first conclusion. For Dawn to have been trapped by the fire and then mown down by a hit-and-run driver was a huge coincidence, and I didn't like coincidences. Either Dawn was incredibly unlucky, or there was a link. And I was no nearer to finding out what it was.

'So though she had doubts about Brian Jennings being the culprit, Dawn still gave evidence at his trial?' I said.

'Only about him stalking her.' Grace was twisting her wedding ring round and round on her finger. 'She did say she couldn't see him being the fire raiser. But I don't remember his barrister ever asking her about that in court, I must confess.'

So, poor Brian Jennings had been represented by a lazy lawyer who hadn't really fought his case properly. Well, that happened – in fact it was what I'd suspected all along.

'Did Dawn ever mention anyone else who might have wished her harm?' I asked.

Grace shook her head vehemently.

'Dawn was really popular. She was a lovely girl – you know that.'

It didn't quite tally with what I'd heard of Dawn in Stoke Compton, but I wasn't about to upset Grace by saying so.

'You said she was frightened,' I said instead. 'Do you know who, or what, she was frightened of?'

Grace shook her head again.

'Not really. She didn't want to talk about it.'

I decided to take the bull by the horns.

'Could it have been Lewis Crighton?' I asked.

'Oh – no, no!' Grace sounded quite shocked. 'She was very fond of Lewis. He was a wonderful employer. And he thought the world of Dawn.' She broke off, her forehead creasing beneath her neat blonde fringe. 'I do think it had something to do with her work, though,' she went on after a moment. 'Not the estate agency – the auctions. And Lewis's partner. She did once say she didn't trust him . . .'

'His *partner*!' I repeated, startled. 'I didn't know he had a partner. I thought it was his own business.'

'Well, yes, as regards the estate agency, it is. Certainly he's the front man, and runs everything on a day to day business. But the auction side of it is a different matter. There's definitely someone else in the background.'

'Do you know who?' I asked, holding my breath.

'I'm sorry, no. I don't think Dawn ever mentioned a name, or if she did, I don't remember it.' She broke off, thinking. 'I don't suppose there would be anything in her diary that might give a clue?'

'Her diary?' I sat forward eagerly. 'Dawn kept a diary?'

'Always. From the time she was a little girl. She wrote it up every night without fail – sometimes I had to get cross with her when I'd find her scribbling away when she should be asleep. It was a ritual with her, right down to the book she wrote it in. She'd buy exercise books, then cover them with fancy paper and attach a sticker with the dates and something pretty to decorate it – a star, or a flower . . . the very first one, when she was about six or seven, I remember, was a picture of a puppy, and the gold paper was the wrapping from a birthday present . . .' Her eyes were misting as she remembered her little girl. A little girl who had grown up, but still stuck to the childish ritual of decorating her diaries as she always had.

'And she kept on writing them up after she came home?' I asked.

Grace recovered herself with an effort.

'Oh, I think so. I must say I haven't looked – I couldn't bring myself to. It would have upset me too much. But they're all in a shoebox on top of her wardrobe Even after she went to live in Stoke Compton she would bring each one home when it was completed and store it with the others.'

My heart was thudding with excitement. Was it possible the key to all this was here, in a shoe box, in Dawn's own hand writing? There was just one problem, though.

'Presumably the one she was keeping at the time of the fire will have been destroyed, though,' I ventured.

'Funnily enough, no,' Grace said. 'She was here the weekend before the fire, and I remember her taking it out of her bag and up to her room. Her dad was teasing her about it, saying she'd be able to write a book one day. She must have just started a fresh volume, so it would only be a couple of days' entries that will have been lost.'

'Mrs Burridge – Grace . . .' I hesitated, almost afraid to ask. 'I don't suppose . . . would you let *me* look at them?'

'Oh, I don't know . . .' She looked uncertain suddenly.

'I know how precious they are to you,' I said, 'and private, too. But there might be a clue in what Dawn wrote, and if we're both right, and her death was no accident, I'd really like to be able to get justice for her.'

I paused, wondering how far I could take this. Could I mention that Alice, who had also been frightened, was missing, and appeal to Dawn's mother on the basis that if I could find out from the diaries what was going on it might give some clue as to her whereabouts? I really was seriously concerned about her. But bringing her into the equation was a risk. I didn't want Grace to think I was doing this for any reason other than to get to the bottom of what had happened to Dawn.

I waited, saying nothing, and after a moment Grace's eyes met mine.

'You would . . . treat them with respect, if I was to let you have them?'

'Of course I would. I just want to find out the truth of what happened, Grace. If she was killed because of something she knew. And I think you want that too.'

'Very well.' She got up and left the room, a slim, pretty woman whom Dawn would have resembled in years to come,

I imagined, if she had lived, and I heard her footsteps on the stairs.

Rachel and I exchanged a look, but neither of us said a word.

A few minutes later she was back, clutching a silver-covered exercise book, but looking flustered.

'This is really peculiar . . .'

I looked at her questioningly, and she held the book out so that I could see the date on the cover.

'This isn't Dawn's latest diary – the one she brought home with her when it was finished, just before the fire. This is the one before. And the one she would have started just before she died isn't there either. They're missing. The diaries you wanted are missing!'

Seventeen

'She must be making a mistake,' Rachel said. 'The poor woman is obviously in an awful state – of course she is. Why on earth would Dawn's diaries go missing? They couldn't have been here in the first place.'

We were on the way home; if we didn't encounter any delays we'd make it in time for Rachel to pick up the children from school, and Steve wouldn't have to interrupt his work flow to collect them.

'You're probably right,' I said. But whereas once I would have agreed with her wholeheartedly, now I wasn't so sure. Too many sinister things were happening.

'There's no other explanation.' Rachel pulled out to overtake a lycra-clad cyclist and swerved back in violently as she saw a car come over the brow of the hill ahead of us, though he was still miles away. 'If Dawn had ever brought them home with her, they'd be there now. Grace *thinks* she did, but she's confusing it with another time. The last diary will have been destroyed in the fire, and she's never started another.'

'Well, at least I've got this one.' I glanced down at the exercise book, carefully covered with silver wrapping paper and with a scattering of gold stars stuck around the date in the shape of a heart, which Grace had allowed me to borrow. 'And it covers the early part of Dawn's time in Stoke Compton, so it's possible there might be something in it that's useful.'

I hadn't so much as opened it yet; to flip into it at random seemed disrespectful. Dawn's life was in these pages, things she'd never meant anyone else to read, her thoughts, her hopes and fears, a record, perhaps, of her most private moments. And, if I was very lucky, some clue as to what it was that was going on at Compton Properties. What it was that had cost her her life.

'Fancy Brian Jennings working for Lewis Crighton!' Rachel's

butterfly mind was skimming all Grace had told us. 'Now that is a turn-up for the book.'

'I'm surprised no one has mentioned it before,' I said. 'It explains how he came to latch on to her, doesn't it?'

'And gives him another reason for having it in for her,' Rachel pointed out. 'If she got him the sack.'

She was right, of course. Not only spurned by the object of his desire, but losing his job because of her, perhaps Brian Jennings' sense of being wronged against had festered and grown until he could think of nothing but revenge. Perhaps he *had* started the fire, and Dawn's accident was just that – a tragic accident. But Grace didn't think so, and neither did I.

'Why on earth doesn't that motorbike overtake me?' Rachel's exasperated voice cut into my thoughts.

'What?' I murmured distractedly.

'That motorbike. He's been right up my boot for miles . . . why doesn't he just get past and have done with it?'

I glanced over my shoulder, couldn't see anything, and turned further. A big motorbike was maybe thirty yards behind us. The rider, clad in black leather, and wearing a full-face dark crash helmet, was bent low over racing handlebars. Not the sort of bike you'd expect someone who was content to tootle along at forty mph to be riding.

'Anyone would think he was following me!' Rachel said, and her remark, meant as a light-hearted quip, set alarm bells ringing.

Suddenly I was remembering the car that had tailed me from South Compton the first time I went to a meeting of the Compton Players . . . and something else. A big, powerful motorbike, the rider all in black with a full-face helmet. That was exactly how Sam had described the motorcycle that had panicked Dad's cows into stampeding. Oh, there must be millions of motorbikes and riders on the roads fitting that description, but still . . .

'Slow down,' I said to Rachel. 'Give him the chance to pass.'

'He could pass anyway if he wanted to,' Rachel pointed out; we were on a straight stretch of road where he could easily have got by.

'Slow down anyway. Perhaps he's one of the cautious ones. They do exist.'

Rachel raised an eyebrow, but she did slow right down. For a few moments the following bike slowed too, and my heart came into my mouth. Then, suddenly, he accelerated, roared past us, and away.

'You were right,' Rachel said.

No, I was wrong, I thought. Getting paranoid in my old age.

Except that a few miles further on, he was behind us again – well, either him or an identical motorcyclist! I spotted him in the wing mirror and went cold, but said nothing. I didn't want to alarm Rachel – she was a nervous enough driver at the best of times – but my thoughts were racing. Was it the same man? He was further back this time, and it was hard to be absolutely sure. Had he pulled into a turning and waited for us to go by? We certainly hadn't passed him on the road. Who was it? And why was he following us?

At last, on a straight stretch about twenty miles from home, he overtook us and roared away into the distance.

'Wasn't that . . .?' *The same bike that overtook us before,* she was going to say. But I cut in quickly.

'Shouldn't think so, Rach. He'll be long gone.'

'I suppose. They all look the same to me.'

'Me too.'

But I had a bad feeling about this. And what was especially worrying was that if there *was* something sinister about the motorcyclist, he now knew Rachel's car, and that she had been to Dorset with me. I absolutely must not involve her again. If I was taking risks with my own safety, it was one thing. To put Rachel in danger was something else entirely.

Without a doubt the time was coming when I would have to go to the police with my suspicions. The trouble was I still didn't have any concrete evidence to back me up, and I rather thought they'd laugh me out of court. But I'd come too far to give up now. Quite apart from my overwhelming curiosity, and a desire to see justice done, I really needed, for my own sake, to get to the bottom of what was going on. Unless I did, I'd never be able to stop looking over my shoulder. Even when I left Stoke Compton and went home I wouldn't be safe. Dawn had left and gone back to Dorset, but, if I was right, someone had followed her there and made sure she couldn't blow the whistle on what she knew, or suspected. It was a worrying thought.

We made it home without further incident; there were no more black-clad motorcyclists anywhere to be seen.

'Thank you so much, Rach,' I said when she dropped me off. 'You really are a star.'

'No probs.'

Oh, I certainly hoped not!

'You take care,' I said, and for once, instead of a stock phrase, trotted out automatically, I really meant what I said.

Naturally, I could hardly wait to have a look at Dawn's diary. Mum wasn't yet back from visiting Dad, so I put some chops in the oven, prepared vegetables, and then sat down at the kitchen table and opened the silver-covered exercise book, which appeared to cover the period when Dawn had first arrived in Stoke Compton.

Her writing was rounded and childlike, neat and easy to read, but she did have a habit of using initials rather than names, which made it a little difficult to follow at first, and on the whole she didn't go into much detail.

Saw G, went to cinema and for a drink, was a typical entry, recording a date with Gorgeous George.

I was glad of that – it would have been horribly embarrassing if she had poured out her emotions, or described intimate moments, and I would have felt like a voyeur. But it meant it was unlikely she'd recorded her suspicions either, even if she'd begun to have them at this early stage.

Perhaps keeping the diary had become a bit of a chore, something that she no longer really had the time or enthusiasm for, but which had become too much of a habit to break.

I skimmed on through the pages, and noticed the Gs for George appeared less frequently, whilst LC – Lewis Crighton, presumably – figured more and more. Then, before long, LC became simply L – a sure sign of their growing intimacy, though there was no salacious detail beyond the odd *Can't get L out of my head*, and *Two whole days before I'll see L again. Torture!*

No doubt about it, the sketchy shorthand was charting an affair.

Besides the budding romance, I could see the story of Brian Jennings' obsession with Dawn playing out.

BJ gives me the creeps. He just stares at me, she had written. And: *Hate having to go to the warehouse. I don't want to be alone with BJ.*

A little further on there was mention of his sacking: *L has given BJ his cards. Hurray! The freak won't be staring at me any more.*

Some hope! I thought. Brian Jennings might have no longer been at her place of work, but he'd far from given up on the staring, and things were about to get a lot worse.

Sure enough, it wasn't long before Dawn started recording the times when Brian Jennings followed her, or stood on the pavement on the opposite side of the road to the flat she and Lisa shared, simply staring up at the windows.

BJ is really freaking me out! He's been there an hour or more. Lisa thinks I should go to the police, says if I don't, she will.

And: *Police don't seem interested. Say there's nothing they can do. If it wasn't for L I think I'd get out of this place. But nothing on earth is going to make me leave him! Think I'm in love!*

The affair was clearly hotting up. There were mentions of clandestine meetings, and even a weekend away.

Two whole nights with L! Bliss! He promised me again that he'll leave B soon. That he wants to be with me all the time, always, and she makes his life a misery. But I think she put a lot of money into the business, so that will have to be sorted first.

Oh Dawn, Dawn, I thought. Falling for the age-old lies of the philandering married man. It could well be, of course, that it had been Bella's money that had enabled Lewis to set up his own business, but I'd bet anything that money considerations or not, Lewis didn't have the slightest intention of leaving Bella for Dawn, or anyone else.

The clock struck five, reminding me that Mum would be home soon, and I skipped on quickly through the pages. I'd read them thoroughly later, but I was really anxious to see if I could spot anything more revealing. I wasn't disappointed.

Haven't seen L all day. Phone call (from his partner, I think), and he went out, taking warehouse keys. Puzzled. No house clearances to do, and auction not due for another three weeks. Why does he need to go to the warehouse?

Ah! I sat up straighter, excitement quickening. Dawn's mother had said she thought that whatever was worrying Dawn was connected with the warehouse, rather than the estate agency, and to Lewis's mysterious 'partner'. Might Dawn have recorded more in her diary than she had been prepared to tell Grace? I turned the page, tingling with anticipation, but at that moment I heard the door open, and Mum's voice calling.

'It's only me! I'm back.'

Burning with frustration, I closed the exercise book.

'Hiya, Mum. How's Dad?'

'I can see an improvement every day.' Mum was unbuttoning her coat. 'And how did you get on?'

'Very well, actually. Would you believe that Dawn's mother doesn't think her death was an accident either?'

'Really?' Mum sounded surprised. 'Let's put the kettle on – I'm dying for a cup of tea – and you can tell me all about it.'

I did. The one thing I didn't mention was the motorcyclist who had seemed to be following us on the way home – the motorcyclist who could very well answer the description of the one who had made the cows stampede. I didn't want to alarm her. Didn't want to think about it, even. And not just because if it was one and the same man it could mean that I, and possibly Rachel, too, were in dangerous territory. The fact was that if he was connected in some way to my investigation, then that could mean that I was to blame for Dad's accident. If it hadn't been for me, the motorcycle would never have been in the lane. And that was something I couldn't bear to contemplate.

I didn't mention it to Josh either. He rang just as we were eating; Mum put my plate in the Aga to keep warm while we talked. Another day's walking, another B & B, another much-needed beer waiting for him, he told me.

'Haven't you had enough yet?' I teased.

'Beer?'

'No – walking. You must be getting tired, doing all those miles day after day.'

'Funnily enough it gets easier. You get into your stride, I suppose.'

'You might. I don't think I would.'

'Of course you would! When you're skiing you do it every day, don't you?'

'Well, yes, true . . . but there's the ski-lift to take you uphill. Then all you have to do is coast down again.'

'Each to his own. What have you been up to, anyway?'

'Rachel and I have been to Dorset to see Dawn's mother.'

'And? What did she have to say?'

'Some very interesting things. I'll tell you all about it when you get back.'

'Which isn't long now. We'll hit Stinchcombe where we left Paul's car, and then all we have to do is drive back to the start point so I can pick up mine. Then I'll be heading home. A hot bath, a couple of beers, and I'll be all ready to cook that meal I promised you.'

'Oh Josh . . . you aren't going to feel like cooking . . .'

'No, but I do feel like the beers, and if we go out, I won't be able to drink and drive.'

'So I'll drive! It's got to be my turn, anyway.'

'Could be a plan. I don't like the thought of you haring about those country lanes on your own late at night though.'

'Well . . . I could always stay.'

'Why didn't I think of that?'

'You probably did. I've got to go, Josh. My dinner is going to be as dried up as the Sahara.'

'I'll ring you tomorrow.'

'I may stay at Josh's tomorrow night,' I said, retrieving my plate from the Aga. Mum had already finished her dinner, but was still sitting at the table, waiting for me. 'You wouldn't mind, would you?'

'Oh Sally, for goodness sake!' Mum smiled. 'I think you're a bit past the age when you need to ask my permission, don't you?'

But I wasn't altogether sure how pleased she was at the prospect. Whilst she was glad he made me happy, and though they'd got on really well when he'd taken the two of us out for a meal, I couldn't help feeling she still thought I was rushing into things a little faster than she'd like.

When we'd finished clearing away, I returned to examining Dawn's diary, and the more I read the more I became convinced – as Dawn had been – that something very shady was going on and it centred around the warehouse where the auctions were held. At the time of writing Dawn had seemed not to know what it was, and so, of course, neither did I, but I got the definite impression that she thought it was something illegal.

L won't talk about it at all, she jotted down. *Can't understand why he should be so secretive. Unless . . .??!?*

What did those question and exclamation marks hide, I wondered? *Did* Dawn have some inkling, something she wasn't prepared to put into black and white?

It seemed, though, that she was still in the dark about Lewis's so-called 'partner'. His identity was something else Lewis wasn't willing to discuss, and that, too, was niggling at Dawn.

It was all highly suspicious, but it seemed to point to one thing. The auctions, and the warehouse, were a blind for some questionable goings-on. What had Grace said? *Lewis is the front man*. A telling phrase. But what *was* the illicit business?

Something a lot more profitable than an estate agency, if Lewis's lifestyle was anything to go by. And if I was right, and Dawn had died because of what she knew, that was further evidence that it wasn't just a two-penny-halfpenny fraud, but something very lucrative indeed.

What I really needed to find out was who Lewis's partner was. He was the one who, according to Grace, Dawn had been afraid of. But how?

I talked it over with Mum when I eventually surfaced, though I was careful not to let her think I might be treading dangerous waters, and she had a suggestion to make.

'Jeremy might know who Lewis's business associates are,' she said thoughtfully. 'He's in the Chamber of Commerce, after all, and the Rotary Club.'

'That's true. And he knows Lewis,' I said. 'It's definitely worth a try. I'll give him a ring.'

'Not tonight, though, Sally – it's much too late.'

I had to smile. 'It's only half past nine.'

'You can't bother someone at half past nine at night.' Mum's tone was decisive. 'Do it in the morning.'

I couldn't imagine that Jeremy would be so early to bed, but this was the countryside, and it had its own conventions.

'All right, I'll leave it until the morning if that'll make you happy,' I agreed.

In the event, I didn't have to telephone Jeremy; he turned up at the door while I was still helping Mum with the chores.

'Just checking on that man of mine,' he said breezily. 'He's not slacking, is he?'

'I haven't had any complaints from Sam,' Mum assured him.

'And the computer programme I set up is going OK?'

I hardly liked to admit I hadn't yet used it, so I just smiled and nodded.

'Actually, there was something Sally wanted to ask you, Jeremy.' Mum set the kettle to boil. 'I'll make a cup of tea, and she can tell you all about it.'

This was a bit awkward, I realized. I didn't want to go into detail about the reason I wanted this information.

'It's nothing, really,' I said lightly. 'I understand Lewis Crighton has a partner, and I just wondered if you might know who it is.'

A look of astonishment crossed Jeremy's face.

'Lewis Crighton has a partner? I thought the business was his and his alone.'

My heart sank.

'Oh well, never mind. It was just a thought. It doesn't matter.'

'That's not what you said last night!' Mum declared. 'You told me you thought it might be really important.' She turned to Jeremy. 'I had to stop her from ringing you there and then – at going on for ten o'clock. Not important, my eye. She thinks her story might depend on it.'

'Your story . . . the one about the fire . . .'

'And Dawn Burridge's death.' Mum was in full flow now. 'She went to see Dawn's mother yesterday, and it seems this secret partner might be the one behind it.'

'Mum – I don't know anything of the sort,' I protested. 'You'll be having me charged with defamation of character if you're not careful!' I turned to Jeremy. 'I'm just curious, that's all. A shadowy figure in the background whets my appetite.'

Jeremy smiled wryly. I had the feeling he could see right through me.

'Leave it with me, Sally.'

Jeremy hadn't got back to me by the time I left to drive over to Josh's cottage, and to be honest, all thoughts of my investigation had gone on the back burner, so excited was I at the prospect of seeing Josh again. He'd phoned me around lunchtime to say he and his friend had finished their walk and were now driving back to where Josh had left his car when they'd set out four days ago. He should be home by late afternoon, and would expect me at around seven.

I was feeling on top of the world as I drove. I'd only been to the cottage once before, in the dark, and he'd been driving, so I wasn't confident I'd be able to find it again, and I'd put the post code he'd given me into the satnav. Soon it was informing me that I'd reached my destination.

'I don't *think* so,' I replied, just as if the disembodied voice could hear me. I was indeed outside a house, but it looked more like a farm than Josh's cottage, set back from the lane, with big gates and outbuildings. I drove on a little further, then pulled into a gateway to a field and rang Josh.

'I'm lost,' I said, when he answered.

He chuckled. 'How can you be lost?'

'I don't know, but I am. The satnav sent me to a farm.'

'Ah, that's happened before. It's OK, I know where you are.'

'Which is . . . where, exactly?'

'Only a few hundred yards away. Just keep going until you come to a T-junction and you'll see the cottage on your right.'

'I shall be ringing you again if I don't see it,' I warned.

'You will,' he assured me.

He was right. After just a short distance I spotted the cottage. The front door was open and Josh was looking out. Feeling a little foolish, I pulled on to the gravelled area in front of a small garage, and beside Josh's car. Why didn't he keep it in the garage? I wondered, and then remembered. Of course, he had a motorbike. Perhaps there wasn't room for a car as well.

'You found me in the end, then.' Josh was opening my driver's door, helping me out. And then I was in his arms, and as he kissed me, white-hot desire pulsed through me; I was thinking of nothing but him.

We were rather late making it to the pub for our meal; we'd had better things to do. Josh was a wonderful lover, generous and tender as well as passionate, and he aroused in me emotions and responses I'd almost forgotten I could experience. The touch of his hands and his lips stirred my soul as well as my body, the feel of the long hard muscles in his shoulders and back beneath my hands thrilled and delighted me, his heart beating next to mine and our breath rising and falling in unison made me feel as if we were somehow one, not two separate people at all.

'I hope the pub is still serving food,' Josh said after we'd showered and dressed again.

'I don't care much if they're not,' I laughed.

'Speak for yourself! I'm starving! Josh retorted. 'If we're too late we'll just have to find a fish and chip shop.'

'As long as that doesn't mean driving around for miles. I haven't got that much fuel. I should have filled up, but it's such a hassle and I thought I had enough for what I needed tonight.'

'No problem.' He picked up his car keys. 'I'm driving anyway.'

'But we agreed . . .'

'I know, but I've changed my mind. When I take a lady out I don't like being in the passenger seat. And if you're low on fuel, that settles it. Come on, don't argue. Just do as you're told.'

I shook my head in mock exasperation, but there was a warmth inside me that would not be denied. I felt cherished, protected. It was a good feeling.

We were in luck – the pub was still serving food, albeit a limited menu. I chose lasagne, and Josh had steak pie with a huge bowl of chips on the side, and a pint of locally brewed beer.

'I should be all right if I stick to just the one,' he said, licking foam from his lips. 'So, you were going to tell me how you got on in Dorset yesterday.'

Between mouthfuls of lasagne I filled him in, though I

avoided mentioning the motorcycle that had appeared to be following us on the way home. I still wasn't sure if I was being paranoid, and in any case I didn't want to get into another argument about the risks of what I was doing.

'Something is definitely going on at the warehouse, I'm sure of it,' I said. 'I don't know yet what it is, but I'm guessing it's something like drugs – that's how Lewis is making his money. And I don't know where the mystery 'partner' fits in, or who he is. But I've asked Jeremy, and he's going to try to find out.'

'You think he'll be able to?' Josh asked.

'There's a pretty good chance, I'd say. He's well in with the business community. And once I know that, I'm going to go to the police with my suspicions.'

'I thought you were dead set on getting to the bottom of it by yourself.' Josh took a judicious pull of his beer – making it last, I guessed.

'To be honest, I don't think there's much more I can do,' I said. 'And besides, I'm thinking about Alice. I don't know whether she's still missing, or ever was, but if she is, then I owe it to her to go to the police with as much as I know. No, I'm afraid I'm out of my depth here, Josh.'

'Which is what I've been saying all along.'

I ignored that.

'At least I'll have an insider's take on the story,' I said.

When we'd finished our meals we lingered for a little longer, enjoying cups of frothy cappuccino, then headed back to Josh's cottage and went to bed, where once again we made wonderful, exhilarating love.

Afterwards I felt replete and happy. Whether anything came of my story or not, at least investigating it had been the cause of my meeting Josh. If I hadn't gone to the *Gazette* office to research the fire, I'd never have met him, and I'd have missed out on something wonderful.

The word 'serendipity' floated into my mind; it was still there, warming me, as I fell asleep in his arms.

It must have been an hour or so later when I woke with a raging thirst – the result of drinking too much wine, I thought. Josh was fast asleep and snoring gently; I slid out from beneath the duvet and crept downstairs in search of a glass so that I could get a drink of water.

Josh's kitchen was at the back of the cottage. I padded across the open-plan living room, where moonlight made silvery pools and shadows on the woodblock floor, and pushed open the door. I hadn't been in the kitchen before – had had no cause to. Now I took in the shaker-style cupboards and work-tops, the free-standing cooker and fridge, the microwave propped on a shelf, and imagined myself cooking for Josh here. At the moment it was typically a man's domain – basic and a bit untidy – but nothing that wouldn't be improved by a few pots of herbs on the window sill and perhaps a string of garlic bulbs and bunches of dried flowers hanging from the beams between the copper pans. I smiled to myself – how presumptuous was that?

I found a glass in one of the wall cabinets, filled it at the big stone sink, and sat down at the small, rickety table to drink it. My elbow brushed a pile of what looked to be motorcycling magazines stacked on the corner, and as I moved them aside so as not to drip water on them they slipped a bit, revealing . . .

I froze, unable to believe what I was seeing.

In the middle of the stack were two exercise books covered in silver paper and decorated with stickers bearing the dates, and a sprinkling of gold stars.

There was no mistaking what they were: Dawn's missing diaries! But what on earth were they doing in Josh's kitchen?

Eighteen

For a moment my mind was a total blank. I think I even stopped breathing! I flipped open the first of the exercise books, and recognized the rounded, childlike writing. It certainly was one of Dawn's missing diaries. But that made no sense at all. If she'd taken it to Dorset before the fire, as her mother had said, then that explained how it had survived when most of her possessions had been destroyed. But how had it come to be in Josh's possession? He hadn't known Dawn; he'd only taken the job at the *Gazette* in the last year – after Dawn had left Stoke Compton.

Or at least, that was what he'd told me.

Now I came to think about it, though, I realized it was one of the very few things I knew about Josh – or *thought* I knew. He'd given me the impression that he'd come here from another provincial newspaper, but he hadn't provided any details. He'd always been vague, and whenever the subject had come up he'd sidestepped it. Now, suddenly, I was wondering why. Mum and Rachel had both mentioned the fact that I knew next to nothing about him, and I'd pooh-poohed their doubts. But had I been so blown away by him that I simply hadn't wanted to allow myself to think it was a little odd? Perhaps, after all, they had been right to be cautious.

Who *was* Josh? In reality, I didn't have a clue. I'd taken him totally on trust, and now that trust had been well and truly shaken. If he had known Dawn – and with her diary staring up at me, I thought he must – but had led me to believe he had never met her, what else was he keeping from me?

My thoughts whirling in a muddy maelstrom, I glanced down at the pages.

I'd become familiar by now with Dawn's style of writing. I read a couple of entries, but registered nothing beyond the fact that this volume was clearly a continuation of the one that Grace had allowed me to borrow. The abbreviated names were the same, the secret meetings with Lewis were still continuing, and there was the occasional mention of some unusual activity at the warehouse – the dates underlined in red – and the mysterious 'associate' as Dawn was now referring to him.

Then one entry leaped out at me.

More action at the warehouse – it's all happening again. Now know Lewis's associate is JW – the last person I'd have thought was a crook! He's so charming! JW of all people!

JW. I went cold all over. JW – Josh Williams. Oh surely – surely not! Even when I'd found Dawn's diary here in his kitchen it hadn't for one moment occurred to me. Josh wasn't a criminal, or even a crooked businessman. He was a newspaper photographer! Or was that just a cover? An excuse to be here in Stoke Compton, close to the hub of whatever it was he was involved in?

Suddenly I was remembering the day I'd driven round the industrial estate and seen what I'd thought was his car parked outside the warehouse. I'd told myself it couldn't be, that he was off walking the Cotswold Way. But was that another lie? Another part of the smoke and mirrors? How did I know for sure that that was where he'd been? When he'd phoned me each evening, he could have been calling from anywhere. Just because he'd told me he was in a B & B somewhere in Gloucestershire didn't mean he was.

My thoughts were racing now, keeping pace with the thudding of my heart. I thought of all the times Josh had warned me off pursuing my investigation. He'd led me to believe it was because he was concerned for my safety, but could it have been that he'd been worried I might learn the truth about what was going on? The very first time we'd met had been in the *Gazette* office when I was researching all I could about the fire. He'd been really helpful then, but was that because he'd wanted to worm his way into my confidence so that he would be aware of what progress I was making? Had he cultivated me for the same reason?

I thought back to the first time he asked me out – he'd been following me down the High Street, seen me heading for Compton Properties. 'So – you're still on the trail,' he'd said. I'd thought nothing of it at the time. Now it struck me as very odd. If he hadn't known Dawn, how had he known there was a connection? The last thing I wanted to believe was that the reason he'd been dating me was so that he could keep an eye on me and keep himself informed of what I was finding out, but there was no escaping the horrible suspicion. Oh, surely I couldn't have been so wrong about the electric attraction between us, his tenderness towards me, my own feelings for him? Or had it all been an illusion I'd conjured up because, as Mum and Rachel had said, I was on the rebound from Tim?

If the JW mentioned in Dawn's diary was indeed Josh, then I'd been wrong, so wrong about him. The man I'd fallen in love with didn't exist. I'd never known the real Josh at all. The thought was devastating – and not just because my dream of a very special relationship was falling into ruins. If Josh was the shadowy figure behind what was going on at the warehouse, then he wasn't just a fraud, he was a highly dangerous man. The man who had been behind the fire, behind Dawn's death, behind Alice's disappearance, perhaps. He'd known she had agreed to meet me – I'd told him myself. Who else would have known about it? I couldn't think of a single person except Mum. Certainly Alice had been anxious not to talk about Dawn in front of Lewis Crighton, and she had been so nervous about the whole thing I couldn't imagine her telling anyone. But I'd trusted Josh implicitly – and I'd played right into his hands.

Little as I wanted to believe it, the evidence was stacking up, one awful realization after another rushing at me now in a dizzying stream. Josh had Dawn's diary. His car had been outside the warehouse. He'd done all he could to stop me investigating, yet followed my progress every step of the way. Then there was my missing laptop. I'd been so sure it hadn't been stolen in the burglary – I'd mentioned to Josh that it hadn't been. And then, after he'd spent the night with me, it was gone, and the case zipped up again so I wouldn't notice the difference. But what about the original burglary? Had he known the house would be empty that night? Had I told him about Dad's accident? I couldn't remember for sure . . .

Oh my God! The terrible thought struck me with all the force that the avalanche had done, whipping my feet from under me, the breath from my lungs. Suppose he'd *known* we'd all be at the hospital because it was he who had caused the accident? Suppose it had been a deliberate ploy to get us out of the way? Josh owned a motorcycle. A Ducati, he'd told me. Ducatis were big, powerful machines with racing handlebars. Just like the one Sam had described. Just like the one that had followed Rachel and me back from Dorset. And how did I even know it hadn't been a motorcycle that had hit Dawn and killed her? I'd assumed it had been a car or a van, but no one had ever said so.

I was shaking now from head to foot. Somehow I had to be sure. I remembered seeing all Josh's outdoor gear in the little lobby as we'd stumbled through in one another's arms, but only as a jumble of boots, and jackets hanging on the pegs, one on top of the other. Sick with dread I crept across the living room to the lobby. Moonlight was streaming in through the glass pane in the front door, and moments later I'd seen all I needed to. Black leathers underneath a waxed jacket. And a full-face crash helmet on a shelf above.

There was no getting away from it. Josh was JW. Josh was the one who was behind everything that had happened.

I'm not a person given to panic, but for a few horrible moments I was like a fly caught in a trap, the electronic flashes of blue sparking and sizzling all around me. Then the instinct for self-preservation kicked in.

I had to get away from here, away from Josh. I couldn't risk going back upstairs for fear of waking him, but luckily we'd shed some of our clothing in our eagerness for one another; it lay scattered about the living room. My bag was in the living room too. I pocketed my car keys, and stuffed the diaries into my bag.

The key to the front door was still in the lock, a heavy, old-fashioned key. My hands were shaking so much it took long, panicky moments before I could turn it. There was also a Yale; again I fumbled, then it turned and I yanked the door open and stumbled outside, hoping against hope that Josh's car was not blocking me in. But fortunately the gravelled area looked just about wide enough for me to squeeze through. I banged Dad's car into reverse, terrified that either the sound of the front door closing or the engine firing would have disturbed Josh, and swung the steering wheel too quickly. My wing connected with Josh's with a horrible scraping sound, but it was the least of my worries. I cleared the entrance and whacked the gear lever into 'drive'.

I'd made it – so far. But if I had woken Josh he might well come after me. My heart in my mouth, I pressed down hard on the accelerator and shot off up the lane. At that moment I wasn't thinking where I was going, or what I was going to do next beyond putting distance between me and Josh, and it took all my concentration just to keep the 4 x 4 on the road round the bends in the narrow lane.

I passed the farmhouse the satnav had sent me to; it was all in darkness. I hurtled on. Would the police station in Stoke Compton be open at this time of night? Time was when there was a twenty-four-hour presence, but I had a horrible feeling I remembered Mum complaining that nowadays it was manned only during office hours. Should I drive into Porton, then? Or go home and leave calling the police until the morning. More than anything, I wanted to go home. But I wasn't sure that was a very good idea. When he realized that both I and the diaries were missing – if he hadn't already – home was the first place Josh would look for me. I wouldn't be safe there, and I didn't want to put Mum in danger either. If Dad and his double-barrelled shotgun had been in the equation it would have been a different matter, but he wasn't. A dangerous man on a big black motorcycle had made sure of that.

Porton it was then. I racketed on, checking my mirror every few seconds to make sure Josh wasn't following me, and expecting to reach a junction with the main road around every bend. But I didn't come across one, only high hedges on each side of the lane and turnings that didn't look as if they led anywhere. Panic began to stir inside me once more, reducing me to a quivering wreck.

I was lost. Hopelessly lost. I'd have to risk stopping some-where to programme the satnav. But I didn't dare pull into a gateway; if Josh was following me he could box me in and I'd be trapped. I ground to a halt right in the middle of the lane, took Dawn's diaries out of my bag and thrust them out of sight under the passenger seat. As a hiding place it wasn't great, but if Josh did catch up with me, I didn't want to hand them to him on a plate. Then I grabbed the satnav to programme in Porton.

It was then that I noticed the fuel gauge was flashing a warning, and my heart sank. Why, oh why, hadn't I filled the tank yesterday? Now I wasn't sure I'd make it all the way to town before it ran out. What the hell was I going to do?

Jeremy. Out of the maelstrom of my racing thoughts he popped into my mind like the answer to a prayer. Jeremy wouldn't let Josh do me harm. Jeremy would know what to do.

Home was already programmed into the satnav; I punched it in. Once I was on familiar roads I could easily find Jeremy's farm. Then, while I was waiting for the satnav to work out where I was and give me instructions, I fumbled in my bag for my mobile. Thank goodness I'd put Jeremy's number into the directory when he'd been ferrying Mum and me to the hospital to see Dad. I clicked on it and waited for what seemed interminable moments while it connected, then rang.

Please, please don't let it go to voicemail. Please let him have it by his bed and switched on . . .

'Hello?' Jeremy sounded puzzled and a bit sleepy, but at least he'd answered!

'Jeremy!' My voice was shaking with relief as well as tension. 'Oh, I'm really sorry . . . at this time of night . . . but please . . .'

'Sally? Is that you? What on earth . . .?'

'I have Dawn's diary,' I gabbled. 'The last one before she died. And I'm in shock. Look . . . I'm on my way now . . .'

'On your way where?'

'To you.' I was checking my mirror all the while – no lights yet – but I was afraid to delay here any longer. 'I can't talk now, but I really have to see you.' The satnav had planned a route; it was there on the screen in front of me. Unbelievably I was only a few miles from home. 'I'll be there in about ten minutes,' I added, and disconnected. Then, still shaking from head to foot, I stuck the gear lever into 'drive' and sped away.

In no time flat I was in familiar territory and had no more

need of the satnav. I could scarcely believe I'd been lost so close to home, but I suppose at night all lanes look alike, and in my panic I'd been heading cross-country without realizing it.

I reached the entrance to Jeremy's farm and turned into it – a wide private road with his fields, which would soon be planted with barley and sweetcorn, on either side. Then I turned off on the track that led to the barn he'd converted into a residence for himself. Lights were burning at the small, evenly spaced windows, and a larger rectangle of light showed the front door, standing open. As I drew up, Jeremy came out to meet me. He was wearing a thick Aran jersey and jeans – presumably he'd got dressed after taking my phone call.

'Sally!' he greeted me. 'What on earth is wrong?'

'I . . .' Words failed me.

'Come on, let's get you inside.' Jeremy helped me out of the car, and, not bothering with my crutches, supported me to the front door.

'I think a stiff drink is called for. No . . . don't even try to talk until you've had one.'

'I really don't want . . .'

'You, young lady, will do as you are told.'

The barn conversion had been very tastefully done, the vast interior kept as an open-plan living and dining room, with the kitchen, also open-plan, on a little mezzanine above it. There was a central log-burning stove, its chimney creating a focal point to the room, a glass dining table and chairs of a modern geometric design, and leather armchairs and sofas in natural shades. Had I not been so preoccupied I might have thought it looked like a show house; as it was, I was simply glad to be here, and safe.

Jeremy installed me on one of the dining chairs – easier for me than the soft, deep sofas, and poured me a whisky.

'Drink that, and I'll make some coffee.' He went up the three stairs to the kitchen area, and I sank my head into my hands, massaging my temples where a headache had begun.

'Here we are.' Jeremy was back, placing a mug at my elbow. 'Only instant, I'm afraid, but hot, strong and sweet. Hey . . . you're not drinking your whisky.'

'Not my bag.' I managed a weak smile.

'Come on, it'll do you good.' He nudged the glass closer to me and I took an obedient sip, quickly followed by a gulp of coffee. After the strong spirit, it tasted oddly bitter.

'So. Tell Uncle Jeremy what this is all about.'

I was a little calmer now, sipping whisky and coffee alternately, and finding it surprisingly comforting. But I still barely knew where to start.

'You said you had a diary belonging to Dawn, so I take it this is all connected to your story about the fire,' he prompted me.

'Yes, but it's much more than that. The fire is just part of the big picture,' I said, and explained about my visit to Dorset, how Dawn's mother had let me borrow some of her diaries, and discovered that the latest ones were missing. 'The thing is, I'm pretty sure Dawn was targeted – and I don't just mean the fire,' I went on. 'I don't believe her death was an accident either. From the diaries I've already studied it's pretty clear she'd begun to suspect something illegal was going on at Compton Properties, though she didn't know what, or who else, besides Lewis, was involved. But later I think she did find out, and it cost her her life.'

'This is pretty startling stuff,' Jeremy said. 'Are you sure you aren't seeing conspiracies where none exist so as to make a good story?'

'I don't blame you for thinking that,' I said. 'I sometimes wondered myself if I was chasing rainbows, and everything that was happening was just coincidence. But now I have Dawn's latest diaries. I haven't had a chance to read them properly, but I'm pretty sure they contain what she discovered about what was going on – she was really meticulous about keeping them up to date – as well as who it was she was afraid of: Lewis's partner in crime.'

'Where did you get them?' Jeremy asked.

I lowered my eyes, staring at the half-empty coffee mug that I was gripping tightly between both hands in an effort to keep them from shaking.

Josh. Josh had them. But somehow I couldn't bring myself to say it aloud – I could scarcely bear to think about it, shrinking from the pain of knowing how he'd deceived me, ashamed of what a fool I'd been.

'I was going straight to the police when I realized what I had, but I didn't have enough diesel to take me to Porton and there's no one at the station at Stoke Compton overnight,' I said instead. 'I'm going first thing in the morning, but I'm really frightened, Jeremy. And I wanted to ask . . . will you come with me?'

For a moment Jeremy said nothing. He was looking at me narrowly, almost as if he was trying to read my mind. Then he stood up.

'I'll do better than that. I'll ring them now.'

'But . . . they're closed . . .'

'Stoke Compton, maybe. I'm ringing Porton. The divisional commander is a good friend of mine. A mention of his name will ensure this is treated with the seriousness it deserves. If you're right about all this, Sally, then you could be in the same danger as Dawn. You need to tell the police all you know, and hand over the diaries as soon as possible.'

He was right, I was sure, but the thought of going through everything again tonight was a daunting one. I was beginning to feel dreadfully tired – it was, after all, the middle of the night, though how I could sleep after all that had happened, I couldn't imagine.

The telephone was at the far end of the living room, and Jeremy's back was towards me, so I couldn't hear what he said, but after a few minutes he was back.

'Now that's what I call action,' he said, with a look of grim satisfaction.

'They're coming now? Tonight?'

'They want us to meet them at the warehouse.'

'The warehouse?' I repeated stupidly. 'But why . . .?'

'It seems they've had their suspicions about the place for some time. They want to strike while the iron's hot.' He glanced at me narrowly. 'Are you all right, Sally?'

'Not really.' I did feel very peculiar, totally devoid of energy, and my eyelids heavy.

'Come on. You can't fall asleep now. We've got to get going.'

He put a hand beneath my elbow, helping me up, and as I stumbled against him he supported me.

'Hey, Sally, you can do this. It'll soon be all over. Do you have the diary? They'll need to see that.'

'Yes . . . yes, in my bag . . .' I realised immediately that this wasn't true – I'd hidden it under the passenger seat of Dad's car – but I was too drowsy to correct myself.

'Good. That's the most important thing. Don't you have your crutches? Never mind, lean on me . . .'

I did. I had to. The plaster on my leg and the drowsiness tugging at my eyelids left me no option.

Jeremy installed me in the front passenger seat of his car and helped me fasten my seat belt.

'You can do this, sweetheart,' he encouraged me. But his words were cold comfort.

I'd wanted to unravel this mystery. But now that I had I wished with all my heart that I could turn back the clock. And terrible as the things that Josh had done were, I was wishing too that it didn't have to be me who was going to expose him.

The cold night air revived me a little, but with the heater running at full blast in Jeremy's car it was all I could do to stay awake.

'Have a little nap if you want to, Sally,' he said. He must have noticed me nodding. 'Don't fight it.'

'I've got to be awake to talk to the police,' I mumbled, but my eyes were closing. Dimly I was aware that we were driving along the rutted lane to the industrial estate and pulling into the yard outside the warehouse, then – I have no idea how much later – of lights cutting through the darkness. I fought my way back through layers of muzziness that seemed to be weighing me down.

The police were here. I must wake up.

Except that something was wrong. The beam of light didn't come from two headlights, but one. Puzzled, I struggled to keep my eyes open and to catch the thoughts that were trapped as if in thick treacle.

'I don't understand . . .' My lips felt numb and rubbery, my words were slurred.

'Don't worry about it, Sally. Go back to sleep.' Jeremy's voice seemed to be coming from a long way off.

Go back to sleep . . . But . . .

I could feel alarm now, not sharp and focused, but a sort of foreboding that was permeating my stupor like a bad dream. Half-formed thoughts whirled inside my head like trapped birds. This wasn't right. It never had been . . .

The passenger door opened; the interior light of the car came on, and my vague alarm became real fear.

The man standing beside me wasn't wearing a police uniform, but black motorcycle leathers and a full-face crash helmet.

As if from a long way off I heard Jeremy's voice.

'What kept you? Well, you're here now. Let's get her inside.'

And in spite of my muzzy state the realization hit me like a blinding flash.

Josh Williams wasn't the JW Dawn had been referring to at all.

Those initials also stood for Jeremy Winstanley.

Nineteen

I really don't remember much of what happened next, just fragments, like old snapshots, some faded to sepia, some in the sharp relief of black and white. A word here and there in the exchange between the two men, a dull pain in my shoulder as they manhandled me roughly out of the car and half carried me towards the warehouse, my fear – and the realization that this wasn't normal sleepiness. Jeremy must have put something in my coffee. I'd been drugged.

And something else, something that, given all the circumstances, was really bizarre. Though cohesive thought was still beyond me, though I hadn't seen the face beneath the visor of the crash helmet, or even heard his voice properly, I was absolutely sure the man in black leathers wasn't Josh. And ridiculous as it sounds, I was experiencing something that might almost have been elation.

I remember the scrape of the warehouse door against the concrete floor. I remember the musty smell that hit me in a nauseating wave. I remember the hard edge of the seat of a chair cutting into the back of my knees as I was pushed roughly on to it, my ankles bound and my arms yanked behind me and fastened together. And I remember Jeremy's voice, apologetic, regretful.

'I wish it hadn't come to this, Sally. But really you left me no choice.'

And then, once again, I must have drifted into unconsciousness.

When I surfaced once more through the layers of nightmare-hued muzziness, the cold grey light of morning was filtering in through the small, dirt-encrusted windows of the warehouse. By it, I could see the furniture stacked untidily around the walls, small tables piled on top of sagging sofas, a huge oak dresser, a couple of beds, dark clusters of shadows that hemmed me in like a pride of wild animals waiting for the signal to pounce.

My head was throbbing painfully, my mouth parched, my arms and legs numb. For a moment I thought I was alone, then I sensed the presence of another human being and turned my stiff neck a little to see Jeremy sitting in a polythene-covered easy chair to my left. He appeared relaxed, arms outstretched along the arms of the chair, one jean-clad leg crossed over the other with the ankle resting on his knee, but his eyes were on me, narrowed and watchful.

'You're back with us then, Sally.' The normality of his tone was somehow more chilling than any threat could have been.

'You drugged me,' I accused.

'I'm afraid so. It seemed the best way of dealing with the situation. Oh Sally, Sally, why did you have to be so persistent? You just wouldn't be frightened off, would you? I did hope the silent phone calls and having you followed would be enough to make you realize you were getting out of your depth, but you're too good a journalist for that, aren't you? You just had to go on digging until you discovered the truth.'

'Except that I hadn't!' I protested. 'I had no idea you were involved. I certainly wouldn't have come to you for help if I had. And I still don't know what's behind all this. Is it drugs?'

Jeremy looked affronted. '*Drugs*? Oh Sally, what do you take me for? Fine art and antiques are much more my style, don't you think? I *deal* in them, I suppose you could say. Their original owners might have another word for it, I suppose, but I much prefer to think of it as dealing. And where better to hide the precious artefacts whilst they're waiting to go to their new homes than an auction house? Gems among the junk. The perfect solution.'

He levered himself up out of the chair, solicitous suddenly.

'I expect you're thirsty. Would you like a drink of water?'

Thirsty was an understatement. My mouth felt as though it was full of sawdust and my throat was dry. But how did I know if he was going to put another dose of whatever he'd given me before into it? As he returned with a cracked mug and held it to my lips, I turned my head away.

'It's just water,' he assured me, reading my mind. 'There really is no need for you to be sleepy and easy to handle now. Jason is very good with knots – I think he must have been a boy scout.' He chuckled at his own joke.

'Jason?' I managed. I was still too muzzy to be thinking straight – then, even before Jeremy explained, it came to me.

Jason Barlow. The beefy, tattooed porter I'd seen at the auction on Tuesday. The witness who had given evidence against Brian Jennings. And the mysterious motorcyclist.

'Jason is a very useful addition to the team,' Jeremy said smoothly. 'I'd really prefer not to work with thugs and bully-boys, but sometimes it really is necessary to have some fire power on side. And Jason is extremely good at doing what is asked of him.'

He held the mug to my lips once more.

'Do drink some, Sally. I don't want you to be uncomfortable.'

How bizarre was that? Jeremy didn't want me to be uncomfortable, but he had me trussed like a chicken.

'Can't you at least untie my hands, then?' I asked.

'Sorry, but no.' Jeremy sounded regretful. 'I don't want you doing anything silly. I'm afraid you'll have to be restrained until I decide what to do with you.'

What to do with you . . . The words hung in the cold, musty air, and a fresh wave of fear washed over me.

'What do you mean?' I whispered stupidly.

'I can't possibly let you go, can I?' Jeremy's tone was eminently reasonable.

'I wouldn't say anything, I promise!' I blurted desperately.

'Unfortunately, Sally, we both know that isn't true,' Jeremy said sadly. 'No, something will have to be arranged – an accident of some kind, perhaps, or . . .'

'You mean like Dawn.' It was out before I could stop it.

'Mm, poor, foolish Dawn. She couldn't leave well alone, either. She was in love with Lewis, of course. Wanted to know all about him, be part of his life. Except that when she did find out she really didn't like it one little bit. She became far too dangerous and she had to be dealt with. Just as you will have to be too, I'm afraid. Jason has gone to fetch your car. I can't have it discovered outside my home. When he gets back, we'll arrange something.'

Then, suddenly, chillingly, he was solicitous once more.

'Do have something to drink, Sally. You'll feel a lot better if you do.'

He held the mug to my lips again, and again I twisted away, spitting out the few drops that had spilled into my mouth. I absolutely could not reconcile this monster with the man I'd known since I was a child, the man who had been so kind the last few days. But I knew now that it had been nothing but false concern, a way of keeping an eye on me and limiting any damage I might do. And I'd played right into his hands, going to him, of all people, with the evidence that would send him to jail for a very long time.

Fear was running ice-cold waves through my veins now, but somehow I managed to meet his eyes defiantly.

'How can you do this to me, Jeremy?' I demanded. 'I thought we were friends!'

He smiled sadly. 'We were. In fact, I hoped we might be more. If that had happened, Sally – you and me – there'd have been no need for all this . . .'

'And you were Dad's friend!' I went on. 'How could you have got your . . . your henchman . . . to start a stampede that nearly killed him?'

Jeremy sighed. 'I was very sorry to have to do that. But I had to get him out of the way, don't you see? I had to get hold of his computer to see just how much you'd found out, and also, hopefully, to hamper your investigations. To do that I needed the house to be empty,' Jeremy explained in that same reasonable tone. 'Jack, I'm afraid, was collateral damage.'

Collateral damage! The ruthlessness of the man was terrifying.

'Except, of course, unknown to you I'd bought myself a laptop,' I said, ridiculously pleased at that one small victory.

'Which I was able to take without much trouble, since you'd kindly let me have a key to the house.'

'And I'd also transferred it all to a memory stick.'

For the first time Jeremy looked thrown. Then he recovered himself.

'We'll talk about that later. For the moment let's concentrate on Dawn's diary. You told me it was in your bag. I've checked, and you were obviously lying to me. Where is it, Sally?'

I held his gaze defiantly. Dawn's diary, detailing the criminal activity at the warehouse and also incriminating Jeremy, was the one card I held. 'You really think I'm going to tell you?'

'Oh yes, you'll tell me.' He tangled his fist in my hair, jerking my head back. 'Where are they?'

I gritted my teeth against the pain, but kept silent. Jeremy jerked again on my hair, so hard that I thought my neck would snap, but stared up at him, mute and defiant. After a moment, he released me.

'You really are a very stubborn young woman, Sally. But we'll see how stubborn you can be when I let Jason loose on you. He doesn't have my sensibilities when it comes to violence. Ah . . . that sounds like him now.'

In my determination to resist Jeremy's attempts to force me to reveal the whereabouts of Dawn's diaries, I hadn't heard the car driving up. Now, however, the warehouse door was scraping open and a big burly figure came in. He was still clad in black motorcycle leathers, but he was no longer wearing his crash helmet, and I could see it was indeed the same man who had been working at the warehouse on the night of the auction. I hadn't taken much notice of him then, but now everything about him alarmed me – the bullet-shaped, close-cropped head, the heavy eyebrows meeting across the bridge of a nose that looked as if it had been broken more than once, the earring and the stud in his lower lip. Jason Barlow looked every inch a thug. I could well imagine that not only would he have no qualms about hurting me, he'd positively enjoy it.

Worse. He'd enjoy staging my death, too. Hot and cold waves of fear washed over me. Josh had been right when he'd warned me I could be tangling with very dangerous characters. Why, oh why, hadn't I listened to him? Against Jeremy's ruthless cleverness and Jason's brute force, I didn't stand a chance.

'Right, her car's here then.' Jason's voice was gruff, as if he smoked too many cigarettes, and he had a marked local accent. 'Have you decided what you want to do with her?'

'Pretty much.' Jeremy's tone was dismissive – he didn't care to discuss his plans with underlings, I thought; simply giving orders was more his style. 'But first we have to persuade Sally to tell us where something rather important can be found. I've already warned her that you will be very good at extracting information. You won't let me down, will you?'

Jason smirked.

'Right up my street, guv'nor. Where d'you want me to start?'

Jeremy shrugged.

'I'll leave that up to you, though perhaps that broken leg might be a good place.' He took a step or two away, distancing himself, then turned back. 'Are you sure you aren't going to be a sensible girl and tell me what I want to know without any of this unpleasantness, Sally?'

I was shaking from head to foot, so violently that the ropes binding my wrists and ankles cut into the flesh. But one thought was uppermost in my mind – Jeremy wouldn't want me killed before he knew the whereabouts of the diaries so that he could destroy them. But the moment I told him I would be signing my own death warrant.

'Jeremy, this is crazy!' I said, desperately trying to delay the moment the pain would begin. 'We've known each other since I was a little girl. You taught me to ride – have you forgotten all that?'

'Of course not.' Unbelievably, he was the same suave character he had always been, except that now I'd seen the ruthlessness that lay beneath, driven, no doubt, by greed. 'But it's a long time ago now, Sally. Believe me, I am sorry, but I can't take the risk of too much interest in me, or the warehouse. It's too important to me.' He smiled slightly. 'Would it surprise you to know that there are treasures worth many thousands of pounds not more than a few yards from where you are sitting? This operation is a very profitable one, which is more than I can say for my investment business. But that makes a very good cover for my travels.'

'When you arrange the transportation of stolen treasures.'

Jeremy smiled slightly. 'Something like that. But please, don't let's waste any more time. I need the diaries, Sally. And I will have them, one way or another, make no mistake of that.' He turned to Jason. 'I'll leave this to you. Let me know when Sally decides to give us some answers.'

He moved away, out of my line of sight, towards the rear of the warehouse, and Jason came closer. He was grinning, getting out a cigarette and lighting it.

'First things first . . .' He yanked open my top, exposing my décolletage, drew on his cigarette and brought the glowing tip close to my face, so close I could no longer see it, but could feel the heat.

He was going to burn me. This couldn't be happening . . . it couldn't! But it was. I squeezed my eyes shut, gritting my teeth, determined, even now, not to crack, but more terrified than I had ever been in my life as I waited . . . waited . . .

The crash of the warehouse door bursting open made me jump so much that the burning cigarette did actually make contact with my skin, and I screamed. But the pain lasted a few seconds only.

Startled, I opened my eyes. Two uniformed policemen were running across the open space, and Jason was diving for the open door. But a tall figure was barring his way.

Josh. Oh my God, it was Josh.

What happened next is all rather a blur to me. I remember screaming Josh's name, as he and the two policemen grappled with Jason Barlow. I remember struggling frantically and futilely against the ropes that were binding me. I remember trying to tell them that Jeremy was somewhere in the warehouse. Later I learned that he had escaped through a rear door and driven off, but he didn't get far. In the narrow lane he had met another police car racing to the scene and when he tried to squeeze past it he had run into the ditch and been apprehended.

I remember Josh freeing me from my bonds, chafing my wrists and ankles, calling for an ambulance that I was trying to tell him I didn't need. And I remember his arms around me, holding me close, whispering against my hair. Of all my memories of that awful day, it is that one that I want to hug to me and cherish forever.

'I'm sorry, but I can't come with you, Sally,' Josh said when the ambulance arrived and the paramedics insisted on taking me to A & E to have me checked over. 'I'm afraid there are things I have to do, and I'm needed here.'

He nodded in the direction of the warehouse, where no fewer than three distinctive police vehicles were now drawn up at crazy angles in the parking area outside, hemming in Dad's car, Josh's and Jeremy's, and Jason's motor bike. I looked at him blankly.

Needed here? What was he talking about?

Josh grinned faintly. 'I know, I've got some explaining to do. But I expect you've realized by now that newspaper photographer isn't my usual day job.'

'Well, yes, but I thought . . .' I broke off. I didn't want to admit what I'd thought – how could I ever have suspected for a moment that Josh was an international criminal? But my brain still wasn't working properly – I was still a bit woozy from the drugs Jeremy had given me, and reaction to what I'd just been through had kicked in too, so that I was shaky and confused.

'I'll fill you in properly later,' Josh went on. 'But the fact is the job at the *Gazette* was just my cover story. Actually, I'm afraid, I'm a policeman with the regional crime squad. We've known for some time there was a clearing house in the locality for art and curios coming in from the continent – stuff worth millions that's been stolen to order. I've been working under cover, gathering information, and waiting for the evidence – a big shipment and the brains behind the outfit both to be in the same place at the same time.'

'Oh!' I was too startled to say more, but suddenly things were falling into place. The very things that had made me suspicious of Josh when I found Dawn's diaries in his cottage were pointing now in exactly the opposite direction.

'I'm really sorry I had to deceive you, Sally, but I absolutely couldn't blow my cover. Too much depended on it – not to mention the best part of a year's work,' Josh went on. 'And now, I'm afraid I've got a full day's work, and the rest, ahead of me tying up my side of things. I'll see you just as soon as I can – OK?'

I nodded. 'OK.'

The paramedics were hovering, anxious to get me to A & E.

'Off you go then. See you soon.' He gave my hand a quick squeeze.

As I climbed into the ambulance I glanced back. Josh was still standing there, watching me. 'I love you,' he mouthed. Then the doors closed, and though I could no longer see him the look on his face as he said it remained with me.

Twenty

'You've no idea the trouble you caused me, Sally,' Josh said. 'Quite apart from worrying me half to death, I was afraid you were going to blow the whole job wide apart with your investigations.'

'Well, that's nice!' I said, mock-sarcastically.

It was early evening. It was some hours now since I'd been sent home from A & E with a clean bill of health, but only twenty minutes or so since Josh had arrived to see me. He'd been kept busy all day working on his case and still had to go back to the police station to complete yet more paperwork, but he'd snatched a break of an hour or so, and now he was sitting at the kitchen table with me and Mum.

'You just wouldn't be warned off, would you?' Josh chided. 'Wouldn't accept the danger you were in, even though you were convinced Dawn had died because of what she knew. At least Alice had the sense to realize the gravity of the situation. When I learned she was about to talk to you I had a word with her, and she agreed straight away to let me get her to a safe house until it was all over. But you . . . no, you had to go right on, ploughing in deeper and deeper. If I hadn't found you when I did, I dread to think what might have happened.'

I shuddered. I didn't want to even think about that.

'How *did* you find me?' I asked.

'When I realized you'd gone I went out looking for you. I passed your car heading for Stoke Compton, but I was pretty sure it wasn't you driving it, so I called for reinforcements and turned around myself. By the time I caught sight of it again I guessed it was heading for the warehouse and radioed in. The local officers and I arrived at more or less the same time and the rest you know. It was a bit of gamble to come in with all guns blazing, but it paid off. We caught the man behind the operation and one of his goons red-handed, and there'd been a shipment just a couple of days ago – art and curios worth a king's ransom that had been stolen to order on the continent and were stored in the warehouse awaiting delivery to the collectors in this country who had placed orders for them. Result. Though I have to say at the time we barged our way in I was thinking more about you than the job. Jeremy Winstanley would have had no more scruples about dealing with you than he did in disposing of Dawn when she became a threat to the operation. There was just too much at stake.'

I closed my eyes briefly. I knew all too well how close I had come to ending up as Dawn had.

'I just can't believe the Jeremy I knew could be so evil,' I said. 'To dispose of anyone who got in his way without a second thought . . . risking Dad's life by stampeding the cows, having Dawn killed . . . I know he was squeamish about actually doing the deeds himself, but that thug was acting on his instructions, which is just as bad.'

'And what about the fire?' Mum put in. What wickedness is that – trying to have her burnt in her bed and then getting Brian Jennings blamed for it! Or was it Brian Jennings all the time? He used to work for Lewis Crighton, Sally said . . .'

'He did, yes, but it wasn't him who set the fire, and it wasn't directed at Dawn,' Josh said. 'In fact, at the outset, the fire was totally unconnected to Jeremy Winstanley's operation. He simply hijacked it for his own ends.'

'You mean it was local louts all the time?' Mum asked.

'Not unless you count Paul Holder in that category,' Josh said.

'Paul Holder. Lisa's husband.' It had occurred to me when I'd sensed Lisa was hiding something that he might have been responsible – it had, after all, been very convenient that he had been on the scene so quickly with a ladder, and that Lisa had been jumpy all evening, and awake when the fire started, but, unable to see a link, I'd dismissed it.

'Paul and Lisa were desperate to get their hands on the shop to start a business of their own,' Josh went on. 'But it was on a long lease. They knew the shopkeeper was struggling and wasn't insured, and came up with the idea that if he lost everything and couldn't afford to start again they'd be able to step in. Paul was friendly with Jason Barlow – he enlisted his help, and through him, Lewis Crighton got to hear of what they were planning. It was he who suggested they frame Brian Jennings. He had become something of a danger to Lewis and Jeremy – Lewis thought he knew too much about what was going on at the warehouse and couldn't be trusted. Seeing him charged with arson seemed a good way of getting him out of the way. Not only was he locked up, he'd been portrayed as a complete nutter – if he did ever start talking about what he'd seen no one would pay him any credence. Framing him was easy. It was already well known that he was obsessed with Dawn – she'd actually gone to the police about him stalking her. Jason Barlow came forward to say he'd seen him hanging about outside on the night of the fire, and just to make sure he would be charged and convicted, managed to plant a handkerchief with traces of petrol on it in the pocket of the jacket he always wore.'

'How on earth do you know all this?' I asked incredulously.

'From Dawn. At the time of the fire, she had no idea what Lisa and Paul were planning, and although she knew by then that Lewis was involved with Jeremy Winstanley in his international art and curio robberies, and was worried about it, there was no way she'd have given him away. She was still completely under Lewis Crighton's spell, though he was tiring of her and the affair was past its heady heights. But afterwards, when she went home, she began to wonder. She came back to Stoke Compton to see Lisa, and discovered the truth – that she had been implicit in sending an innocent man to jail. That was something she couldn't stomach. Whereas she had been prepared to keep what she knew about Lewis to herself so long as it was only about stolen property, now her conscience wouldn't allow her to keep silent. And the last straw, I think, was when Lisa told her that Lewis had a new love – Dawn's replacement at the estate agency, a girl called Sarah.'

'Sarah. Yes.' I nodded. 'I knew they were carrying on. So in the end it was Lewis's wandering eye that was his undoing.'

'That certainly had a part in it, though I don't think Dawn's conscience would have allowed her to leave Brian Jennings in prison for something he didn't do for very long. Lewis must have thought so too. He contacted Jeremy Winstanley and told him there was a problem, and Jeremy organized the accident to silence her. Not knowing, of course, that he was too late. Dawn had gone straight to the police, handing over her diaries as evidence, and it was passed to the regional crime squad. Which is where I came in.'

'How did you manage that, though?' I asked. 'I've heard of undercover officers posing as all kinds of things, but a newspaper photographer! I don't know how you pulled that off.'

Josh grinned. 'It came as second nature really. That's exactly what I was before I joined the force. When a vacancy occurred on the *Gazette* it was the perfect cover. I could nose about without arousing anyone's suspicion. Strings were pulled in high places – and I got a new persona. So I'm afraid we're not actually in the same line of business at all, Sally. Though if you fancied a change of career, I reckon we still could be. You'd make a better detective than some I know.'

'I'm perfectly happy as I am, thank you!' I retorted. 'And while we're on the subject of deceit, I suppose you didn't walk the Cotswold Way either.'

Josh held up his hands in surrender.

'Not last week, no, though I did do it a couple of years ago. In actual fact, I was at headquarters, reporting on the latest developments. I am really sorry about keeping you in the dark, but I had no choice. I couldn't risk being unmasked.'

'You could have trusted me,' I said. I was feeling a little miffed, actually, that Josh had kept me in the dark.

'It's the nature of the job, I'm afraid. Living and breathing the assumed identity, and getting enough evidence to secure a conviction.'

'And so you cultivated me in case I found out anything useful to you, or did something that threatened to upset your operation.'

Mum got up and excused herself. She was a bit uncomfortable with the personal way the conversation was going, I guessed.

'Well?' I said bluntly when she was out of earshot. 'Is that how it was?'

'In the beginning, yes, I suppose it was,' Josh admitted. 'It was no hardship, though.' He gave me a wicked grin. 'I fancied you right from the off. Crutches and all.'

'That's all right then,' I said sharply. I wasn't in the mood for his banter. 'At least we know now where we stand.'

Josh reached across the table for my hand; I jerked it away. He grabbed it again, more securely.

'Come on, Sally, surely you know better than that. Yes, I admit, I did ask you out at first so that I could keep an eye on you. But it wasn't long before I was having feelings for you that really didn't help with what I was supposed to be doing. You worried the life out of me, damn it! You were so stubborn, you just wouldn't listen when I told you that you were playing with fire. And you were a whole lot too friendly with Jeremy Winstanley, too. For all I knew you could have been playing a double game – trying to get the low-down on who I really was, and what I was doing.'

'You couldn't really have thought that!' I said, shocked.

Josh pulled a face.

'In my game you can't be too careful. A pretty girl is often the downfall of an undercover officer – well, never mind the undercover officer, the downfall of a man, full stop.'

'Hmm.' Something about the way he was looking at me was making my anger dissolve, starting the treacherous warmth deep inside me once more. 'So what are you saying?'

'You know very well. Now this is all over, we can start again. If you want to, that is.'

Oh I did, I did. But I wasn't going to let him off the hook so easily.

'I'll have to think about it.'

Josh glanced at his watch.

'I'm going to have to go. I'm afraid a normal working day doesn't exist for a policeman. But I reckon I can drop by again tomorrow evening. Will that give you enough time to think?'

I had to laugh. There was absolutely no thinking to be done.

'I should think so, Officer,' I said mischievously.

Mum was in the doorway.

'Oh – are you going?' she asked.

''Fraid so. I've got a whole load of reports to write. And Sally needs an early night too after all she's been through today.'

He squeezed my shoulder, dropped a kiss on top of my head, and made for the door.

'Take care of her,' he said to Mum. And was gone.

'Well, well, what a turn-up for the book!' Mum said. 'A policeman! Perhaps he'll be able to keep you in order.'

I grinned.

'I wouldn't hold my breath if I was you,' I said.

Postscript

Josh had his own idea of a way to 'keep me in order' – he wasted no time in asking me to marry him. And I wasted no time in saying 'yes'. What would have been the point? We are both absolutely sure of our feelings, and old enough to know our own minds. I had no wish to get into another long-term live-in relationship as I had with Tim, and besides, all the things that have happened have convinced me life is for living – now. You never know what tomorrow may bring.

We're planning a September wedding, though the honeymoon may have to be delayed for the various court hearings Josh is going to have to attend. Jeremy, Jason Barlow and Lewis Crighton are looking at very long jail sentences – especially Jeremy and Jason, who has admitted being the hit-and-run driver responsible for Dawn's death. And of course Paul and Lisa Holder will be charged too with various offences. Muffins is closed and shuttered and I can't see it opening again any time soon, if ever. I do actually feel a bit sorry for Lisa; it must be devastating for her to see her dream destroyed – she had made a very good job of the café. But even if she was talked into the arson plan in the first place by her unscrupulous fiancé, to remain silent when poor Brian Jennings was sent to prison for something he didn't do was unforgivable. Whatever the outcome for Lisa and Paul, they brought it all on themselves.

The good thing is that poor Brian Jennings is free, and will probably be able to claim a lot of money in compensation for wrongful imprisonment. I sincerely hope he has learned his lesson and won't ever stalk another girl as he did Dawn. But weird and unsavoury as he may be, he was innocent of arson, innocent of wishing her harm. Just a fall guy of whom everyone was only too ready to believe the worst.

But back to our forthcoming wedding. I'm out of plaster now, and my leg is almost as good as new, so I will be able to walk down the aisle unaided, albeit with a bit of a limp. And when we were discussing the honeymoon I had a suggestion to make.

'If we left it until next winter we could go skiing.'

Josh raised his eyebrows in utter disbelief.

'After what happened last time?'

'They say lightning never strikes in the same place twice, and I suppose the same thing goes for avalanches,' I said breezily.

'I wouldn't want to take bets on it.'

'And besides, I'm sure you'd enjoy it. Quite apart from the actual skiing, it's really beautiful. I'd love you to see the crimson sunsets over the snow, and the après-ski is pretty good, too.'

Josh sighed deeply.

'Oh – if you're really set on it – we'll see. But I'm making no promises. Personally I'd rather be somewhere hot. Snorkelling, water sports, a cold beer on a sun lounger listening to the surf and getting a decent tan . . .' He put his arms round me. 'Not so many layers of clothes between us, either . . .' he added wickedly.

'If it hadn't been for my skiing accident we'd never have met,' I pointed out.

'True. It still doesn't make me want to take up the sport,' he said.

I pulled a face, pretending to be deeply upset. But to be honest, I don't much care where we are as long as we are together. Some things, it would seem, are meant to be.

Josh and I together are just one of them.